Seven F... ...DERS
OF THE ANCIENT WORLD

THE GREAT PYRAMID OF GIZA

THE HANGING GARDENS OF BABYLON

THE TEMPLE OF ARTEMIS AT EPHESOS

THE MAUSOLEUM AT HALICARNASSOS

THE STATUE OF ZEUS AT OLYMPIA

THE COLOSSUS OF RHODES

THE PHAROS AT ALEXANDRIA

for my father

For more information about Katherine Roberts, visit
www.katherineroberts.com

First published in Great Britain by CollinsVoyager 2003
CollinsVoyager is an imprint of HarperCollins*Publishers* Ltd,
77-85 Fulham Palace Road, Hammersmith,
London W6 8JB

The HarperCollins website address is: www.harpercollins.co.uk

1 3 5 7 9 8 6 4 2

Chapter quotations reprinted by permission of the publishers and the Trustees
of the Loeb Classical Library from LUCIAN: VOLUME VII. Loeb Classical
Library Volume L 431, translated by M. D. Macleod, Cambridge, Mass.:
Harvard University Press, 1961. The Loeb Classical Library ® is a registered
trademark of the President and Fellows of Harvard College.

Illustrations by Fiona Land

ISBN 0 00 711281 5

Katherine Roberts

‹THE›
MAUSOLEUM
MURDER

Collins
VOYAGER

An imprint of HarperCollinsPublishers

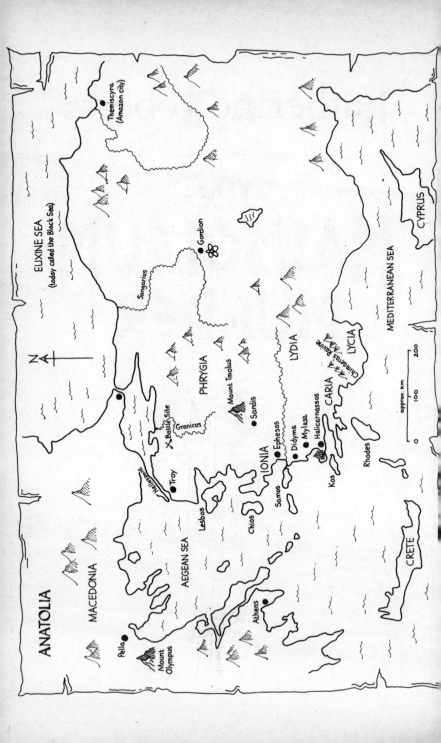

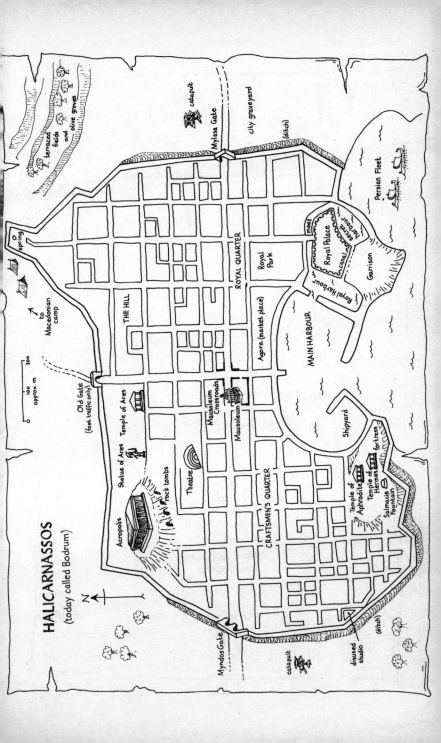

HALICARNASSOS
(today called Bodrum)

N

0   100   200
approx. m

to Macedonian camp

spring

terraced fields and olive groves

catapult

Mylasa Gate

city graveyard

(ditch)

Persian Fleet

Old Gate
(foot traffic only)

THE HILL

ROYAL QUARTER

meet

Acropolis

Statue of Ares

Temple of Ares

Rock tombs

Theatre

Mausoleum Crossroads

Mausoleum

Royal Park

Royal Palace

Second Harbour

canal

Royal Harbour

Agora (market place)

MAIN HARBOUR

Garrison

Myndos Gate

CRAFTSMEN'S QUARTER

Shipyard

catapult

disused studio

(ditch)

Temple of Aphrodite

Temple of Hermes

fortress

Salmacis Fountain

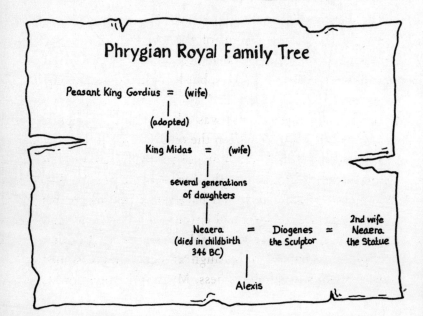

Carian Royal Family Tree

Hectomnus = (wife)

Queen Artemisia (died 351 BC) = King Maussollos (died 352 BC)

Idrieus (died 344 BC) = Queen Ada

Pixodarus (died 335 BC) = (Persian wife)

1st rulers of Halicarnassos

2nd rulers of Halicarnassos

King Orontobates Satrap of Caria = Ada the Younger

Princess Phoebe

Phrygian Royal Family Tree

Peasant King Gordius = (wife)

(adopted)

King Midas = (wife)

several generations of daughters

Neaera (died in childbirth 346 BC) = Diogenes the Sculptor = 2nd wife Neaera the Statue

Alexis

Chapter 1

ATTACK

DIOGENES: Why, Carian, are you so proud, and expect to be honoured above all of us?

The day the Macedonians attacked Halicarnassos, Alexis was in the narrow streets of the Craftsmen's Quarter looking for his father. Not that there was any real hope he'd find him after all these years, but habit kept him looking, just in case.

This morning's excuse was a bent chisel. By rights, Kichesias should have been the one running to borrow a replacement chisel from one of the other sculptors in the Quarter, since he was the one who had bent it. But, as a slave, Kichesias would have got a beating for his carelessness. So Alexis had covered for his friend, and was in no hurry to return to the studio where the other apprentices would only laugh at what they assumed was Alexis's usual clumsiness. Making the most of his freedom, he'd taken a detour, and was on the far side of the Quarter when everyone began running for cover.

Women screamed and dropped their hydria, men and slaves shouted, and the streets filled with people tripping over broken pots and dodging loose donkeys in their rush to reach the Acropolis where they would be safe. Heart thudding with a mixture of excitement and fear, Alexis abandoned his errand and fought his way back to the cluster of sculptors' houses where he lived.

"The Macedonians are coming!" he shouted, crashing through the doors.

The studio was quiet and dark, making Alexis feel a bit foolish. Master Pasion must have already heard the news and sent everyone home. Rough, half-finished statues watched from the gloom as he caught his breath and tried to think where Kichesias might be.

Halicarnassos had been preparing for an attack most of that year, ever since the Macedonian army had crossed the Hellespont back in the spring. The other apprentices delighted in taunting Alexis about the coming invasion. They said he would be made into a slave like Kichesias along with the women and children if the city were captured, whereas they would sign up with General Alexander, who was sure to want more brave young men to join his army when he marched on Persia. Alexis was looking forward to seeing how brave the others were now.

The back of his neck prickled and he blinked round at the statues, uneasy, imagining a Macedonian hiding in every shadow. Marble dust hung in the air and a hammer lay abandoned on a battered stool. Kichesias had worked on the face of their statue while Alexis had been gone, and the delicate features of a girl with big Persian eyes were starting to take shape. Alexis's own efforts were ugly by comparison. He wondered if the Macedonians would care if the slaves they took from Halicarnassos could make lifelike sculptures or not, and was seized by a sudden fit of shivering.

"Where have you been?" snapped his stepmother's voice from the shadows behind him. "Gawking at the soldiers with the other boys, I suppose?"

Alexis whirled, his sweat breaking out afresh. His stepmother Neaera must have been there the whole time, standing among the statues, silent and still. Waiting for him.

"Where's Kichesias?" he said, still breathing hard.

Neaera laughed softly as she stepped into the light. She was wearing her travel cloak and sandals, and had tied up her hair in an orange headscarf. A tall and robust woman, she was still very beautiful, though lately age creases had begun to mark her face and strands of silver had invaded her dark ringlets – just one of the things she blamed Alexis for.

"Is that any way to greet your mother?" she said. "I warned you what I'd do to him if you tried to leave home, didn't I?"

Alexis's stomach twisted in sudden fear for his friend. "But I wasn't running away! Master Pasion sent me to borrow another chisel, that's all. The city's under attack. Everyone's trying to get up to the Acropolis. I came back as quickly as I could."

Neaera laughed again, and her fingers stroked Alexis's cheek. They were cold and smooth, not soft and warm like the fingers of other people's mothers. "Pasion's a fool if he thinks you bent a chisel all by yourself. What's wrong, Alex? You look pale, and your tunic's soaked. I hope you're not coming down with a fever at such an important time. Our careless slave is out in the courtyard loading the mule. Oh, don't worry, I haven't beaten him – wouldn't be much point, would there? Or are you worried I'll hurt him, just because you lied to Pasion and were a little late back from your errand? No point in that, either. I know how the magic works. You can't leave me, any more than I can leave you."

"That's not true," Alexis mumbled, bolder now that he knew Kichesias was safe. "You could leave if you wanted to. You're not my real mother."

But Neaera's attention had moved on. She reached behind her and picked up an empty basket. "We need supplies," she said, holding it out. "We've a long way to go tomorrow, and none of us can survive on fresh air, not any more. You'll have to go to the agora."

Alexis stared at her in disbelief as he realized what she must mean. Every year since his father had disappeared, Neaera had taken him and Kichesias on a pilgrimage to Phrygia. It was all to do with his stupid magic. The only good thing about the Macedonian invasion was that this year's pilgrimage had been delayed. "But we're being attacked!" he protested. "We can't possibly go travelling, not now! There's an *army* out there, in case you haven't noticed."

A frown creased Neaera's forehead. "That's enough of your cheek. You will do what I tell you." She thrust the basket at him and threw in a handful of coins. "We're leaving today, before they close the gates. That young upstart Alexander and his ragtag army won't bother stopping us. We're going to Mount Tmolus, like we always do, and you are going to wash in the river and ask the river god to reverse your magic so it's more useful. Then we'll see who rules in Caria." Her eyes gleamed, staring past Alexis at a future only she could see.

"But—"

"Don't argue with me!"

Neaera's hand darted out and closed about Alexis's wrist. Her fingers might have looked pale and soft, but her grip was like stone. She squeezed until tears sprang to Alexis's eyes, before letting him go.

Her tone softened. "I don't like having to hurt you, Alex. Go and buy our supplies. You know what to get – dried fruit, goat's cheese, salted fish – anything that'll keep for the journey. If they're panicking in the agora as much as they are around here, I expect you'll find most of what we want abandoned for the taking. Kichesias and I will meet you at the Mausoleum Crossroads. I've something to take care of before we leave." Unexpectedly, she smiled. "I've a good feeling about this year. You're growing up, and I think the god will recognize that."

Alexis studied his dirty toes as more people ran past the door shouting warnings in case anyone hadn't heard about the attack. He tried not to imagine what it would be like outside the city walls in the midst of the fighting, or how horrible it would be if the river god actually came this year and did what Neaera wanted. He had no illusions that he and Kichesias would be any freer of her once his magic was reversed – if such a thing was even possible.

"Hurry up, then." With one of those motherly gestures that always seemed so stiff and awkward, Neaera picked a strand of hair out of his eyes. "Don't want the Macedonians to catch you and steal your magic for themselves, do we? It's mine, Alex. You chose me, remember?"

How could he forget? The route to the agora took Alexis past the Mausoleum, where eight years ago Neaera had entered his life and changed it for ever. As he fought his way through the crowds, flattening himself against the wall whenever a troop of Persian soldiers or Carian mercenaries galloped past, he relived the memory, clinging to every detail because his father was a part of it.

He'd been four years old, and Diogenes was taking him to the Mausoleum as a birthday treat. With Alexis's short legs, the walk to the centre of the city seemed endless. But he held tightly to his father's hand with its familiar calluses until they came to the crossroads at the centre of the city. Tourists were everywhere, whole families come to see the famous tomb. Alexis remembered being sad that he didn't have a mother like the other boys. Then they passed through a pair of high, ornate gates, and he forgot his sadness as they entered another world.

They walked across a sea of white marble, warm underfoot and gleaming in the sun, and climbed some steps between two life-sized statues of prancing horses ridden by men in Persian uniform. "They're guarding the dead King Maussollos," his father explained. "The Mausoleum is his tomb, and Master Pytheos designed it to be the best tomb in the whole world. Do you like the statues?"

He pointed to the building before them, but Alexis couldn't see properly past all the people. He was more interested in the horses, which seemed to whinny at him. *Please, please, we want to gallop away from this place. We want to be free.* He reached out a hand towards the nearest horse statue. But before he could touch it, his father bent down and lifted him on to his shoulders so he could see over the heads of the crowd.

That had been his first proper view of the Mausoleum with its brightly painted statues of people standing on three tiers around its base, and to the four-year-old Alexis it seemed the largest and most magnificent building in the whole world. On the platform above the tiers, yet more statues stood between the marble columns, and at the top of the columns were rows of golden lions, and above the lions, right up on the roof against the blue of the sky, four more horses of white and gold reared towards the sun.

He remembered stretching up his arms, wanting to ride them, but his father laughed. "They're much too big for you, Goldenhands! They just look small because we're down here. I'll take you up on the platform so you can see the giant people, how about that?"

Alexis was carried, jolting through the crowds, up some more steps, closer to the huge statues of men and women standing between the pillars. They looked down at him as if they knew what he could do, and he clutched his father's curls, suddenly terrified.

"What's wrong, Goldenhands? Don't hold so hard, you're hurting me."

"Giants!" said Alexis. "Giants kill me!"

"They're only statues, silly." His father swung him off his shoulders and set him down gently. But Alexis clasped his legs and buried his face into his father's stained apron. Diogenes chuckled and ruffled his hair. "All right, we'll go down if you want. They are rather overpowering, aren't they?"

As they left the platform, his father told him how the architect Pytheos had commissioned four skilled sculptors to work on the four sides of the Mausoleum, and how he'd made the work into a competition so that each craftsman would do his best. But when the time came to judge, he had to split the prize four ways because all four had sculpted with equal magic. "Who would you give the prize to?" he asked, leading Alexis round the base of the huge tomb. "Shall we look for the best statue?"

Alexis was still a bit frightened of the giants. But the statues looked smaller from the ground, and the ones on the first tier were much nicer because they were life-sized like real people. He reached up the wall of the tomb, trying to touch the gilded toes that poked over the ledge above his head.

"I'll lift you up again, shall I?" Diogenes said, hoisting him back on to his shoulders. "All right, how about this man? He's pretty good, don't you think?"

Alexis had eyes only for the lady statues. Some were prettier than others, some young, others older, but none seemed quite right. He'd never known his mother, but his father had told him about her so many times that he had a clear picture of her in his head. Strong. Beautiful. Not that old, but not too young either. Some of the mothers in the Craftsmen's Quarter acted more like big sisters, giggling and being silly with each other. He liked the older mothers who would hug him and make him feel safe.

They had walked round three sides of the Mausoleum before he found her. She was tall and wore an elegant, old-fashioned peplos dress gathered at the shoulders with long pins covered in gold leaf. Her hair had been sculpted in ringlets and painted a rich, dark brown. Her eyes were brown as well, and looked down calmly at him.

He tugged his father's ear and pointed. He distinctly remembered calling the statue "Mama".

Diogenes stiffened and stared up at the statue. He gave a wry chuckle. "No," he said softly. "No, she's not much like your mother. I know I probably told you your mother was a goddess, but my Neaera was a Phrygian girl. She was shorter, and not so pretty – except to me, of course. To me, she was the most beautiful woman in the world. You'll understand that one day, Goldenhands."

He sighed sadly. At the same time, Alexis reached over his father's head to touch the statue's painted toes.

LIVE, he willed. *LIVE AND BE MY MOTHER.*

Chapter 2

MAUSOLEUM

MAUSSOLLOS: I was King of all Caria,
ruler also of part of Lydia.

That was how he'd chosen Neaera to be his stepmother –
part of a childhood game, awarding a prize for the best
statue. It was the first time Alexis had tried to use his
magic on the image of a living thing, and at four years old
he'd had no idea of the trouble it would cause. If only he
could go back and change what he'd done that day. But
life wasn't like that.

By the time he reached the agora, the merchants were
frantically packing up their goods, spilling things in their
haste to escape the city. Loose donkeys and mules added
to the confusion, trotting through the overturned stalls
and braying at the tops of their voices. Some of the ships
in the harbour had already hauled up their anchor-stones
and were hurrying to leave before someone tried to stop

them. Over by the food stalls, partial order had been imposed. Guards had been posted around the colonnade, and soldiers were clearing the quay for military traffic. The merchants were reluctantly obeying orders and loading their foodstuffs into carts commandeered by the soldiers. Bags of coin, embroidered with the Carian Royal Lion, changed hands in payment for the food, which was quickly transported under guard back to the garrison on the headland.

Alexis watched the process in frustration. It would be impossible to get close enough to snatch anything from those carts. The guards carried spears, while Persian bowmen knelt on the roof of the colonnade watching the streets.

He glanced back at the Mausoleum. The chariot on its roof glittered white and gold in the autumn sunshine, deceptively beautiful. He couldn't return to Neaera with an empty basket. Gritting his teeth, he ducked behind the nearest cart. It had been loaded with baskets of salted fish that rocked gently as the ox shuffled along, but to Alexis's disappointment none fell out.

"You, boy! Get away from there!" One of the soldiers pushed him roughly. "Get on home! Didn't you hear General Memnon's announcement? Everyone is to return to their homes and stay there until we've dealt with the invaders."

Alexis kept his eyes on the cart and the swaying baskets of fish. He assumed his poor-little-orphan expression, which, when he'd been younger, used to make the women of the Craftsmen's Quarter take pity on him and give him treats. "Please, sir, my mother sent me to buy supper. We've nothing to eat tonight. Can I have a fish? Just one? I can pay for it." He showed the soldier the coins Neaera had given him.

The soldier grunted. "You'll need more than brass to buy food after today, boy! If this business turns into a siege, you'll get your rations same as everyone else. Get on home and stop botherin' me. I've important work to do." He slapped the ox on the rump, and the cart jolted forward again.

Alexis ran after the soldier and tugged his sleeve. "Please, sir! You don't understand! I *have* to buy some food!"

"Oh, for Ares' sake! I don't have time for this." The soldier snatched the basket from Alexis and replaced it with the point of his spear, bringing him up short with a gasp.

But the soldier's attention was diverted by a sudden commotion from the eastern wall, where the Macedonian attack was in progress. Shouts of alarm were followed by a deep *boom* that shook the agora, inciting fresh panic among the people trapped in the streets. "Earthquake!" someone yelled, and those under the colonnade ran into the open so that they wouldn't get hit by falling columns.

With a silent prayer of thanks to Poseidon for shaking the earth, Alexis sidestepped the spear and examined his chest for blood. But it quickly became obvious the vibration was no quake sent from the gods. A cloud of dust drifted across the city from the direction of the

Mylasa Gate, and a second *boom* brought a shower of tiles sliding off the roof of the colonnade. The bowmen crouched up there jumped down in alarm, the ox took off in panic with the cart jolting wildly behind it, and a muddy child wearing an oversized woollen cap took advantage of the confusion to dodge through an unguarded gap into the agora.

"They've got this huge, great catapult!" the mud-caked apparition yelled excitedly. "It can throw stones bigger than a house! They're knocking down our walls!"

"Shut up, you!" The soldier who had nearly speared Alexis swung the child off its feet. "No one's knockin' down our walls, don't be so silly! How many more times do I have to tell you boys to get on home— Ares' great beard!" He dropped his captive as the child's cap fell off. A mass of long, tangled, dark hair tumbled out.

Alexis hardly noticed or cared that the muddy apparition was a girl. His whole attention was on the trail of spilled food the bolting ox had left behind. Before the soldier could recover from his surprise, he had retrieved Neaera's basket and filled it with gritty fish and bruised fruit. He fled for the Mausoleum Crossroads, head down, shutting out the noise of the battle and the outcry behind him.

There were more soldiers at the Crossroads. A whole troop of them blocked the entrance to the Mausoleum courtyard, stopping people from going in. Others could be seen inside, poking around the outlying buildings and swarming over the Mausoleum itself, dwarfed by the enormous statues that stood between the columns on the main platform. There seemed to be a lot of activity around the drain covers at the edge of the enclosure, where an officer with a scarlet crest on his helmet strode up and down barking orders.

Alexis spotted Kichesias waiting quietly with their mule at the edge of the main road, and his heart lifted with the relief and pleasure he always felt upon seeing his friend. Kichesias was the perfect model of Greek youth with good looks and an athletic body that made Alexis seem puny. His golden curls gleamed in the sun, and his eyes were the deep turquoise of the sea on a summer's day. But his lower lip was scabby because he bit it such a lot, and his shoulders hunched as if he were permanently afraid of being hit.

"What's happening?" Alexis asked, hurrying across. "Where's Neaera?"

Kichesias pointed silently to the Mausoleum.

Alexis searched the enclosure. Although he knew what he was looking for, it took him several moments to spot Neaera up on the lowest tier of the Mausoleum, standing among the life-sized statues. She'd chosen the sheltered side so her cloak didn't blow in the wind, and she was so perfectly still that even the soldier working his way around that tier passed her without a pause.

Alexis experienced a pang of unlooked-for memory. He frowned at his stepmother. "What's she doing in there? I thought she wanted to leave before they shut the city gates? Down in the agora, they're saying there's going to be a siege. We ought to hurry, if we're going at all."

Kichesias chewed his lip some more. "She never tells me anything, you know that. But she went a bit pale when she saw the soldiers poking about in the drains." He glanced around and lowered his voice. "Maybe it's because she's... you know."

Alexis watched Neaera uncertainly. Had she decided that it wouldn't, after all, be a good idea to travel with the Macedonian army so close? He didn't know whether to be relieved or not.

"That's past," he said firmly. "She's flesh and blood now. It doesn't matter to her any more what happens to the Mausoleum. What are the soldiers doing in there, anyway? Are there Macedonians inside?"

He looked anxiously over his shoulder, but the dust and noise of the battle still seemed to be safely outside the eastern wall. From their vantage at the Crossroads, part of the Macedonian army was visible on the hill beyond the city – Alexis could see the glitter of their long pikes and a lone horseman silhouetted against the sky behind them. Was that General Alexander himself, overseeing his troops? The wall hid the actual fighting, so it was difficult to tell how the battle was going. His father would never have let Neaera take them outside the walls at a time like this.

"Is it true they're knocking down our walls?" Kichesias asked, interrupting his memories.

"Who told you that?" Alexis said.

Kichesias pointed to a muddy figure stroking the neck of their mule. "She did."

With a start, Alexis recognized the girl from the market place. "You followed me!" he said, annoyed.

She turned a dazzling smile towards him. "Of course I followed you! I lost my cap when that brute of a soldier grabbed me, didn't I? Girls on their own in the streets attract unwelcome attention. I needed a brother."

"I'm not your brother!" Alexis spluttered, still distracted. "Haven't you a home to go to?" He studied her more carefully. She was older than he'd first thought – but that was when he'd thought she was a boy. She was slim, dark-eyed, maybe even pretty, though it was hard to tell under all the mud.

Kichesias was gazing at her with a soft look in his eye. "She looks a bit like our statue," he whispered. "Alex, you didn't—?"

"No, I did not!" Alexis scowled at the girl. "You shouldn't be out on your own. How come you got so muddy, anyway?"

The girl kept stroking the mule, still smiling. "Fell in the ditch, didn't I? The Macedonians really *did* knock down part of the wall, and they knocked me down with it." She laughed a little. "I was a bit scared, to tell you the truth. But it was exciting! Much better than being locked up in the Palace with all those stupid women. Anyway, I got back into the city easily enough. The soldiers out there were all too busy fighting and running about to notice me."

"You live in the Palace?" Kichesias breathed, clearly impressed. "Are you one of the royal slaves? What's your name?"

The girl gave him an amused look and treated them both to another dazzling smile. "If you tell me the name of your mule, I'll tell you mine." She kissed the animal's neck and fondled its long ears. "He's such a darling. I've got ponies of my own in the Palace stables, of course, but I'm not allowed to groom them, and they're no fun to ride because they're so expensive and spoilt. I like mules. They're so sensible."

Alexis sighed. "He hasn't got a name. We just call him The Mule."

The girl looked shocked. "Hasn't got a name? Oh, you poor thing!" She flung her arms around the surprised creature's neck and hugged it. "I'm going to call you Pan, after the wild goat-god, because there's such panic in the city today."

"I like that," Kichesias said. "Hello, Pan."

"Oh, for the gods' sake, you two!" Alexis said, the tension of the past few hours making him irritable. "Haven't you noticed we're being attacked? There are soldiers everywhere. My stepmother wants to take us on a pilgrimage to Mount Tmolus, even though I don't know how we're going to get out of the city alive with the Macedonians at the gates. Something's going on in the Mausoleum, and you two are just standing there like... like it's a festival or something, naming stupid *mules*!"

Immediately, Kichesias was serious again. Biting his lip, he touched Alexis's arm. "I know things are crazy today, Alex. But you have to admit it's about time Pan had a proper name."

Alexis frowned at his friend. Then he saw the funny side. He sighed and patted the mule. "Maybe you're right. I'm sorry, Pan. It's not your fault the Macedonians are attacking us, is it?"

The girl was watching them, still amused. "You don't look much like brothers, so I guess that means you're friends?" she said. "You're not fancy-boys, are you? I hate that sort of thing."

Kichesias smiled again. "I'm Lady Neaera's slave," he explained without a trace of bitterness. "She's Alexis's stepmother – his real mother died giving birth to him."

"Ah!" The girl seemed pleased to hear they weren't the sort of boys who preferred men to girls. She turned to Alexis. "And what does your father do?"

"My father's a sculptor," Alexis said with pride. "He was apprenticed to the great Pytheos, who made that chariot up there." He pointed to the gold and white horses on the roof of the Mausoleum.

The girl whistled, impressed. "Then your father must be very good! I'll have to ask Daddy to hire him to make something for my Collection."

Alexis grimaced, and the girl frowned. "What did I say?"

"Alexis's father isn't here any more," Kichesias said gently. "He vanished five years ago and no one's seen him since."

"Vanished?" The girl's dark eyes widened. "How exciting! Is that why you're going on a pilgrimage? To find him?"

"It's none of your business," Alexis muttered. "Go

back to your palace, or wherever you live, and leave us alone. We've got things to do."

The girl pulled a muddy face at him. "I'll go back when I'm ready. You haven't even introduced yourselves properly yet." She looked thoughtfully at Alexis. "But you're Alex... I assume that's short for Alexander, like the Macedonian General? What's your friend called?"

"It's *Alexis*, not Alexander," Alexis snapped. "And our names are none of your business, either."

"I'm Kichesias," Kichesias said quickly.

"I see." The girl narrowed her eyes at them. "I could make enquiries about your father, Alex, if you're nice to me. Get Daddy to put someone on the case. Men sometimes go a bit crazy, you know – forget their families and turn up in the strangest places. The Palace women say it happens all the time."

Alexis's head spun. He shoved the girl away from Pan and angrily began to transfer his stolen food into the mule's panniers. "You leave my father out of this! He wasn't crazy. He was kind and good and gentle and the best sculptor in our street. Something serious must have happened to keep him away from home so long."

"Alex..." murmured Kichesias. "It's not her fault. She doesn't know what happened, does she? Besides, if she really does live in the Palace, maybe she can help."

"It's obvious she's lying," Alexis said. "No girl from the Palace goes about covered in mud! Go home," he told the girl through gritted teeth. "And stop poking your nose into things you can't possibly understand. As soon as we find out what's going on in the Mausoleum, we're leaving, so you won't be able to pretend I'm your brother any more. I wouldn't want to be your brother, anyway. I don't like liars."

He meant his words to hurt her as much as her comments about his father had hurt him. But instead of being upset, the girl straightened her shoulders and gave them a cool, haughty look. Despite the mud, she suddenly looked exactly like the Palace-dweller she claimed to be.

"General Memnon is checking security," she informed them. "The Mausoleum drains are more than big enough to hide Macedonian soldiers. If your father studied under Pytheos, I'd have thought you'd know that. And since your friend was polite enough to ask, my name's Phoebe. Daddy's Satrap of Caria now, and King Maussollos was Mummy's uncle, which makes Daddy King, whatever Great-aunt Ada might say. Daddy and General Memnon are good friends, so you'd best watch your mouth, Alex-who-is-not-Alexander." She smiled sweetly at them both.

Kichesias's jaw dropped.

Alexis stared at Phoebe in equal disbelief. "You expect us to believe you're some kind of *princess*?"

"The daughter of the King and Queen of Caria is usually called a princess, yes." Phoebe was still smiling, enjoying their shock.

Kichesias went all shy, blushing when she looked his way. Alexis shook his head. "I don't believe you."

"Believe what you will. Or shall I get old Memnon to come out of there and tell you who I am?"

"That's General Memnon himself in there?" Alexis turned his attention back to the scarlet-crested officer in the Mausoleum enclosure, worried again.

Phoebe laughed. "Not so sure of yourself now, are you, Alex? But don't worry, I don't tell on my friends. I'll be in as much trouble as you will if he finds me out here all covered in mud talking to a couple of rude craftsmen's apprentices."

Alexis opened his mouth and shut it again, not sure whether he should be flattered a princess counted them as friends, or insulted by what she'd called them. Kichesias merely gazed at Phoebe with that infuriating adoration in his eyes.

They'd been so distracted by the girl, they'd almost forgotten Neaera. Her sudden appearance in the road outside the Mausoleum made them jump. Ignoring the mud-covered Phoebe, she seized Pan's halter rope and dragged the animal up the hill towards the Old Gate, which was the most direct route off the Carian peninsula for foot traffic. She didn't even stop to check Alexis had purchased the right sort of supplies. "Come on, you two!" she snapped, "We're leaving right away!"

Alexis and Kichesias hurried obediently after her. Alexis cast a warning glance back at Phoebe, but the girl didn't try to follow them. She was staring at the Mausoleum entrance, where General Memnon and his soldiers bent over something they had dragged out of the drains. Both hands were over her mouth, and her dark eyes were wide.

They've found a Macedonian! Alexis thought with a pang of terror, catching a glimpse of legs and arms in the midst of the soldiers. *The enemy is inside the city already!*

But the man the soldiers laid on the white marble of the Mausoleum courtyard had not been alive in a very long time. His limbs were stiff, and his clothes had rotted away. Rats had eaten some of his toes and nibbled at his fingertips. Most of his body, however, was coated in a strange, black crystalline substance that the scavengers had obviously found hard going, so his features were still recognizable.

Alexis froze in the middle of the road, as rigid as the dead man lying below. He couldn't feel his legs.

"What's wrong?" Kichesias stopped, too. "Oh, how horrible! Is he dead? What's that stuff on his skin? It looks almost like—"

"Don't look! Keep going!" Neaera dropped Pan's rope so she could seize both their wrists, one in each hand. As she hauled them up the hill, Alexis's legs gave way. Kichesias went with her for a few strides then, seeing Alexis's distress, dug in his heels. Despite Neaera's unusual strength, she could not move them both.

"Please stop, Lady," Kichesias's voice came from a long way off. "I think Alex is going to be sick."

The mess ended up over Neaera's sandals. She let go of Alexis in disgust. The white marble around him sparkled fiercely and began to go dark at the edges. He couldn't take his eyes from the crystallized corpse the soldiers had pulled out of the drains. He crawled back down the hill and threw himself on top of it, a great cry rising inside him.

"*Father!*" he sobbed. "Live, Father, *live!*"

But the magic only worked on statues. There was a shocked silence. Then people began to whisper. "What's he doing?" ... "Someone get the boy away from there." ... "Ugh, it's filthy, it must have been down there years..."

A soldier lifted Alexis off the corpse and passed him into Neaera's keeping.

"No," he protested as his stepmother dragged him back up the hill. "Let me go! Father's dead... that's why he didn't come back... someone killed him..."

"Don't be so silly!" Neaera snapped, shaking him. "That body could be anyone's. Behave! Everyone's looking at us."

Alexis wanted to tell her that it *was* his father's body, but he couldn't get his breath. His heart was beating far too fast, and there was a rushing noise in his ears. Even as Kichesias hurried forward to catch him, the world slid away.

Chapter 3

MURDER

*MAUSSOLLOS: I was handsome
and tall and mighty in war.*

Alexis was having a terrifying dream. He was seven years old, tucked up in bed in the smallest of his family's rooms in the sculptors' court, and a woman was screaming in the street beneath his window. The blanket Neaera had wrapped around him was too thick and tight. It trapped his arms and legs and lay heavily across his throat so he couldn't raise his head. His whole body was drenched in sweat. He wanted to go to the window and look out, but was afraid of what he might see.

His father and Neaera were both out. They'd been arguing earlier. Diogenes had just completed a commission for a rich Persian who lived on the Hill, and had walked out halfway through the argument saying he was going to collect his fee. Neaera had stayed to put

31

Alexis to bed, but left the house shortly afterwards. They'd been gone ages.

Alexis fought off the blanket and crept to the window. The narrow sculptors' street was bathed in silver moonlight. Neaera stood in the middle of it, sobbing that she'd been attacked. She was splattered in blood, her chiton had been ripped to shreds, and her hair frizzed wildly out of the demure scarf she'd taken to wearing since his father had married her. Their bleary-eyed neighbours emerged from their houses and gathered around her, the women trying to calm Neaera, the men shaking their heads and muttering. Someone put a blanket around Neaera's shoulders, and one of the men hurried off to fetch the authorities.

"He just went mad!" Neaera sobbed. "He had a dagger, and I swear he'd have killed me if I hadn't run away... I should never have married him... I knew there was something strange about him right from the start, the way he always went on about statues having spirits... all I did was follow him to the Mausoleum and say something about his precious work... Oh, gods, if you find him, keep him away from me! I never want to see him again! Poor little Alexis, having a father like that... I'll have to look after the boy now. I'm all he's got."

She sounded really upset, tearing at her hair as she spoke, her words interrupted by wild sobs. But when the other women helped her into the house, she looked up at Alexis's window, and her lips curved into the cruel smile she reserved for when they were alone.

"She was acting!" Alexis cried, sensing someone else in the room with him. "She wanted to get rid of Father so she could take me to Mount Tmolus! Father would never have attacked her like that! He was good and kind. He wouldn't do anything horrible to her, he just wouldn't..."

"Shh, Alex." Kichesias's voice steadied him. "It's only a dream. A bad dream, that's all. Get back into bed. Lady Neaera says you've got a fever. She purchased a special potion from the physician for you. I'll pour you another dose, shall I? It's supposed to help you sleep. Come on, Alex, calm down..."

His friend's words helped banish the final echoes of the nightmare. A strong, cool arm lifted Alexis's head, and something bumped his lips. Sweet liquid bubbled on his tongue. He almost swallowed. Then he remembered what he'd seen at the Mausoleum before he'd fainted – the sight which must have brought on his dream.

He spat out the potion and knocked the cup away.

"No! I don't want to sleep! Father's dead, and I think I know what happened... oh, Kichesias, I've been so *stupid*."

"Lady Neaera said the potion will stop your nightmares." His friend sounded worried. "Please, Alexis. If you don't drink it, she'll only punish us. It's for the best, really it is. You were raving, shouting all sorts of things in your sleep. The neighbours complained."

Alexis focused on his friend's face. The scabs on

Kichesias's lower lip were bleeding again. He was chewing them as he stared at the door, as if expecting Neaera to march in at any moment. Alexis realized he was lying on the floor, twisted in the same old blanket that had covered his bed since childhood. But it was daylight outside, not night, and this time he wasn't alone.

"What happened?" he asked. "Why are we still at home?"

Kichesias smiled tightly. "You fainted. Lady Neaera said it was the shock of seeing the dead man. She was still determined to take you on the pilgrimage, but the Gate was shut and the guards wouldn't let us through. Lady Neaera was furious. She couldn't do much about it, though – there were too many soldiers around."

Alexis's sweat was cooling in the breeze coming through the window. He sat shakily on the edge of the bed and took deep breaths, trying to think.

"Where is she?" he said.

"Out." Kichesias glanced at the door again, still chewing his lip. "Don't ask me where. She didn't say. She just told me to stay here and make sure you drank the potion, and not to speak to anyone. No one's supposed to go out without good reason – there are soldiers all over the streets. You were right, we're under siege. It's official now. We have to ration our food, and no one's allowed to leave the city. No one can get in, either, so we don't really know what's going on. The Macedonians didn't manage to get through the wall, but they've made camp up in the hills, and everyone's saying there's going to be another attack before long."

"Then Neaera can't flee the city. Good." Alexis tried to stand, but had to sit down again as the room swayed horribly around him. He shook his head but it only made the swaying worse. "What's in that stuff? Is she trying to poison me?"

"It's only a sleeping potion." Kichesias frowned. "You know she can't really hurt you, Alex. That's the way the magic works."

Alexis sighed. The magic, always the magic. "How long have I been asleep?"

"Three days, on and off."

"*Three days!*" No wonder he was feeling so weak. He tried to stand again. "Quick, Kichesias, help me dress! We have to tell the authorities what Neaera did, before she starts spreading her lies again."

"Tell them what?" His friend looked puzzled as he helped Alexis into his day-tunic.

"That I think she murdered my father," Alexis said through the folds of linen, a coldness coming over him. "That must be why she was so worried when General Memnon's men started checking the drains. She knew they'd find his body in there, because she was the one who put it there."

Kichesias stared at him. "Alex," he said gently. "I know it must have been a terrible shock for you to see that man they dragged out of the drain. But Lady Neaera said it wasn't your father."

Alexis closed his eyes. "Of course she'd say that. My father's dead, Kichesias. I know it now. It was definitely him. I think I know when she did it, too. Five years ago, the night she came back from the Mausoleum screaming that he'd attacked her. You weren't here then. You didn't see how pleased she looked after everyone left. I knew she was lying about the attack. I just didn't realize how much."

He felt sick all over again as the image of his father's crystallized corpse formed behind his eyes. What had Neaera done to him, to make his body look like that?

"The face was a bit disfigured," Kichesias said after another pause. "Maybe you just thought you saw your father's body because we were talking about him earlier? The physician who made up your potion said the human brain plays funny tricks like that sometimes."

"I know what I saw," Alexis said stubbornly. "Neaera was covered in human blood when she came back from the Mausoleum that night. Statue blood is black, isn't it? So it wasn't hers. She must have murdered Father and stuffed his body into that drain so no one would find him. She obviously spread about the story that he'd attacked her and run off so everyone would search for him elsewhere. Oh, she's clever all right! Even I half believed her! I never believed Father would attack her for no reason, but I knew how she never respected him like women are supposed to. They had an argument that night. I thought maybe he'd tried to make her come home, and she'd run off and got herself attacked, and afterwards he'd been too scared to come back in case he really did get in trouble for attacking her. I kept hoping he'd come home eventually when things died down. All these years I've been looking for him, and the whole time his body was lying there in the drains..." He choked. "Oh gods, Kichesias, why did she have to kill him? I hate her! We can't let her get away with it."

Kichesias frowned. "All right... assuming that body was your father's, there's still no proof Lady Neaera killed him. More likely, they both got attacked by a gang of ruffians and Lady Neaera just took advantage of the situation. After all, if people had known your father was dead and she was a widow, they'd have made her marry someone else. The way I see it, with her story she got to stay in Diogenes' house with no man to tell her what to do."

"That's stupid—" But Alexis broke off, wondering if Kichesias could be right. By law, women were not allowed to run households themselves. In the absence of any known living male relations, their neighbour Pasion was officially responsible for Neaera, by virtue of the fact he had taken on Alexis as an apprentice. But it had never been more than an arrangement of convenience, and Pasion had long ago given up trying to control Diogenes' strong-willed wife.

Alexis sat down again to wait for his head to stop spinning. "I'll prove it," he said quietly. "Somehow, I'll prove that body was my father's and Neaera killed him. Then I'll make her pay."

Kichesias sat beside him, chewing his lip again. "Do you think you can?" he asked, just as quietly.

Alexis knew what his friend meant, but he chose to misunderstand the question. "This city has laws, doesn't it? The Macedonians haven't changed that – not yet, anyway. But we'll need another look at that body. I... I want to be sure, and we have to work out how she did it."

Kichesias frowned. "How are we going to do that? We're not allowed out, remember? And Lady Neaera's sure to stop us if she finds out what we're trying to do."

His friend's blue eyes widened as Alexis seized the sleeping potion, took it to Neaera's room, and poured the remains carefully into her amphora of best wine. He shook the amphora and tasted a small sip to check the sweetness wasn't too noticeable. He smiled tightly at Kichesias's questioning expression. "If she can do it to me, I can do it to her. Be ready to move when she gets back – I'll pretend to be asleep again so she doesn't suspect anything. In the meantime, I need something to eat. How rationed are we?"

Silently, Kichesias reached under his sleeping mat and unrolled the cloak he used as a pillow. Some dried figs and a piece of goat's cheese fell out.

"I kept you some of mine," he said. "I couldn't eat much, anyway, with you so sick and all the worry about the Macedonians knocking down our walls." As Alexis forced the food down, still trying to think of a way to get another look at the body from the Mausoleum, his friend glanced at the door and lowered his voice. "What do you think they'll do to us if they capture Halicarnassos? What if they find out about your magic and try to separate us?"

"They won't," Alexis said, only part of his mind on what Kichesias was saying. "We've half the Persian fleet anchored in the bay, and there are thousands of mercenaries in the city who'll fight for General Memnon. What happened to that girl who claimed she was a princess – what's her name, Phoebe? She might be able to get us into the Palace complex. I assume they took the body to the garrison?"

Kichesias's expression brightened. "I think so. But I don't know what happened to Phoebe after they found the body, and she mightn't want to help us. You weren't that polite to her last time we met."

"Then you'll just have to persuade her, won't you? She seems to like you well enough."

Alexis grinned as his friend blushed. He felt slightly better now that the shock of seeing the crystallized corpse was starting to wear off. Maybe Kichesias was right, anyway, and the body the soldiers had pulled out of the Mausoleum drains wasn't his father's. But one way or another, he had to know.

When Neaera finally came home, the potion worked better than they could have hoped. She slammed the door, yelled for Kichesias to bring her some supper, looked in briefly at Alexis's heavily breathing form under the blanket, and retired to her room where she downed the contents of her amphora in one long draught without even stopping to water it first. A few heartbeats later, she was fast asleep on her couch with her head flopped over the edge at an awkward angle and one pale hand trailing across the rug.

Alexis smiled grimly as he checked her breathing. She'd have a stiff neck when she woke. He started to follow Kichesias down to the studio then paused, fighting an urge to go back. He descended another step and stopped again in frustration. If he left his stepmother like that, he'd only be worrying about her all night. Fists clenched, he hurried back up the stairs.

His friend didn't say anything as he helped lift Neaera on to the couch and arranged a pillow under her head, but his gaze rested briefly and sadly on Alexis's face. This was exactly what Kichesias had been referring to earlier, when Alexis had threatened to make Neaera pay for her crime. The statue magic bound them in more ways than one. Could he really bear to see her punished? Could he stand aside and watch her whipped, or forced to drink poison?

He thrust the unsettling thought away and checked up and down the street, before following Kichesias out into the night.

Chapter 4

PALACE

MAUSSOLLOS: I have lying over me in Halicarnassos a vast memorial, outdoing that of any other of the dead.

The starlit streets were eerily quiet. During the three days Alexis had been under the influence of Neaera's sleeping potion, Halicarnassos had settled into its role as a besieged city. There were no loud groups of young men returning from symposium parties, no night fishermen hurrying to cast off their boats; just the flare of torches above the rooftops as sentries patrolled the city walls, and the fierce sound of skirmishes somewhere out in the darkness. Kichesias was worried they would get arrested for breaking the curfew, but Alexis was filled with determination. At last there was something he could do to clear his father's name and, after all the years of uncertainty, it felt good.

They made it to the Royal Quarter unchallenged and crouched together behind a bush, watching the Palace.

"We're never going to get in there without being seen," Kichesias whispered. "They must have increased security because of the siege."

Alexis was starting to think the same thing. The Palace had been built along the waterfront next to the garrison, and the Royal Harbour was separated from the main harbour by marble quays wide enough to support guard towers. The main gates were closed and heavily guarded, the walls nearest to them were protected by a moat, and all the windows he could see were much too high to climb through. On the headland beyond, protecting the sea approach, General Memnon's headquarters was a blaze of light and activity.

"I could try to get closer – maybe break open that side gate," Kichesias offered.

Alexis considered the gate. Fashioned of solid cedarwood set beneath a stone arch, it closed off a path that skirted the Palace and led up to the garrison. Several flights of shadowy steps could be glimpsed beyond, winding their way around the rocky headland. If they got through, they might have a chance of staying out of sight. But the gate was on the far side of the moat. The men guarding the bridge looked alert, and his friend wasn't as good at playing statues as Neaera was.

He shook his head. "No, it's too dangerous." Before he could think about it too much, he pulled Kichesias from behind the bush and marched up to the bridge.

"HALT!" Two soldiers came running across, spears levelled at the boys' chests. "Identify yourselves!"

Alexis took a deep breath. "We're from the Craftsmen's Quarter," he said. "We've important information about the body you found in the Mausoleum."

The men relaxed slightly when they saw the boys were unarmed. They exchanged glances. "What body?" asked the younger of the two, who looked only a few years older than Alexis.

"General Memnon pulled it out of the drains when he was checking security," Alexis explained. "It was covered in some kind of crystal, and we think we know how it happened."

The older man laughed. "Only body in that old tomb is King Maussollos's, and he was cremated. You've got your facts wrong, boy! He'd be ashes by now, not crystal. Don't you know General Memnon's ordered a curfew? You're lucky no one thought you were Macedonian spies. Get on home before we decide to arrest you." He gave them both a gentle prod with his spear.

Alexis frowned. He hadn't counted on the guards not knowing what he was talking about. "But there really was a body! We both saw it. General Memnon must have brought it here. I think it was a murder, but we'll have to see it again to be sure."

Kichesias nodded. "Please sir, it's the truth. Ask Princess Phoebe. She saw it, too."

The young guard looked impressed. "You know the Princess?"

"Yes!" Alexis said, seizing this unexpected opening. "She was there. Ask her where they took it – please."

But the other man grunted, "The Princess is not allowed out of the women's quarters. She can't have been out in the streets. Don't be so stupid."

An officer with grey streaks in his hair, who had been standing on the bridge listening, marched up. He gestured the other two guards aside. "This is no time for adolescent pranks!" he snapped, scowling down at them. "If you don't get on home right now, I'll have to report you. I've quite enough security headaches as it is, with the Macedonians camped outside our gates. The last thing I need is irresponsible youths like you, who seem to think this war is some kind of game, causing trouble. What are your names?" He eyed Kichesias, obviously deciding that because he was the biggest he must be the ringleader. "How old are you, boy?"

Kichesias glanced helplessly at Alexis.

"Come on, speak up! Or have you lost your wits? It's a simple enough question, surely?"

"I don't know," Kichesias whispered, hunching his shoulders like he did when Neaera shouted at him. "Maybe as old as the city, but I can only remember the last four years..."

Alexis gave his hand a warning squeeze. The officer scowled. "Right, that's enough! You'll answer my questions sensibly, or I'll arrest the pair of you as spies, underage or not." He turned to Alexis. "Name?"

"Alexis, son of the sculptor Diogenes, sir. I think my father's body is the one they—"

"And your name?" The officer snapped at Kichesias, cutting Alexis off.

"Kichesias, sir."

"Son of?"

"I d–don't know, sir. I haven't got a father."

"He's our slave," Alexis said quickly, seeing the officer's expression darken. "He'd lost his memory when we got him, which is why he doesn't know how old he is." It was the story they told everyone to avoid awkward questions.

Kichesias's trembling had grown worse. He was chewing his lip again.

"Oh, for Ares' sake!" The officer jerked his head. "Escort these two back where they came from, and make sure whoever's responsible for them knows what they were up to."

Kichesias stiffened as the young guard took hold of his elbow. But the one who had made the Mausoleum joke pulled a face at the officer's back. "Don't worry, lads," he said. "Old Cleon will have forgotten all about you by morning. He's always threatening to report people. Makes him feel like he's doing his job— Hey! Where do you think you're going?"

Since they obviously weren't going to be allowed in the official way, Alexis dodged past the guards and raced for the bridge. Kichesias wrenched his elbow free and followed. They had surprise on their side and made it across before anyone thought to stop them. The guards shouted a warning to the sentries at the main gate, who drew their swords. But when the boys swerved along the Palace wall and headed for the side gate, they didn't bother to chase them. They knew the gate was locked.

Alexis flattened himself against the wall, breathing hard, while Kichesias put his shoulder to the gate. He seemed simply to lean against the wood. But Alexis knew how much effort his friend was putting into it, for his face assumed the frozen expression it had displayed the first time he'd seen him, standing under the vines in the public park. With a massive CRACK followed by a loud splintering noise, the gate gave way. Kichesias disappeared after it, sprawling in a heap of broken planks and powdered wood. He scrambled up, and Alexis leapt through after him. They paused only long enough to throw the splintered pieces of the gate back into the gap to slow the guards. Then they were racing along the path into the shadow of the headland.

By the time the guards had cleared the gateway and clambered over the debris, Alexis and Kichesias were inside the garrison, Kichesias having broken down the first door they came to. As the sounds of pursuit faded, they stopped to catch their breath and grinned at each other.

"Well, we got in," Alexis said, bending over a stitch in his side, panting.

Kichesias looked round at the flickering torchlight. "Now we just have to find the body and get out again – do you suppose Officer Cleon will leave that gate open for us?"

They stopped laughing abruptly as the seriousness of their situation hit them.

"We'll get out another way," Alexis said, trying to sound more confident than he felt. "Come on."

They ventured deeper into the garrison, choosing turnings at random and praying they wouldn't meet any soldiers. As they went, Alexis tried to think where General Memnon might keep a crystallized corpse. The garrison was a lot bigger than he'd imagined, a real maze of torchlit tunnels and spiralling stairs. No windows, of course – they were deep in the rock of the headland. The walls were getting wetter, and he had a horrible feeling they'd made a mistake. Eventually they came to some dark steps that spiralled downwards. A rotten smell rose from the depths, and – oddly – they heard the echo of water against wood.

They crept down, wary of the torchlight that flickered below. The strangest sight met their eyes. Scraping along an underground canal that crossed the bottom of the steps was a full-sized warship, its masts almost touching the rocky roof. The ship was being hauled along on ropes pulled by two teams of barefoot slaves.

"All those stories about the King's secret harbour must be true!" Alexis breathed. It was too good an opportunity to miss. They crouched on the steps until the slave teams had passed, then jumped aboard and hid under the folded sails.

The slow, creaking journey gave Alexis plenty of time to worry about what might happen if one of the slaves had seen them creep aboard and decided to report them. But it seemed no one had noticed. Finally, the ship stopped moving, the shouts and tramp of feet across the deck faded, and all went quiet. They counted to a hundred before they dared lift the sails to peer out.

Their ship was moored in a grotto full of reflected ripples, surrounded by several more unmanned warships with folded sails and neatly-stacked oars. Grey light filtered down through ventilation holes high overhead, and vast cedarwood struts rose out of the water like trees, holding up the roof.

Kichesias gazed round in amazement. "I think this was a bad idea, Alex," he whispered. "We'll be in real trouble if we're caught in here."

Alexis had been thinking the same thing, and the daylight above reminded him of how much more trouble they would be in if they didn't get home before Neaera woke up. They had to find that body, and quickly.

He led the way across a quay of green marble, every nerve prickling. Surely there would be guards in such a place? Or did the King think his underground harbour so secret as to be safe from intruders? From the quay, polished green steps ascended through an archway into a vast hall. Marble benches were arranged between the columns around its edge, shaded by potted palms and exotic ferns. Reflected light from the underground harbour cast ripples across the floor, adding to the illusion of an indoor garden.

They were halfway across the hall before they realized they weren't alone. A man with dark Persian skin, wearing a plain purple robe and threadbare slippers with upturned toes, was sitting on one of the benches with his head in his hands. Across his lap rested a golden sword with rubies set into a hilt shaped like a lion's head. The blade had been carved with the old Carian script and shimmered eerily in the green light. Scarlet tassels dangled from the lion's neck over the man's knees to brush the floor.

The Persian blinked at Alexis and Kichesias in confusion, while they slithered to a halt and stared back at him, their hearts pounding. He recovered quicker than they did, grasped the sword in both hands and blocked their way with the blade raised threateningly. "Who are you?" he demanded. "What are you doing down here?"

Alexis froze, his eyes on that golden blade, desperately trying to think up an excuse. But all he could think was, *Gold, it's gold...* Somehow, he had to find a way to change that sword into a less dangerous substance before the Persian tried to use it on Kichesias. At his side, Kichesias froze too, playing the statue game. But since they'd been caught halfway across the empty floor, it was a pathetic attempt at concealment. His friend's curls were full of splinters from the gate he'd broken, and both he and Alexis had picked up slimy marks on their clothes from the tunnel walls.

"Please, sir!" Alexis said desperately, still eyeing that golden sword. "Don't call the guard. We're..." What could two scruffy boys possibly be doing in the secret harbour of the Royal Palace so early in the morning? "...cleaning the ships," he finished lamely.

The Persian frowned. "Cleaning my ships?" he repeated, taking in their dishevelled appearance. "Are you new slaves? I don't remember giving an order for anyone to clean my private fleet."

Alexis blinked. *My private fleet*. He'd assumed this man was some minor noble. He was dressed quite casually for a Persian, and his beard wasn't even oiled. He had no servants or slaves attending him, not even a guard, and the way he'd been sitting when they first saw him suggested he was in some kind of trouble. But there was the valuable sword... Alexis had a sudden, interesting thought. Maybe the Persian had stolen it and shouldn't be down here, either?

Before he could explore this further, a soldier hurried into the hall and saluted smartly. "Your Excellency, forgive me! I know you asked not to be disturbed, but there has been a minor breach of security and—" His eyes widened as he caught sight of Alexis and Kichesias. "These are the very boys! Thank Ares you caught them before they got any further!"

Alexis's heart sank as he recognized Officer Cleon, the man who had interrogated them at the main gate. As he wondered whether to run or try to bluff it out, Cleon clapped his hands and two guards with the Carian Royal Lion embroidered on their tunics hurried in.

"I'm sorry, Your Excellency," he continued. "I've no idea how these boys found your secret harbour. I apologize for putting you in such grave personal danger. I thought they were playing a stupid prank, but now I fear their intentions are more serious. They'll be properly interrogated, you can be sure of that. If they're Macedonian spies, we'll find out soon enough." He gestured curtly to the guards.

Kichesias paled. Alexis tensed as the guards moved towards them. The Persian's sword had lowered. If he moved fast, he might be able to touch it before the guards seized them. But even as he was readying himself for this desperate act, a slender figure emerged from behind the ferns and called, "No, Daddy! Let them go!"

Alexis relaxed slightly, relieved he wouldn't have to put his magic to the test. It was Phoebe. He wondered how long she had been watching them.

"Princess Phoebe!" Officer Cleon exclaimed, taken aback. "What are you doing down here?" He looked at the King for an explanation. The guards glanced at each other in confusion. Kichesias actually smiled.

Alexis had to admit the Princess looked quite impressive. She was a lot cleaner than the last time they'd seen her. Her dark hair tumbled down her back in oiled ringlets threaded with tiny rubies. She wore a long, floating skirt of crimson silk spangled with gold and a little coat of Persian beads over the top. Her feet were bare, but her toenails were painted crimson to match her clothes. Her eyes had been carefully outlined with kohl, making them seem huge.

The King – there was no question now that Phoebe had been telling the truth about being a princess – seemed equally surprised by his daughter's appearance. But he drew her protectively under his arm and pushed a dark curl behind her ear. "You shouldn't be here, Phoebe," he said gently. "Let these men do their job. They have to find out if these boys are Macedonian spies."

Phoebe wriggled out from under his arm and gave Alexis a sideways look. "They're not spies, Daddy! I know them." She addressed the guards in the same haughty tone she'd used on Alexis at the Mausoleum. "Return to your posts! These boys have come to help me clean my Monster Collection."

The guards glanced uncertainly at the King. Taking advantage of their hesitation, Phoebe grasped Alexis's hand and pulled him and Kichesias firmly across the hall.

Cleon scowled after them. "The blond boy is dangerous, Excellency. He tore down a locked and barred cedarwood gate with his bare hands!"

The King frowned at Kichesias. "Is this true?"

Kichesias licked his scabbed lip and bowed his head. "I'm sorry for damaging your gate, sir, but it was locked and Officer Cleon wouldn't let us in."

Unexpectedly, the King chuckled. "Wouldn't let you in, huh?" He turned to Cleon. "You tried to keep out the boys my daughter had sent for? Why?"

"They didn't say anything about helping the Princess, Excellency," Cleon said, flushing. "They were going on about some body that was supposed to have been fished out of the Mausoleum drains. I haven't had time to check with General Memnon, but—"

The King laughed. "Then they spoke the truth! I gave the horrible thing to Phoebe for her Collection. Memnon's got quite enough to bother him, without worrying about centuries' old corpses. It was obviously a failed mummification experiment someone stuffed down the tunnels way back before Halicarnassos was built. Probably got washed into the drains by one of the summer storms."

"It wasn't an experiment, sir!" Alexis said, seeing his chance. "You have to let me see it... I mean..." He glanced at Phoebe, who was smiling encouragement, and remembered what she'd said about them coming to clean her Collection. "We must clean it at once! It's bound to be filthy if it's come out of the drains. I'm sorry we broke your gate, Officer Cleon, but we knew the Princess wanted her new exhibit cleaned right away. Only we went through the wrong door, and we got lost. I promise we won't tell anyone about the secret harbour."

Cleon shook his head. "This boy is just as dangerous as his friend. He has the serpent's sly tongue. He's obviously lying to save his own skin. Your Excellency, I strongly recommend these boys should be taken to the garrison and—"

Before he could say any more, Phoebe marched up to Alexis and slapped him across the cheek. "I told you I'd send someone to escort you through the Palace!" she said in her haughty princess voice. "Why didn't you wait for the lily-hand like you were supposed to?"

Alexis was filled with fury. That slap had *hurt*.

"Play along, you fool!" Phoebe mouthed, pushing her face close to his. "I'm trying to help, can't you see?"

She stepped back and whirled on the guards. "Well?" she said. "Why are you still here?"

The guards looked at the King, who nodded. "You can go. If my daughter says she sent for these boys, I believe her. I'll be responsible for them now."

Cleon narrowed his eyes at Alexis. But he dared not question the King. With a final frown at Phoebe, he strode stiffly from the hall.

Alexis let out his breath in relief. He looked uncertainly at the King of Caria, still a bit worried about the golden sword. But the King laid the weapon on the bench he'd vacated and spoke sternly to his daughter. "Phoebe, you really mustn't let the guards see you when you leave the women's quarters. It creates a bad impression."

Phoebe lowered her eyes and peered up at him through her kohl-heavy lashes. "I know, Daddy. But I couldn't let them arrest poor Kichesias and Alex, could I? That horrible Cleon was going to *torture* them!"

The King let out a long-suffering sigh and glanced back at the two boys. "You should have made sure the lily-hand was at the gate to meet them, and you should have informed Officer Cleon they were coming. He was only doing his job."

"They were late," Phoebe said, smirking over her shoulder at Alexis. "I did send a lily-hand, but he must have given up waiting for them. So I came myself to see where they'd got to."

The King sighed again. "Phoebe, what am I going to do with you? How long have you been hiding back there?"

"Long enough to see you and Great-aunt Ada, when she came down here earlier!" Phoebe's voice took on a fierce note. "If she helps General Alexander like she said, I'll... I'll set my monsters on her!"

The King glanced at Alexis and Kichesias again. He rested a hand on his daughter's head and steered her across the hall. "Shh, Phoebe, not so loud. I know Ada sees this siege as an opportunity, but she wasn't the one who brought the Macedonian army here. She's got a right to be bitter. Technically, her claim to the throne is stronger than mine. She's King Maussollos's sister, after all, and your mother was only his niece..."

There was more, but they were too far away for their words to be heard clearly, and it was all boring stuff about politics, anyway. Alexis stopped listening, suddenly nervous. "Do you think Phoebe really has got my father's body?" he said. "What's this Monster Collection of hers, anyway?"

Kichesias smiled, still watching the Princess with that soft look in his eye. "I think we're about to find out."

Chapter 5

MONSTERS

*MAUSSOLLOS: Don't you think I have
a right to be proud of these things?*

The Palace was a blur of marble, rich furnishings, Persian
rugs and gilded ornaments, through which Alexis and
Kichesias followed the King and the Princess in nervous
silence. Finally, the King stopped before a pair of heavy
doors guarded by two massive slaves with oiled skin and
lily-flower designs burnt into the palms of their right
hands.

Seeing the Princess, one of the slaves silently opened
the door. Phoebe stood on tiptoe and kissed her father on
the cheek, then beckoned to Alexis and Kichesias and led
them past the impassive guards. The door thudded shut
behind them.

Alexis didn't know what he'd been expecting.
Giggling women, maybe, with pale, sun-starved flesh.

But the corridors and rich furnishings continued on this side of the doors just as they had on the other. The only differences were the lily-branded slaves standing with folded arms at every junction, female voices rather than male ones drifting out of the shadows, and some small children playing chase around the statues. Phoebe cast a furtive look around and hurried them up a small staircase and along an upper corridor until she reached a door locked with a complicated bar mechanism. She produced a key from under her skirt, quickly unlocked the bar, and pushed them through into an unlit hall filled with peculiar silhouettes and an unpleasant, musty smell. She pulled the door closed and applied a rope lock across the handles.

As soon as they were alone, the princess's manner changed. She hitched up her long skirt and grinned broadly at them. "It's all right, we're safe in here. This is my private place. The other women are too scared to come up here. Well? Aren't you going to say thank you?"

Alexis grimaced. "Did you have to slap me back there? That hurt, you know."

Kichesias elbowed him. "Princess Phoebe just rescued us from being interrogated," he hissed. "We're really grateful," he added, smiling at her. "Thank you."

Alexis sighed. "Thank you," he said grudgingly. "But we can't stay long. My stepmother will be wondering where we are. We just want a look at that body, and then we'll leave you in peace."

Phoebe wasn't listening. She moved through the hall,

lighting lamps, while the silhouettes took on three-dimensional forms around her. Kichesias caught his breath. A chill crept over Alexis.

Crouched on the floor of the hall, as if they'd been surprised there and turned to stone, were some of the ugliest statues he'd ever seen. Some had been clumsily painted in lurid colours, with glowing emeralds or amber for eyes and gold-plated claws. Others had what looked like real blood on their teeth and around their snarling lips. There were centaurs – part man and part horse with long, scowling faces and curly beards. There were harpies and sirens, dragons and gryphons, and many more creatures so beloved of the storytellers who entertained the crowds in the agora. Some were as small as his hand, others life-sized, and there was one massive white monstrosity, still raw and unpolished, with the forepart of a lion, a goat's head growing out of its back, and a snake for a tail. Someone – maybe Phoebe – had painted its three pairs of eyes red.

Between the statues were other, more horrible things, the things that were making the smell. Mummified cats, a stuffed peacock with its tail spread permanently in a fan, a mangled thing that might once have been a fish but had frog's legs and human hair sewn on to it... and in pride of place, lying on a bench in the centre of the hall, was the corpse the soldiers had pulled out of the Mausoleum drains. Its dark, crystallized limbs glittered in the light of the lamps that Phoebe was carefully placing around it.

Alexis felt bile rising in his throat. "You can't keep my father's body in here!" he cried, squeezing past Phoebe's monsters and rushing to the bench. He pushed the Princess aside and touched the dark crystal that coated the dead man's limbs. He closed his eyes, fighting another wave of sickness, opened them again and made himself look more carefully.

Back at the Mausoleum, he'd been certain he'd seen his father's features in the twisted, crystallized thing. But the dead man lying on the bench had no face. It had been sliced off, as a sculptor might chisel off a face that wasn't working from a practice stone so that his apprentice could start again.

Alexis took deep breaths, knowing he should be relieved. Kichesias was right. He must have imagined he'd seen his father's face on the body pulled from the drains, because they'd been talking about him before it had been discovered. His mind had been playing tricks on him that day, after all.

"Oh, no!" Kichesias breathed, peering over his shoulder. "Who did that to him?"

"Neaera," Alexis whispered, though he was no longer sure. Without a face, there was no proof. The horrible crystal coating might have been the result of some failed mummification technique, as the King had said. It just looked like Neaera's statue blood, that was all. This thing wasn't his father, never had been...

It was only when Phoebe rushed forwards with a little cry and held her lamp near the sliced-off face, that he realized Kichesias wasn't talking about what had killed the man.

"Someone's been in here!" Phoebe hissed, running her finger across the smooth place where the face should have been. "They've ruined him! They've broken off his face!"

Alexis's stomach fluttered.

"Phoebe," Kichesias said quietly, seeing Alexis's expression. "Alex thought this might be the body of his father. It might still be his father, though I don't see how we can tell for sure, now the face has gone. But it's definitely the body of some poor man. It should be out in the city graveyard, not kept in here among all these..." He glanced around. "...creatures."

Phoebe blinked at him. "You don't like my Collection?"

"No," Alexis said, his initial sickness turning to disgust. "We don't."

She frowned. "But I thought boys liked this sort of thing. That's why I brought you here. Don't you like any of them? The Chimaera took ages to make – it's only just finished." She laid a tender hand on one of the three-headed monstrosity's legs.

Alexis had eyes only for the crystallized body on the bench. "I think they're horrible," he said. "Those dead things are going rotten. I assume you got the cat mummies and the false mermaid-thing at the market? I've seen the merchant who sells them. He's a crook. They're not real. Who did you persuade to make the statues for you? My father would never have made anything so ugly.

I can't believe your mother lets you keep these things in here."

Phoebe's jaw clenched. "I thought you'd be interested! You don't even care that someone's broken in here and damaged my new monster. And for your information, my mother's dead so she never saw any of them!" She slammed down the lamp she was holding and marched to the other side of the room, where she stood with her back to them and her fists clenched.

"Let's go home," Alexis said, wishing they'd never come. "We're wasting our time here. No one's going to believe this is my father's body, not now."

But Kichesias shook his head, biting his lip. "I do. I'm sorry I didn't believe you before, Alex, but there was such a lot of confusion when they dragged it out of the drains, and Lady Neaera wouldn't let me get a good look. But that's definitely statue blood on his skin, so Lady Neaera must have been involved somehow. And whoever broke off his face obviously did it because they were afraid of the body being recognized. Phoebe's a witness. If we can persuade her to help us, we might still be able to prove it's your father, even without a face."

Alexis stared at the corpse, unable to think straight. He glanced uncertainly at Phoebe. "We can't tell her the whole truth," he whispered.

"Why not? She can keep a secret. She's already proved that. She could be really useful to us, Alex. She's got powerful connections."

Alexis frowned. It was true that it would strengthen

61

their case to have a royal witness on their side. "Maybe she'll agree to be a witness anyway," he said. "She doesn't need to know everything."

"Shall I go and ask her?" Kichesias's face brightened.

"No, I'll do it."

Alexis squared his shoulders and approached the Princess. "Phoebe?" he began. "I'm sorry..."

She turned wet eyes towards him. Tears had left dark lines of kohl down her cheeks. He blinked at them in surprise. He hadn't expected her to be the sort of girl who cried.

She sniffed. "I'm sorry, too, Alex. I thought you'd like my monsters. Everything's so boring in here, it sends me crazy! That's why I go out into the city and listen to the storytellers whenever I can. I only want to know what life is like outside the Palace, but no one ever lets me go anywhere, and the storytellers tell such wonderful tales!" Her eyes brightened. "So I ask Daddy to hire the best sculptors for me, and then I get them to make me the creatures and other magical things from the stories – not boring statues of men and women and horses and lions like everyone else has. He doesn't know I go outside the Palace, of course. He thinks I've heard the stories in the women's quarters. He'd have a fit if he knew I actually went into the city." She giggled a little. "Please don't tell him, Alex. He wouldn't believe you, anyway."

Alexis regarded her awkwardly, wondering how to bring up the subject of his father. "Don't worry, I won't tell. But these things aren't real, Phoebe. They're only monsters invented by the storytellers to scare people."

"I've got some nice things in here, too." She pointed at the statue of a winged horse, gleaming white and gold among all the monsters. "See? That's Pegasus, the horse Bellerophon rode when he killed the Chimaera! Isn't he beautiful? And over there is King Gordius's cart with the famous Gordion Knot on the shaft that only kings are supposed to be able to untie – only it's not very good, because the sculptor didn't have a clue what the actual Knot looked like. He said it didn't matter because no one would ever manage to unravel the real one. But it does matter, doesn't it?" Her look challenged him to deny it.

"They're all stories, Phoebe," Alexis said more gently. "Just stories."

She sniffed again and pointed to the cat mummies and the stuffed peacock. "What about them, then?"

Alexis grimaced. "They're dead."

For a moment he thought she was going to cry again. But she nodded and said fiercely, "I know. So are the statues, or as good as. But I don't *want* them to be dead! I want them to come alive and attack Great-aunt Ada and General Alexander and the whole Macedonian army! I want them all to go away and leave Daddy alone. I love him, Alex. I love him so much... General Memnon says that if General Alexander wins, he'll put Daddy in prison, maybe even kill him!" She peered up at Alexis. "Are you *sure* there aren't any creatures like these in the world? You go on pilgrimages to other countries. Don't you ever see any magic?"

Alexis stiffened. "No."

"Phoebe..." Kichesias came across. "We'd like to stay and help you clean your Collection, but we're going to have to go home soon, otherwise we'll be in a lot of trouble with Alex's stepmother. What Alex wanted to ask you is, will you be a witness for us? Say that the body found in the drains did have a face when you first saw it, but that someone broke in and damaged it. Maybe describe it, if you can remember what it looked like?"

Phoebe eyed Alexis sideways. "At a murder trial, you mean?"

Alexis stiffened again. "How do you know I want a murder trial?"

Phoebe smiled. "I'm not stupid! I saw your reaction up at the Mausoleum. You think this body is your father's, and that your stepmother killed him, don't you? Daddy will do anything for me. I could get him to order the Assembly to vote for a trial. But if you want me to help you, you've got to tell me everything." She folded her arms.

"There's really not much to tell," Alexis said. "Neaera never really loved my father. They had an argument one night. My father went out to collect his fee for his latest commission, and she went after him and killed him and hid his body in the Mausoleum drains. Probably stole the money, too."

Phoebe shook her head. "You'll have to do better than

that, Alex-who-is-not-Alexander! How did she do it, to make his body go black? Surely he was stronger than her? Did she use poison?"

"Yes!" Alexis said, seizing on this half-truth. "I don't know what she used, though..."

"Statue blood, maybe?" Phoebe said, raising her eyebrows.

She laughed when Alexis and Kichesias looked at each other in despair. "I've got sharper ears than you think! I heard what you were whispering about over there. So tell me the rest, and then I'll decide whether I'm going to help you. On the other hand, I could tell Daddy you're Macedonian spies after all, and you can stay in the garrison with old Cleon until he drags the truth out of you the hard way."

Kichesias glanced worriedly at the door. "Hurry up, Alex. We've been ages. Lady Neaera's going to be *furious.*"

Alexis sighed. Maybe it would be safer to trust the Princess than make an enemy of her. She seemed to know half of it, anyway. He took a deep breath.

"My stepmother Neaera is a statue," he began. "Or, at least, she was one until I touched her. Now she's like a real person, but with unusual strength and black blood that's poisonous to humans and crystallizes like that stuff on my father's body. You see, I'm descended from King Midas who had the gift of turning everything he touched into gold. That's why Father used to call me Goldenhands. Only, if you remember the story, when

King Midas turned his daughter into gold by accident, he begged the river god on Mount Tmolus to reverse his gift. So although I inherited his magic, it's in reverse. I can't turn things to gold, but I can turn gold into other metals... and I can bring statues of people to life, as long as they have gold on them somewhere. It isn't a very useful gift. My father got a gold coin once as payment for a statue, and I turned it into brass because I thought it wasn't real money unless it looked like all the other coins we had. Neaera was furious. That's why she takes me on pilgrimages to Mount Tmolus so I can wash in the same river King Midas washed in. She hopes the river god will come and reverse my magic back again, so I get the golden touch and she can be rich. That's why I think she killed my father. He would never let her take me there. Now she can do exactly what she likes."

"Except when the city's under siege," Kichesias added.

"Except when the city's under siege," Alexis agreed. "Is that good enough for you, Princess? Will you help us?"

Phoebe's mouth had dropped open. She stared at Alexis's hands and glanced uneasily at Kichesias. Finally she laughed. "You expect me to believe that? It's crazier than the stories they tell in the agora! Try again."

"But it's true, Phoebe," Kichesias said. "Alexis really can change gold and make statues live. He made his stepmother come alive when he was only four years old... and after his father disappeared, he woke me to be his friend."

Phoebe looked uncertainly at Kichesias. "You expect me to believe *you* were a statue?"

Kichesias nodded. "That's why I was strong enough to break down that gate with my bare hands, and that's why we were so scared of your father's sword. Alex didn't tell you, but gold is the only thing in this world that can really hurt us, and unless it was part of our statue when we were woken its presence weakens us. I think it's something to do with the original Midas touch."

Phoebe made a small noise in her throat. "But... you seem so real."

Kichesias smiled. "I am real – at least, I used to be. Sometimes I remember bits of my past life. I think I had an accident in the Royal Park when I was small. There's this dream I get, of horses' hooves and a chariot rushing towards me and my mother screaming... Alex thinks he somehow captured my spirit and put it into this statue-body. Something similar must have happened when he woke Lady Neaera at the Mausoleum."

Phoebe looked at Alexis's hands again, and her eyes narrowed. "All right... prove it."

"What?" Alexis said, caught off-guard.

"I said, prove it! Touch one of *my* statues and make it come alive." She looked at the huge, three-headed Chimaera, then changed her mind and pointed to a small centaur. "Touch that one!"

Alexis backed away from her, a chill coming over him. He should never have told her. He might have known she would want something like this. "Oh no, no Phoebe, you don't understand... it doesn't work like that. I have to really *want* the statue to be alive, I have to get a spirit from somewhere. It was easier when I was younger. You want things badly when you're little, and you believe in the magic without needing to know how it works. I don't think I could do it now, even if I wanted to."

Phoebe frowned, obviously still trying to decide whether they were making it all up to tease her. "When was the last time you tried?"

"Well, I haven't. Not since I woke Kichesias."

"Not even on something that won't come alive? That doesn't need a spirit?"

"No." Alexis thought it best not to mention his thoughts about her father's sword.

"Then try now." She wriggled a golden bracelet off her wrist. "Try it on this!" Before he could protest, she'd jammed the bracelet into his hand and closed his fingers around it. She stared at it with a fierce, hopeful look in her eye.

Alexis shook his head and placed the bracelet on a statue plinth. "It's not something you go around doing for fun, Phoebe! I know that now. I was wrong to wake Neaera. And it wasn't really fair on Kichesias, either. He's not had an easy time of it as Neaera's slave." He glanced at his friend. "I'm glad I woke him, though."

He and Kichesias exchanged a smile, which Phoebe must have mistaken for them making fun of her. She snatched up her bracelet and gave them a furious look.

"You're just like all the other boys! You think that

because I'm a girl, I'm stupid! Go home to your stepmother, then. Have a good laugh at me. But don't try coming back here. I'll not save you from Cleon next time. I'll tell a slave to show you out."

She marched to the door, wrenched it open, and called something in Persian. One of the big lily-hands came running. He looked impassively at Alexis and Kichesias as the Princess explained what she wanted him to do. When she'd finished giving the slave his orders, Phoebe stiffly turned her back and disappeared into the shadows of her Collection. Alexis stared after her, rather relieved she hadn't believed him. Kichesias sighed like someone who has just lost something.

The slave escorted them silently out of the women's quarters and through the maze of corridors to a side door that opened on to an unexpected blaze of sunlight. The guard on duty at the door gave them a strange look when their escort showed him the lily-brand on his palm, but nodded and ushered them out into the street. He ignored their protests that they could find their own way home and insisted upon marching them all the way back to the Craftsmen's Quarter.

Chapter 6

PUNISHMENT

DIOGENES: But, my handsome
Maussollos, the strength and beauty you mention
aren't still with you here.

Neaera was very much awake when Alexis and Kichesias
arrived home. She marched downstairs to meet them in
the studio, where Pasion was working on a statue with a
class of younger apprentices. Master and boys stopped
work and held their breath, chisels poised, watching to
see what would happen.

Alexis braced himself. But when Neaera saw the
Palace guard standing in the doorway, her furious
expression melted into one of motherly concern. She
rushed across and hugged Alexis, squeezing him a little
too hard. "Where have you *been*?" she exclaimed. "I was
so worried! There was a raid up on the Hill last night.
The Macedonians were virtually in the city! I thought

you'd been captured or killed!" She glanced at the guard and sniffed back a theatrical tear. "Thank you for bringing my boys home. I'm very sorry they broke the curfew. You can be sure I'll discipline them. It won't happen again."

The guard nodded. Without a word, he turned on his heel and headed back to the Palace.

When he'd gone, Neaera released Alexis and shook her head sadly at him. "Upstairs," she said in a dangerously quiet tone. "Both of you."

Ignoring the younger boys' sniggers, they obeyed. As they climbed the narrow stairs to the smallest room, Alexis tried to think of a good excuse for them having been out when his stepmother woke. Kichesias followed with hunched shoulders, chewing his lip as if he had already been punished. Below, they heard Pasion mumble something about going easy on them.

"Boys their age can't be allowed to get away with pranks like this!" Neaera snapped back. "The next thing you know, they'll be out murdering people in the streets. Get back to your work, and let me deal with this."

Her tone chilled Alexis. He touched Kichesias's hand. "Don't worry," he whispered. "I won't let her hurt you. If she does, I'll threaten to go to the Assembly and ask for a murder trial. That'll make her stop."

Kichesias shook his head. "The Assembly won't listen to you, Alex. Without Phoebe's help, we've no proof that body is your father's, not with its face gone."

"Neaera doesn't know it was damaged, does she? If we..."

But they didn't have time to get their story straight, because Neaera had reached the top of the stairs. With her in the room as well, there didn't seem to be enough air to go around. Alexis's breath came faster, and Kichesias turned pale when he saw what she was holding.

Balanced between Neaera's fingers was a long, golden pin that glittered in the morning sunlight. It was one of the pins that had fastened the shoulders of her old-fashioned peplos dress, which she'd been wearing eight years ago when Alexis had touched her statue and worked the life magic for the first time. Like the other women of the Craftsmen's Quarter, Neaera wore the simpler modern chiton now, fastened with brooches or ties. But she'd kept her gold pins, and carried them around in a little casket hidden in a special pocket sewn inside her clothes.

"Sit down on the bed, Alex," she ordered. "Kichesias, come over here and hold out your hand."

Kichesias walked across to her as if she had tied an invisible leash around his neck. He closed his eyes as he obeyed her instructions. Alexis clenched his fists. He imagined himself leaping across the room and snatching the golden pin out of his stepmother's hand, turning it to brass or iron so she couldn't hurt his friend. Fear of failure and of the revenge Neaera would take for his disobedience kept him immobile. "No!" he said. "It's not fair!"

Neaera sighed. "Do you really think I enjoy this, Alex? But you put sleeping potion in my wine and sneaked out of the house without telling me where you were going. That was naughty of you, even though the potion didn't have as much effect on my statue-body as you'd obviously hoped. I assume you went to the Palace, since you were escorted back here by a member of the Carian Royal Guard. I dread to think of the gossip that'll spread around the Quarter once those boys Pasion is supposed to be teaching down there get home. Now then, Kichesias, you know how we do this. Keep very still." She grasped the boy's wrist in her stone-like grip and lowered the pin until it pricked the middle of his palm. Kichesias stiffened.

"No!" Alexis yelled, unable to take his eyes off that sharp golden point. "Punish me, not Kichesias! It was my idea to go to the Palace!"

Neaera sighed. "I know it was, Alex. And I have to make sure you don't go there again."

"I won't! I promise. Please don't—"

With a set expression, Neaera pushed the pin carefully through Kichesias's hand until the point came out the other side. The blond boy bit down harder on his lip. He did not make a sound, but Alexis's head spun and he had to cling to the edge of the bed to stop himself from falling. A sharp, sympathetic pain shot through his left hand. The pain dulled to a throbbing ache as Neaera pulled out the pin and released Kichesias.

"I really hate doing that," she said with another sigh, wiping the pin clean on her skirt before returning it to the casket in her pocket. "But you have to understand who's in charge here. Let me see that, Kichesias."

Trembling with reaction now that the operation was over, the boy held out his injured hand. There was very little blood. Neaera examined the wound and picked off a dark, crystalline scab. "Good," she said. "That'll serve to remind you both what happens when you disobey me. Tonight, I'll decide if we need to repeat the process."

"*What?*" Alexis said. That black crystallized blood had reminded him of his father's body, hardening his resolve. But Neaera's words turned him cold. "You've already punished us!"

He looked desperately at his friend, who was cradling his pierced hand. He still didn't know how much the gold pin hurt Kichesias. Maybe not as much as it would hurt someone with a body that had been born human. But Neaera's grey hairs and age creases proved that statues were human enough in other ways, and Kichesias had been alive long enough to feel pain.

"I punished you for going to the Palace," Neaera said. "You still haven't told me why you went there."

"We..." Alexis decided it would be simplest to tell the truth. "We went to ask if we could see the body the soldiers pulled out of the Mausoleum drains."

Neaera raised an eyebrow, as if she hadn't expected him to be so honest. "Why?"

"I thought it might be the body of my father."

"And did you see it?"

There were shouts outside as a troop of Persian bowmen ran past, followed by the faint booms of the Macedonian siege engines starting up again. Another raid, Alexis thought vaguely. It could have been happening in a different world. Kichesias's eyes were closed again. He looked as if he were having trouble staying on his feet.

"Well?" Neaera snapped, losing some of her cool. "Did you?"

Alexis set his jaw. "Yes, we saw it!"

Kichesias's eyes opened. He shook his head. But Alexis was too furious to heed his friend's warning.

"It *was* my father's body," he rushed on. "And it was covered in statue blood, so we know you had something to do with his death. I'm going to ask the Assembly for a murder trial. You're going to pay for what you did."

Neaera frowned. Briefly, she looked unsure. Then her lips tightened and she felt in her pocket again. Alexis got ready to push Kichesias out of the room and run. He didn't care where. Even climbing the city gates and giving themselves up to General Alexander seemed better than staying in the house a moment longer with his stepmother and her peplos pins.

But Neaera brought out her hand empty. She laughed. "Is that so? Do you really think the Assembly is going to concern itself with a murder trial at a time like this? All the wealthy citizens are hiding up in the Acropolis, afraid for their lives. General Memnon is out on the wall fighting in the name of the Persian Emperor Darius, and the Satrap who likes to call himself our King is far too worried about losing his throne to Queen Ada to think about anything else. The Satrap's too much of a coward to overrule the

Assembly, anyway. Besides, where's your proof? Who are your witnesses? Or were you thinking of testifying against me yourself? Maybe you're planning to stand up before half of Halicarnassos and tell everyone how you can touch statues and make them come alive? They'll laugh you right out of the agora!" She chuckled again.

Alexis stared at her. She hadn't even tried to deny it. Deep down, in the place that had prompted him to wake her statue to be his mother, he'd been hoping that he was wrong and Neaera was innocent – or, at least, might offer some explanation for his father's death that would make her part in it accidental. But he no longer found it difficult to believe that this woman standing before him, laughing at them, could kill a man. "I hate you!" he shouted, springing across the room, fists clenched.

Neaera didn't even bother stepping out of range. "Oh, don't be so silly, Alex! You know you can't possibly harm me, and I'm not going to let you touch my gold pins, so you might as well give up that idea right now. Listen, I've brought you some more sleeping potion. I want you to drink it like a good boy and stay in this room today and rest. You haven't been well lately, and you need to recover your strength for the pilgrimage. This siege will be over soon if Ada's plans work out, but before we go I've a few things to take care of." She turned to Kichesias. "You get washed and put on some clean clothes – you can come with me to carry my parasol. I want to look my best, and I don't want to get sunburnt on my way through the streets. I'm visiting a queen, after all." She smiled as she picked up the amphora of sleeping potion, and Alexis had a sudden flash of insight.

"It was you," he whispered. "*You* were in the women's quarters at the Palace! *You* destroyed my father's face so no one would be able to identify the body!" He couldn't keep the bitterness out of his tone. "How did you get in? Pretend to be a statue again?"

Neaera shook her head as she uncorked the amphora. "Queen Ada and I have come to an understanding. She needs a messenger capable of getting past suspicious guards, and I have special gifts in that direction so she was only too happy to employ me. But I don't know why you keep insisting that body is your father's, Alex. It could be any poor man's. Let's face it, Diogenes abandoned us both and he's not coming back. Men do it all the time. You're my responsibility now. As soon as the river god has reversed your magic so you can make gold for me, I'm going to have a lot of influence in Caria – and when that happens, you'd better learn to behave yourself. Drink up!"

Her voice had hardened to match her grip on his arm. He thought about refusing to drink, but saw the way Kichesias was cradling his pierced hand and changed his mind. He took a large mouthful and held it under his tongue while he turned over on the bed. He curled up with his back to Neaera as if he were sulking.

"Swallow it, Alex." Neaera leant over him and pinched his nose, putting her other hand over his mouth until, despite his struggles, the potion went down. She examined what was left in the amphora and smiled. "Good," she said. "I think you've had enough to keep you quiet until we get back."

Alexis glared at her. "You won't get away with murdering my father," he whispered as she drew Kichesias out of the room. "I'll *make* proof and take it to the Assembly. They'll listen to me, you'll see!"

Neaera merely smiled as she shut the door.

Alexis lay quietly, hardly breathing, fighting the heaviness that was creeping over his limbs. "*I'll make proof...*" He'd said it in desperation, but maybe there *was* a way to make the Assembly listen. All he needed was another body – a body convincing enough for the good citizens of Halicarnassos to believe it was his father's. He was unlikely to find another corpse that looked like his father. But what if he were to sculpt a statue of Diogenes as he had appeared five years ago, and use his magic?

It must have been the effect of the potion, because surely he'd never have dreamt up such a horrible plan with a clear head. But the idea, once born, refused to go away, and Alexis couldn't think of anything better now that Phoebe had refused to help them.

Pushing aside his doubts, he lay with his eyes closed until he heard Kichesias and Neaera leave the house. Then he rolled off the bed and stuck his fingers down his throat.

This was a disgusting way to be sick, but it worked.

Most of the potion he'd swallowed came back up as thin green bile. He spat several times, washed out his mouth with water from the hydria, and looked for something to eat. But Neaera must have already used all their rations for that day, or hidden them somewhere. Still hungry, he drank some more water and changed his tunic, examining his plan from all angles. There was quite a lot that could go wrong, but at least he would be doing something. Before he could have second thoughts, he made his way down to the studio on shaky legs.

Pasion was still there, working quietly in the gloom, though the apprentices had gone. Alexis breathed a sigh of relief. He didn't feel up to facing the younger boys' childish taunts just now.

"Master?" he whispered.

The sculptor jumped. "Oh, it's you, Alex." Pasion's black eyes, that always reminded Alexis of a bird's, examined him anxiously. When he didn't find any obvious signs of injury, the sculptor relaxed. "Lady Neaera told me you were resting and wouldn't be helping me today. Not that anyone can concentrate on work with all that racket going on!" He frowned at the door, where dust from the Macedonian barrage floated in the sunlit street like a veil.

The distant booms as the missiles hit the city wall reminded Alexis of the noise waves made when they broke over the quay during a storm. He wondered what would happen if the Macedonians actually did manage to break down their walls and capture Halicarnassos. He thrust the thought away. He had more important things to think about.

He ran a finger over the rough stone block Pasion was working on. "Master, I've a favour to ask."

Pasion looked surprised. "If there's anything I can do for you, Alex, you know you only have to ask. But I'll probably have to check with Lady Neaera."

"It's a surprise," Alexis said quickly. "I want to make a special sculpture. But I don't want anyone else to know about it, not even Kichesias or the other boys. Otherwise they might tell Neaera, and then she'd stop me."

Pasion frowned, white dust trapped in his wrinkles. "What are you up to, Alex?"

Alexis felt bad about lying to his master, who would be in a lot of trouble when Neaera found out he'd helped with the trick. But he remembered how his stepmother had pushed that pin through Kichesias's hand and hardened his heart. "I want to make a statue of my father," he said quietly.

Pasion was silent a moment. Slowly, he nodded. "In that case, I agree it's probably best if Lady Neaera doesn't know. Once it's done, maybe she'll come round to having it in the house. A son should have something to remind him of his father. I've a nice block of red marble here somewhere that's not big enough for a commission. I've been keeping it for the younger ones to practise on, so you needn't worry about the cost. It'd make a nice little bust of your father's head and shoulders..."

"No!" Alexis said, sickened by the very thought. "It has to be life-sized, just like he was on the night he disappeared."

His master blinked. "Life-sized? Are you sure? That's an ambitious undertaking for an apprentice. A bust would be easier."

Alexis knew his master spoke the truth, but a bust or smaller statue wouldn't do for what he had in mind. "Please, Master, help me?" he said. "I know it's a big project, but I'm willing to work hard. I'll work for you during the day, and I'll work on my father's statue at night. And I'll pay you for the marble. This is all I have right now, but I'll get more." He held out the brass coins Neaera had given him to buy food at the market and which the soldiers had refused to take – a hundred years ago, it seemed.

Pasion folded Alexis's fingers back over the coins with a little smile. "You're a good boy, Alex, despite what Lady Neaera says. But have you any idea how much a block of marble that size is worth?"

"I know it's worth a lot. But I'll save up, I promise. I have to make a start right away, though, or I'll never get it done in time."

Pasion chuckled. "A life-sized image of your father sculpted by your own fair hand? That would certainly surprise her Ladyship! When are you thinking of having it finished? If you told Kichesias, he could help you. He's got all the makings of a fine artist. Such a pity he's a slave."

"Kichesias mustn't know what I'm doing," Alexis said. He'd love to have Kichesias's help with the sculpture, but there was too much danger Neaera would find out – the statue magic linked his stepmother and his friend too closely. "It needs to be finished before the next Assembly," he added.

Pasion set down his chisel and laughed. "Before the next Assembly? Then, Alexis son of Diogenes, you'd better hire yourself a team of master sculptors such as Pytheos had to help him with the Mausoleum, because that's the only way you're going to get it finished by then!" He shook his head in amusement.

Alexis still felt a bit dizzy from the potion. When *was* the next Assembly? He realized he had lost track of the days, and he'd never taken much notice of politics, anyway. He began to see the enormity of the task he'd set himself. But Pasion looked thoughtfully around the studio.

"I wonder..." He pulled a cloth from a partly finished sculpture that had been lurking forgotten in a dusty corner and walked around it, studying it from all sides. "Yes, maybe you could work with this. It'll be much easier and quicker than starting from a raw piece of marble, and from what I remember of your father it's about his height and build. You'll need to give it a new face, maybe work on the hands a bit and tidy up the robes. We can take it out to my old master's disused studio so Lady Neaera doesn't realize what you're working on... Things mightn't be too safe out there, mind!" Pasion cautioned as Alexis started to grin. "His studio is very near the wall, and the last I heard, the Macedonians had filled in the ditch and got their siege engines close enough to demolish half his neighbour's house. But the stubborn old man won't move, and since most people have been evacuated from the area it's the perfect place to keep a secret as long as you're not too scared of the missiles."

Alexis threw his arms around the surprised sculptor's neck and hugged him. Before Pasion could change his mind, he fetched Pan and helped his master carefully wrap the statue and lever it into the sturdy wheeled frame they used for transporting heavy blocks of stone. They were both sweating by the time they'd got it properly balanced and harnessed behind the mule, but they managed it without damaging the sculpture. While his master checked the knots that would keep the statue in place during the short journey, Alexis hurried upstairs and grabbed the amphora containing the rest of Neaera's sleeping potion to add to Pan's panniers.

"You'll stand trial," he muttered under his breath to the empty room. "I promise."

Chapter 7

STATUE

DIOGENES: I can't see why your skull should be thought better than mine.

By a stroke of luck, soon after they'd moved the statue, Pasion was called to work on a big commission that took him out of the studio. His apprentices were given a holiday for the duration of the commission, and since Neaera spent more of her time away from home than ever, Alexis was able to escape to the studio beside the wall and work on his project during the day with no questions asked. But sculpting the statue into an exact image of his father proved a lot harder than he had anticipated. Some days, when he tried to remember the details of his father's face, he saw only the face of the crystallized body in Phoebe's Collection – blank and dark, no longer human.

The constant Macedonian barrage didn't help. The

general opinion in the Craftsmen's Quarter was that the siege would be over before winter, despite Queen Ada's open support of General Alexander and her adoption of the Acropolis as a resistance headquarters within the city. But out here, by the wall, the fighting was as fierce as ever. Alexis lowered his chisel as yet another missile landed close by, shaking the disused studio. A trickle of dust fell from the ceiling, adding to the layer already on the floor. He wiped his eyes and blew debris from the folds of his project's marble robes, glad of the excuse to stop work.

He'd taken to calling the statue "his project" because that was the only way he could trick himself into doing any sort of productive work on it. If he called it "the statue", he saw a lump of marble impossible for him, an average apprentice, to sculpt into a living person. Worse, if he called it "his father", he kept stopping to stare at the emerging features until tears came, which he'd rub angrily away only to end up with dust in his eyes that made them red and swollen. He covered his project's face if he was working on the hands or clothing, but the work became harder as the statue neared completion, and he'd already missed that month's Assembly. Although there was probably no more than a couple of days' sculpting left to do, part of him was reluctant to finish because then would come the most difficult part of his plan.

Wiping his tools carefully, Alexis wrapped them in an oiled cloth and hid them under a bench in the corner of the studio next to the tightly stoppered amphora of sleeping potion and a small pot of gold paint he'd rather guiltily stolen from Pasion's supply a few days ago. As he blew the dust off the amphora, he wondered what would happen if the potion didn't work when the time came. He shook his doubts away, adjusted the sheet over his project, and stretched the kinks out of his shoulders with a sigh.

The next Macedonian missile landed with a crash that shook the whole house. Alexis's heart thumped in sudden worry as part of the ceiling fell down, narrowly missing his project's head. He looked up anxiously. The ceiling had been cracked when he first came, and now there was a jagged hole the size of his hand in the middle of it, through which he could see into the room above. He hurried out to the narrow hall and peered up the stairs into the gloom of the upper storey where Pasion's old master lived.

"Are you all right up there?" he called. "Can I get you anything?"

There was no answer. As Alexis hesitated, wondering if he should try to find someone to help him move his project and the old man to a safer place, a third missile whistled over the wall, its shadow darkening the doorway behind him. He felt a whoosh of air, and the whole world seemed to jump as the boulder hit a corner of the roof.

Tiles exploded in the street outside as Alexis flung himself up the stairs. Incredibly, the old sculptor had slept through the whole thing, curled up in his faded blanket. The room smelled of rotting fruit and unwashed clothes. When Alexis rushed in, the old man blinked grumpily at him. "What do you want?"

"Sir, wake up! The Macedonians are breaking through! You have to get out!"

The old sculptor listened a moment to the noise outside, and turned over with a grunt. "Let me alone, boy. Get back to your work and let me sleep. I already told Memnon's lot. This is my house, and I'm not leaving. You youngsters are so jittery. It's only a little war."

Alexis pulled the blanket off him. "Get up, you crazy old man!" he shouted.

The old sculptor tugged the blanket back. "I already told your girlfriend, I'm not moving."

This made Alexis pause. "Girlfriend?" he repeated. "What girl?"

But the old man had gone back to sleep again. Alexis shook his head. Maybe the sculptor had mistaken him for a girl when he'd shouted up the stairs earlier? He was too worried about his project to be embarrassed that his voice had squeaked. The sheet over its head had collected a new layer of debris in his absence. He shook the dust off and tried to manoeuvre the statue to a safer spot, but it was too heavy for him to manage alone. One place was probably as safe as another, anyway, out here. "Protect my father, Great Ares," he muttered under his breath as he turned to leave.

A figure wrapped in an ankle-length cloak blocked his way, brandishing something that looked like a spear.

Alexis froze, his heart pounding. For a horrible moment, he thought it was a Macedonian. Then he realized the intruder was much too slender and short to be a soldier, and that the thing in its hand wasn't a Macedonian pike as he'd first thought, but an oar.

There was an audible intake of breath as the oar lowered. "Alex! You scared me!"

He knew that voice. Alexis's heart sank as the intruder's hood dropped to reveal a shower of dark ringlets and Phoebe ducked inside, shaking dust off her cloak. She propped her oar against the wall and flashed him a smile. Realizing that she must be the "girlfriend" the old man had been talking about, Alexis scowled. The Princess must have been snooping around the house while he'd been working.

"I scared *you*?" he said warily, remembering their last meeting and how it had ended. "I'm working here. You're not even supposed to be outside the Palace, let alone in the Craftsmen's Quarter! What on earth do you think you're doing, Phoebe? The Macedonians are about to break through the wall!"

"Don't be silly," Phoebe said, coming further into the studio and peering curiously around the shadowy interior. "We're in no danger. General Memnon's sent extra troops from the garrison to make the Macedonians move that siege engine back again – I saw them on my way across the harbour. So, where is he, then?" She raised her eyebrows.

Alexis shook his head, exasperated with the Princess,

yet worried for her at the same time. "You mean Kichesias, I suppose? He's not here. Sorry to disappoint you, Princess. Now get back in your boat and row right back where you came from! If the Macedonians catch you out here, I won't be able to help you."

Phoebe giggled. "Don't worry, the Macedonians won't catch me – though that might be more exciting than being shut up in the Palace! Maybe I should surrender myself as a hostage to General Alexander? I hear he wears a gorgon's head on his breast that can turn men to stone. I wonder if I could get hold of it for my Collection?" Seeing Alexis's expression, she sobered. "I'm only joking, silly! I'd never do that to Daddy. The worry would kill him. I didn't mean your friend. I meant where's your father? I thought he'd be upstairs, but that old man up there is much too ancient... or is that why he's such a great secret?" She looked at him slyly.

Alexis made to push past her. "I don't know what you're talking about! That's Pasion's old master up there. My father's not here. He's dead. You've got his body in your Collection remember? You used to have his face as well, until you let my stepmother knock it off. She's working for Queen Ada, you know – they probably plotted the whole thing right under your father's nose! That's why I'm working out here every spare moment at risk to life and limb, making up for your carelessness!"

Fear – for her, for himself, for his project – made him speak more sharply than he'd intended. Phoebe wrapped her arms about herself and said in a little voice, "Don't be like that, Alex, please. I wasn't looking for Kichesias. I was looking for you. I wanted to tell you I'm sorry. After you'd gone, I thought about what you'd said, and you're right. It was horrible of me to keep all those dead things, and they did smell awful. I only collected them to shock the other girls. I get so fed up with them going on about their clothes and their perfumes and their hair all the time, as if that's all there is to worry about in the world! When you'd gone, I got a lily-hand to help me take all the dead things outside, and I got rid of them. I got rid of the body from the Mausoleum, too. We couldn't take it outside the city to the proper graveyard with the Macedonians out there, so we put it in my boat with the other dead creatures and dropped them all overboard. I hope you don't mind. Daddy says sailors sometimes get buried at sea, so it must be all right. I kept my statues, though. They're not real, so it's all right to keep them... isn't it?"

She gave him such a vulnerable, pleading look, Alexis almost felt sorry for her. But all he could think was: *She threw my father's body into the sea!* Now he had no choice but to continue with his plan.

"It's taken me ages to find this place," Phoebe went on. "I couldn't think what you were doing out here at first, so close to the missiles and the fighting. But I think I know why you chose this place. You're hiding him, aren't you? Your father's not dead, after all, and you're hiding him out here." Alexis realized she must have heard him praying to Ares. He flushed, but Phoebe didn't seem to notice and went on, "Why? What are you trying to do? Get your stepmother in trouble? It'd be much easier if you'd let me ask Daddy to help. If your stepmother really is working for Great-aunt Ada, he'll have every reason to order a trial. He's in a far better mood since she moved out of the Palace, and he even comes into the women's quarters sometimes – not that there are many women left in the Palace now. General Memnon's sent his wife and family to Persia for safety, and we don't get any travellers with this stupid siege, so it's really quiet in there and we're all even more bored than before. Daddy wanted me to go to Persia as well, of course, but I'm not going anywhere without him, no matter how dangerous it gets. I'm not afraid of the Macedonians!" She set her jaw and pulled a face at the door. "Please let me do something to help, Alex. I want to make up for how silly I was when you were in the Palace."

A princess wanted to make up to *him*? But she looked so serious, and her guess was so close to the truth, Alexis couldn't help a harsh laugh. Another Macedonian missile landed nearby, but its aim was off, and the sounds of fighting moving away from the wall seemed to confirm Phoebe's story of backup troops. He breathed a little easier. Maybe he wouldn't have to move his project, after all. Except now he might have to move it, anyway, because Phoebe had found his hiding place.

He gripped her wrist and pulled her further into the studio, glancing anxiously up the dark stair. "Shh! Not so loud. The old man might be half-blind, but he's not deaf.

He's already seen you. If he finds out who you are, we'll both be in a lot of trouble."

Phoebe followed his gaze. "I think he's sweet. I bet he won't give us away. Besides, he's asleep." But she lowered her voice to a whisper, too. "He's not your father, then?"

"No, he's not! I told you the truth in the Palace. My father's dead."

Phoebe smiled. "Then who were you asking Ares to protect?"

"No one." But Alexis couldn't stop his eyes straying to the shrouded statue in the corner.

"Aha!" Before he could stop her, Phoebe darted across the room and twitched the sheet aside. She put her head on one side and gave the statue a long, measured look. "So this is what your father looked like... He does look a bit like the dead man they pulled out of the Mausoleum – before the face got knocked off, I mean. This is good, Alex. Really good." She seemed genuinely impressed. "What are you going to do with him when he's finished?"

"None of your business," Alexis muttered. But, deep down, he was pleased she liked the sculpture, because he knew it was the best work he'd ever done.

Another missile hit the city wall, even further away than the last one. If he could get rid of Phoebe, maybe he'd have time to do a bit more work on his project before he had to go home. Neaera was normally out running errands for Queen Ada until well after sunset. Kichesias would be with her as usual, carrying her parasol, and Pasion's commission kept him away from the studio until dark, so no one would miss him.

But getting rid of Phoebe was easier said than done. "If you don't tell me what you're doing, I'll tell your stepmother you sneak out here when she's away," she said, giving him a sly look.

Alexis scowled at her. "You do, and I'll see you don't leave this house. Princesses who go creeping off alone into the middle of a battle can expect to get into trouble."

She laughed. "You wouldn't dare touch me, Alex. Not with your father watching..." Her gaze fell on the pot of gold paint under the bench, and she sucked in her breath. "So *that's* what you're up to! You weren't joking, were you?"

Alexis stiffened, and Phoebe clapped her hands in delight.

"You're going to use your magic on him. You really are! I thought you were just making it up, all that stuff about King Midas and your gift, but you weren't! You really *do* have the magic touch, and you're going to use it to bring your father back to life! By the Chimaera's fiery breath, this is *amazing*..." She stared at his hands again, as if she might see the magic in them if she looked hard enough. "Can I watch?"

"No, you can't watch!" Alexis's head spun. "Get out of here, Phoebe. Get out and go back to your Palace before I throw you out."

He took a menacing step towards her. Phoebe laughed again, a bit more nervously. She stepped backwards and groped for her oar. He snatched it from her and raised it over her head. He only meant to scare her into leaving him alone. He'd never hit a girl, not even one as infuriating as Phoebe. Her yell frightened him more than the missiles had, earlier.

Before he could react, the doorway was darkened by one of the big lily-hands who guarded the women's quarters in the Palace. The slave wrenched the oar from his grip and jammed it across his throat. The next thing Alexis knew, he was on his knees staring at the Princess through sparkling stars.

"Don't hurt him!" Phoebe said, and the pressure of the oar eased slightly.

Alexis could feel the slave's hot, oiled chest against his back. He had no doubt the man could break his neck, should the Princess give the order.

He glared at her, feeling betrayed. "I thought you were alone," he choked past the oar.

"I never said that. You're the one who said it was dangerous out here."

"I wouldn't really have hurt you." He gasped another breath.

She smiled and said something in Persian.

The lily-hand released Alexis and stepped back, but remained in the doorway. Alexis straightened and rubbed his throat. His legs wobbled, forcing him to sit on the bench. Phoebe came to sit beside him.

"I'm sorry about that, Alex," she said. "But I really thought you were going to hit me. You looked so angry. The lily-hand was only doing his job."

Alexis pulled a face. "I don't know why you came here in the first place! You can't be of any help now you've got rid of my father's real body."

She looked hurt. "You were the one who said I shouldn't keep it. And I told you, I wanted to apologize."

"And pry into my secrets."

Her eyes glittered in the gloom. "I guessed right, though, didn't I? I could tell by your face. You really can make statues live, can't you? Don't worry, I can keep a secret."

"You've already ruined it." He scowled at the lily-hand, wondering how much the big slave had heard. He must have been within earshot the whole time, because he'd come as soon as Phoebe called, and she'd given him orders in Greek as well as Persian so he obviously understood both. "It'll be round the whole palace as soon as you get back. Slaves gossip, you know, and since Neaera's so friendly with Queen Ada she's bound to hear something."

"My great-aunt doesn't live in the Palace any more," Phoebe reminded him. "Besides, our lily-hands don't gossip."

"Ha!"

While Alexis tried to think of somewhere else to hide his project, Phoebe crossed to the door, stood on tiptoe and touched the big man's lips. "Open your mouth," she ordered.

The slave obeyed, and Alexis's stomach clenched. The man's tongue had been cut out.

"They have to be silenced before they're allowed in the women's quarters," Phoebe explained. "This way, they can't talk about what they've seen in there. We don't normally allow men inside, not unless they're visiting their wives – you and Kichesias were lucky to be let in." She giggled at his expression. "Don't look like that! I'm not going to order that done to *you*, silly! You're my friend, aren't you?" She came to sit by him again and rested a hand on his arm, challenging him to deny it. "So tell me, Alex. When are you going to do the magic? Will he really be your father when he wakes up, or just look like him? Do you get his spirit back from Hades somehow? Or will you just get any spirit, like when you woke Kichesias and Lady Neaera? Will he recognize you?"

Alexis's head whirled. The questions she was asking were the ones he couldn't answer; the ones he didn't want to think about too much. "It won't matter," he said through gritted teeth.

"Why?" Phoebe's tone was gentler. She squeezed his arm, sending little shivers through him. "I think it does matter to you, Alex. I think it matters a lot. I think if I had the power to make Mummy live again, I'd want her to be exactly the same as she was before. I know she wasn't perfect. She wasn't a very strong queen. She could never stand up to Great-aunt Ada, and sometimes she rowed with Daddy. But if she were anyone else, she wouldn't have been Mummy. I'd want to make her just right. Can you do all that with a lump of marble and some gold paint?"

Alexis shrugged Phoebe's hand off. He couldn't look at her. "Leave me alone," he mumbled. "You don't understand."

"I want to. Please, Alex. I'm sorry. I shouldn't have asked to watch. I'll understand if you don't want me to. Only..." She hesitated. "Only if you really haven't done the magic for a while, perhaps you'd better practise first? You could come and try it out on the Chimaera in my Collection. I painted its claws gold after you'd gone, so your magic should work on it all right. And if the Chimaera really did come to life, Daddy would reward you, because we could use it to scare the Macedonians away. It's got three heads, one for each of the old countries in this region. The lion part is supposed to defend Caria from her enemies."

Alexis laughed. He couldn't help it. "You'll do anything to get your own way, won't you?" he said. "I told you before. You can't just collect magic and lock it in a room in your Palace. It's not a thing you can own. It owns you."

"What do you mean?"

He thrust his hand before her face, making the lily-hand stiffen. "See this hand?" he said. "This is the hand that touched Neaera when she was a statue on the first tier of the Mausoleum when I was four years old. Three years later, she murdered my father and disgraced his name. This is the hand that touched Kichesias, turning him from a beautiful statue in the park into a slave who can't stop biting his lip because he doesn't know when

97

Neaera will next decide to stick a golden pin through his palm. This hand is magic, and I wish it didn't belong to me!"

Phoebe frowned a little. He could tell she didn't really understand. "But you're going to use it for good now, aren't you?" she whispered. "You're going to try to bring your father back to life. Even if he isn't quite like your father used to be, he'll still be a man in your household and look after you all." She paused. "Does your stepmother really stick pins into Kichesias? At least your new father will stop her doing that."

Alexis shook his head. "Is that what you think I'm going to do? Bring Diogenes' statue to life so he can live with us and be married to Neaera? Do you think I could stand that, even if he turned out exactly the same as my father used to be?"

Phoebe's frown deepened. "Then why...?"

"Evidence," Alexis said tightly. "I need a corpse to convince the Assembly that my father's dead, and the one they dug out of the Mausoleum won't convince anyone without a face. Anyway, you've thrown it in the sea, so I've no choice but to make another one."

Phoebe stared at him, her mouth open. "A corpse? Then after you've brought him to life, you're going to have to..."

"Kill him, yes. Well done, Princess, you've worked it out." Alexis crossed the room and readjusted the sheet she'd lifted from his project. "But he'll never have really been alive in the first place, not in this body. He's already dead, so it's not murder. Besides, I'm not the one who's going to kill him. Kichesias will have to do that. I told you the magic owns me – one of the crazy things is that I can't bear to see a statue I've brought to life hurt, not even Neaera. Anyway, as Kichesias told you in the Palace, people who were once statues have tough skin. Gold is the only thing that can really harm them, and the only gold we have in the house apart from Pasion's paint are Neaera's peplos pins, so it'll be difficult. Kichesias should manage it all right, though. He's strong."

Phoebe was shaking her head, tears in her eyes. "Alex, you can't! That's horrible! What if he's really your father? I mean, what if he has your father's spirit, and everything? How can you even *think* of killing him again?"

"He won't have his spirit," Alexis said stubbornly, trying not to think about it. "And he won't feel anything. Statues are confused when they wake up – at least, Neaera and Kichesias were. I've got a potion to make him sleep, and we'll do it straight away. He'll hardly know he was even alive. When his body's cooled, we'll take it up to the next emergency Assembly in the Theatre and tell everyone what Neaera did. I've sculpted him to appear like he did five years ago, and enough people should remember him from back then, so they won't suspect he died more recently. When the Assembly see the corpse, they'll listen to me and put Neaera on trial for murder."

His voice grew harsher as he explained. It was the

first time he'd told anyone his plan, and speaking the words out loud made it seem more sinister. Also, he could see the flaws. Did they have enough gold paint? Was it possible to kill someone with a peplos pin? How were they going to get hold of the pins without Neaera's knowledge, when she always kept them on her person? And, if he needed to touch them in order to steal them, what if he turned the gold to something else before he could stop himself?

Phoebe was still staring at him in horror. "But the crystal on the body they pulled out of the Mausoleum... the statue blood... everyone saw it."

"There'll be plenty of statue blood if Kichesias is using a pin to kill him," Alexis said, sickened by the thought. He looked her in the eye for the first time since he'd admitted what he was going to do. "I don't care what happens to me afterwards, so you can run and tell your precious Daddy everything if you want. Just don't try to stop me bringing Neaera to trial, because she's going to pay for what she did to my father and for all the years she's been hurting Kichesias. It was my fault for waking her, and now I'm going to make things right." He pressed his lips together. "It's no more horrible than you collecting those monsters of yours."

Phoebe sat very still. To his surprise, she didn't try to defend her Collection. "What does Kichesias think of your plan?"

Alexis frowned. "He doesn't know yet."

"Alex! You've got to tell him!"

"It's safer he doesn't know until the last moment. Otherwise, Neaera might find out. She takes him with her all the time now. I think she's treating him as some kind of hostage so I won't try anything against her. I'll tell him when it's time."

Phoebe twisted her hands together. "I still want to help," she said firmly. "When are you going to do it?"

Alexis stared at her in disbelief. "This magic won't be very nice, Phoebe. Believe me, you don't want to watch."

"I know." She swallowed and looked again at the covered statue. "But that's a strong man, or he will be if your magic works on him. I know Kichesias is strong, too, but he's going to have a hard time killing him with a peplos pin. I can borrow Daddy's ceremonial sword. It's pure gold so it'll be a lot quicker and cleaner, and you might need help if your fa— I mean, if your woken statue refuses to drink the sleeping potion. I could bring some lily-hands to help hold him."

Alexis opened his mouth to say absolutely not. But it was true that, once woken, his father – his *project* – would have the same abnormal strength as Neaera and Kichesias. They couldn't risk him escaping. If he let Phoebe think she was going to see magic, she was unlikely to tell anyone – at least until afterwards, when it wouldn't matter. What decided him, though, was the golden sword. Phoebe was right. It would be a much faster and kinder death.

He closed his eyes and rested a hand against the bulge

of marble muscles beneath the sheet. "The day after tomorrow," he said heavily. "But I'm not letting you watch the second part – only the magic. Agreed?"

Phoebe smiled. She seemed relieved she wouldn't have to see his project die. "Agreed."

Chapter 8

LIFE

*DIOGENES: Perhaps your tomb and
all that costly marble may give the people
of Halicarnassos something to show off.*

Two days later, they met in the old studio by the wall at
dawn. As she'd promised, the Princess had brought her
father's golden ceremonial sword and two lily-hands – the
black-skinned slave who had accompanied her before, and
another man just as big but with oiled bronze skin. It was
barely light outside, chilly with the onset of winter, the sea
a faint gleam lapping the dark hills. There had been another
raid by the Macedonians the night before. Alexis had heard
every shout and sword clash as he lay awake praying that
the raid wouldn't stop the Assembly meeting. But the
fighting had died away before dawn like it usually did, and
all was quiet in the Craftsmen's Quarter in the dead time
before people started to go about their daily chores.

Alexis dragged the cloth from his project's head, and Kichesias stepped forward for a closer look at the statue. This was the first time his friend had seen his project, and Alexis wondered what he was thinking. The gold he'd painted on its stone curls looked wrong, too pale for his father's hair... He firmly thrust the thought away.

None of them spoke. They'd planned this down to the finest detail and everyone knew their tasks. Alexis extracted the sleeping potion from under the bench, beckoned to Phoebe, and carefully poured a small amount into a cup they'd found in the kitchen. He glanced up the stairs. "You shouldn't need to give the old man much – it'll be a test to see if this stuff still works after being stored for so long."

Phoebe nodded. She seemed subdued, and her hand shook a little as she held out the cup. She crept up the stairs and they heard her feet creaking across the floor above. After a moment, they saw her cloak darken the hole in the ceiling. There were a few mumbles, and she came back down smiling. "Sleeping like a baby," she reported. "He really is a sweet old man. I wish he were my grandpa."

"If you're going to be silly, you can go home now," Alexis said tightly. The lily-hands glanced at each other but did not move from their positions at the door.

"Give me the rest of the potion," Phoebe said. "I'll make your statue man drink it, don't worry. I'm good at things like that."

Alexis passed her the amphora, too tense to argue. He

flexed his fingers, took another deep breath, and laid his hands on the statue.

He closed his eyes, trying to remember what it had felt like the last time he'd worked the magic.

He had been eight years old. Old enough to know better, maybe, but so lonely that he'd ignored the little voice in his head that warned he would only be creating more trouble for himself.

Since his father's disappearance the previous year, everyone in the Craftsmen's Quarter had heard Neaera's story of how Diogenes had attacked her that night at the Mausoleum, and the details had been exaggerated and changed by street gossip until even Alexis began to believe some of them. The older craftsmen were more reserved. They had respected Diogenes as a decent, hard-working sculptor. But they also believed men sometimes went crazy for no reason and reminded one another in dark tones that the sculptor's namesake, Diogenes the Cynic, still lived in a barrel somewhere near Corinth, and that Neaera hadn't been the sculptor's first wife. Some of them vaguely remembered the pretty girl he had brought out of Phrygia, his first and deepest love. Seeing your young wife die giving birth to your own son was enough to send any man crazy, they said, and it was a miracle Diogenes had kept his grief locked up for so many years, even going so far as to remarry and take into his house a lady he obviously didn't love, sacrificing his own happiness so that young Alexis could have the mother he needed.

No one blamed Alexis for what had happened – in fact, many of them pitied him – but their explanation for Diogenes' attack on Neaera condemned Alexis anyway. He was shunned by the other apprentices, who didn't want to be seen with a boy whose birth had killed his mother and sent his father mad. After that terrible night, he found himself friendless and lonely, trapped in the little house with Neaera who, relieved of Diogenes's restraint, could do anything she liked to her stepson.

Thoroughly miserable, one night Alexis tied some bread and cheese in a cloth and crept out of the house. He intended to run away, but the magical bond between him and Neaera wouldn't let him leave the city. He ended up getting lost and found himself wandering in the Royal Park with its deep shadows and exquisite statues shining white and gold in the moonlight among the trees. Confused and tearful, he stumbled upon a statue of a boy his age, a sculptor's idea of how a Greek youth should look, who seemed to stare straight back at him and smile in understanding.

It was such a long time since anyone had smiled at Alexis that way, he knelt on the wet grass at the statue's feet and poured out his troubles to the boy. "I wish you were alive," he sobbed. "I wish you could come home with me and be my friend."

That was when he felt the magic stir. He rose to his feet and gently touched the gilded curls. And Kichesias's spirit came.

"Alex? Are you sure you're ready to try this?" Kichesias spoke softly, banishing the memories. "We don't have to do it today if you need more time."

"I'm ready!" he insisted. "Don't interrupt me."

His friend retreated and whispered something to Phoebe. Alexis heard the Princess whisper back.

Trying to ignore his audience, he closed his eyes again. *Live*, he willed. *LIVE.*

He opened his eyes. His project stared back at him, frozen marble as before. He turned away before he could start seeing his father's face in the carefully sculpted features. The sun was coming up. All his efforts had been a waste of time. He must be too old to work the magic.

"Maybe you have to use more gold paint?" Phoebe suggested. "Your stepmother must have been beautifully painted and gilded if she was a statue on the Mausoleum, and you said you didn't have any trouble waking her. If we all helped, it wouldn't take that long."

Alexis shook his head. "Pasion hasn't got any more gold paint. He was angry enough when he discovered this pot had gone – it's expensive, you know. Besides, Kichesias didn't have much gold on him." *And I can't go through another night like last night,* he added silently, avoiding his friend's intense look.

Phoebe narrowed her eyes. "Is this all part of the joke, Alex, like when you couldn't change my bracelet? Because if you can't do magic, you shouldn't go round telling people you can. It'll get you into all sorts of trouble."

"I can do magic!"

He replaced his hands on the rigid folds of his project's robes, filled with fresh determination. But no matter how hard he strained, nothing happened. Finally, Kichesias came across, gently took hold of his wrists and moved his hands up to the statue's face.

Alexis stiffened.

"You're not thinking of him as a person, are you?" his friend breathed into his ear. "You've told me plenty of times that the magic only works if you really *want* it to. Last night, when you told me what you were planning, you kept calling him 'your project'. Try thinking of him as your father."

"No!" Alexis snatched his hands away and stared at his friend in horror. "That's the whole point! If I think of him as my father, I won't be able to—"

"I know. But you might have to think it, just until he's awake. Then you can think of him as your project again, if you like. It's worth a try, isn't it? Close your eyes and imagine he's real. If that doesn't work, maybe we can get Phoebe to show us where she got rid of the body from the Mausoleum. We might be able to find it again if the water's not too deep."

Alexis sighed. "Even if we did find it, which is unlikely, you know it won't convince the Assembly without a face. And if we don't do this today, Neaera will find out – she'll be missing us already."

Kichesias chewed his lip. "I only want you to be happy, Alex. If you don't want to do this, it doesn't matter. We'll just go on as we always have. It's not so bad being Lady Neaera's slave, not really, as long as I do what she wants. At least we're together. She's getting older. One day, she'll die of old age and we'll both be free."

Could statues die of old age? Alexis gritted his teeth. "I don't just want to be free of her. I want to clear my father's name, and I want everyone to know she's a liar. Neaera is going to pay for what she did. This is the only way I can think of."

Kichesias squeezed his shoulder. "Then do yourself a favour and think of him as your father," he whispered as he stepped back.

Think of him as your father. It wasn't difficult. The difficult part had been thinking of the statue as "his project" for so long. Alexis moved his fingers over the statue's face, feeling his father's familiar features and the stone curls of his hair. He breathed faster, remembering how he'd twisted his fingers into those same curls so many times as a boy sitting proudly on Diogenes' shoulders.

LIVE, he willed again. *LIVE, FATHER, LIVE!*

Even through his eyelids, the studio brightened. Warmth flowed into him, as if someone had opened the door of a dark cell to let the sun shine on his back. His fingers tingled as the curls beneath them softened. There was a gasp from Phoebe, a whispered "Shh!" from Kichesias... and something seemed to burst inside Alexis.

It was as if all the tears he hadn't shed when he'd lost his father were pouring out of him, through his fingers and into the statue he'd made, until he could not get his breath.

"Father!" he groaned, sliding down the woken statue until he knelt at its feet with his arms wrapped around the strong, thick legs and his face buried in robes that were no longer stiff and cold, but soft white linen. "Oh, Father, I'm sorry, I'm so very sorry..." He was weeping uncontrollably, and shaking, and the room darkened as the dizziness and weakness that was the price of the magic struck him harder than it ever had before.

Strong hands plucked him away from the newly woken statue as it staggered backwards on to the bench. Phoebe supported the new man and gently put the sleeping potion to his lips, while Kichesias stood behind him with the golden sword.

Still dizzy, Alexis remembered the rest of the plan. "No, don't! You mustn't... you don't understand... it's Father!" He fought to reach the man on the bench, but one of the lily-hands carried him, struggling and sobbing, out of the door.

The last thing he saw was his father's kind eyes, framed by dark curls with those strange golden highlights, blinking at him in confusion over the rim of Phoebe's treacherous cup. "Who's that boy?" the woken statue asked in a cracked voice. "What's wrong with him? Is he sick?"

"*FATHER!*" Alexis screamed, kicking the lily-hand. "It's me! Your son, Alexis! Don't you remember me?"

The face that looked so much like his father's creased into a frown, and the bewildered eyes turned questioningly to Phoebe. "I feel so strange. It's like... I've been away on a long journey, but I don't remember where. Is this my home? What's in this drink? It's very sweet. I'm so tired..."

"NO!" Alexis screamed. "No, Father, *don't sleep!*"

The door closed, and choking darkness smothered Alexis like a shroud.

When he came to himself, Alexis was sitting on a cool marble floor with his back propped against the ornate base of a column. He felt washed out and weak, yet strangely calm. It was enough to rest his head against the column and let his gaze roam around the interior of a large, shady temple. The column he was leaning against soared above his head to a vaulted roof, where swallows swooped through the rafters. The rising sun streamed through a pair of tall doors at the far end, flooding the floor with crimson light. At the other end of the temple, partly hidden by clouds of incense, glittered a huge golden statue.

"The Temple of Aphrodite," he whispered, recognizing the beautiful goddess of love. This was where they'd planned Phoebe would bring him while Kichesias killed the statue. He wondered what would happen if he were to touch the gigantic goddess and make *her* live. The thought brought a harsh laugh that ended with him choking on his own tears.

Phoebe knelt at his side with a brimming cup. The

hood of her cloak was down, and her ringlets fell around her worried face. "Drink!" she commanded. "I thought you were dying. You should have warned me the magic would make you pass out like that."

"It was bad this time," Alexis said, eyeing the cup suspiciously.

Phoebe shook her head, impatient, and put it to his lips. "It's only water," she said.

He drank with a sigh. The worst was over.

He grasped the column and tried to stand, amazed by how weak he still felt. A few people were already in the Temple, come to make sacrifices to the goddess and beg her help in their war against the Macedonians. The Assembly met at sunrise. He didn't have much time if he was going to catch today's session.

Phoebe pushed him back down. "Take it easy," she said. "I told my other lily-hand to help Kichesias take the body up to the Theatre when they're ready. So all you have to do is meet them up there. You need to get your strength back, otherwise the Assembly isn't going to hear a word you say, let alone listen to you."

This was true enough. Alexis saw the bronze lily-hand who had carried him out of the studio standing nearby, arms folded, watching them. The slave's face showed no emotion. He wondered if the lily-hands lost their spirits along with their tongues.

"Thank you," he said, his voice still a little hoarse. "Hadn't you better put your hood up in here? Someone might recognize you."

Phoebe's mouth worked, as if she wanted to say something but couldn't decide how to start. She pulled her hood over her ringlets and sat beside him on the floor, drawing her knees up to her chest and wrapping her arms around them.

"I'm sorry, Alex," she said.

"What for?"

"Not believing you. It was so amazing, what you did. You have a wonderful gift."

Alexis grunted. "It's a curse, not a gift." He didn't want to be reminded of what he'd done.

"He wasn't really your father, you know," Phoebe said gently. "He didn't even recognize you."

Alexis set his jaw, aware he'd made a fool of himself. "I don't want to talk about it. You can tell your slave to relax. I'm not going to try to run back and stop Kichesias, so you needn't worry. It'll be too late now, anyway."

Phoebe's dark eyes flickered. "I expect so." She spoke softly in Persian to the bronze lily-hand, who nodded and silently left the Temple. "I've sent him back to collect Daddy's sword," she explained. "There will be awkward questions if someone at the Assembly recognizes it." She avoided his gaze and stared at the drifting incense, unusually quiet.

While they waited for the lily-hand to return, Alexis eyed the Princess. He wouldn't put it past her to have stayed to watch the killing, despite the plan that she should accompany Alexis and stay away until it was over. But she didn't seem to know any more than he did.

"Have you ever used the magic on an animal?" Phoebe asked suddenly, glancing sideways at him. "I mean, on a statue that's not human?"

"Once," Alexis said, glad to have something to distract him from the thought of what Kichesias and the lily-hands were doing to the woken statue. "When I was about five, I touched the statue of a horse. It was beautiful, white all over with gold hooves, and so gentle even I could ride it. I called it Marble. Neaera hated me riding, of course. She knew all about my magic by then, and I think she was a bit afraid someone would find out about her being a statue. But Father—" He choked and forced himself to go on. "Father said I had to learn to ride sometime, and he'd lead me on Marble up and down the streets of the Craftsmen's Quarter every evening after he'd finished work. I felt so grown up, sitting up there on Marble's back. I loved that horse."

"What happened to it?"

"Neaera sold it to a horse dealer one night. By the time I woke up, Marble was halfway across the Aegean Sea on a ship bound for Athens."

Phoebe touched his hand. "I'm so sorry, Alex."

He shook his head. "It's not the same with animals. I cried a bit, and I don't think Marble would have ever hurt me. But it wasn't anything like the bond I have with Neaera and Kichesias. Or maybe the bond can be forcefully broken. I don't know."

"Or maybe it's only in your mind?" Phoebe said softly. "The women say that sort of bond can sometimes be stronger than a chain."

They were both silent, while the worshippers at the incense-shrouded shrine made little chinks and whispers at the feet of their goddess.

Alexis frowned at the Temple doors. "It's getting late, Phoebe. The Assembly's business will be over soon, and I don't want to have to wait till tomorrow to speak. How long is your lily-hand going to be?"

Phoebe frowned, too. "Maybe he missed them at the studio and had to go up to the Theatre after them? You'd better go, Alex. I'll be safe enough here until my lily-hand gets back."

Alexis scrambled to his feet. He looked back at the Princess and hesitated. "Are you sure?"

She smiled. "This is the Temple of Aphrodite. Women come here alone all the time to pray to the goddess. I'll keep my hood up and I promise I'll wait for the lily-hand. But you've got to tell me everything that happened at the Assembly! Come to the Palace this afternoon. Bring Kichesias, too. I'll tell Daddy you're going to help me clean my Collection again, and I'll send a lily-hand to meet you at the gate this time so you don't get arrested by suspicious old Cleon." She touched his arm. "I think you're very brave, Alex. I wouldn't dare stand up and speak before the whole Assembly."

He gave her a tight smile. "If girls were allowed to speak to the Assembly, I bet you'd be the first one up there! Anyway, I haven't done it yet."

"But you will. And you'll make them listen, Alex, I know it. You're such a good storyteller. Then after it's all over, maybe you can use your magic on some of my statues?" She giggled at his expression, waved him towards the door, and strode off through the columns with her cloak billowing behind her.

Alexis thrust the Princess and her schemes from his mind. He hadn't even thought about afterwards, except that there was sure to be trouble. He opened his mouth to say they mightn't be able to come to the Palace. But Phoebe had already vanished into the incense clouds.

Chapter 9

ASSEMBLY

DIOGENES: And they can boast to
strangers of the magnificent building they have.

On the way up to the Theatre, Alexis rehearsed his
speech in his head. He had to get it right, because he
would have only one chance to put his case to the
Assembly. A ration cart passed him, guarded by soldiers,
and the smell of the freshly baked bread made his
stomach turn. He marched on, head down, avoiding the
soldiers' eyes. He hadn't eaten since yesterday lunchtime,
but the very thought of food made him feel ill.

A small market was in progress at the agora, and some
of the rich citizens from the Hill had ventured down to
shop. Most of them seemed to be complaining about the
quality of the goods, blaming the Macedonians for
everything from their blisters to the fact they couldn't get
the right spices for their wine. Alexis hurried on past and

worked his way around the rocky slopes below the Acropolis.

The Theatre had been carved out of the hillside overlooking the bay. As Alexis entered its bowl, the clamour of hundreds of voices raised in argument struck him like a wave. He stopped to catch his breath. He must have taken the wrong turning off the main street. He'd emerged too high, level with the top rank of seats rather than the stage. Below him, several hundred citizens stood, sat, or reclined on the stone tiers cut into the hillside, their colourful robes glittering in the sun. On the half-moon stage at the bottom of the tiers, a man wearing the speaker's myrtle wreath was opening and closing his mouth and waving his arms in an attempt to make himself heard. He might as well not have bothered, because from where Alexis stood he could not hear a word.

Several arguments seemed to be going on at once, but they were all about the same thing: the war, the siege, the Macedonians, and General Alexander.

"I say we should open our gates and attack with all our troops!" shouted a well-dressed man seated near the edge of the Theatre. "Finish this stupid siege, once and for all."

"Rubbish!" said the man next to him. "We should send an assassin into the Macedonian camp during the night and skewer that upstart Alexander in his bedroll!"

This was shouted down as cowardly by several loud voices, and anyway impossible because the Macedonian camp was too well guarded.

A grey-bearded citizen said, "We should have a single combat like in the old days, General Memnon against General Alexander. The victor wins the city."

This sparked off a new argument about whether General Memnon's experience would beat Alexander's youth, and someone mentioned that they thought Memnon was ill, but was quickly shushed.

"What's the Persian fleet doing, that's what I'd like to know!" someone else called.

"Yes!" agreed a younger man. "We never see King Orontobates with a sword in his hand, do we? Seems to me, the Persians are perfectly happy to take our taxes in peacetime, but at the first sniff of a war they all run back home and leave us to it! Cowards!"

"The King and the fleet haven't run anywhere yet," pointed out the grey-bearded citizen. "General Alexander burnt his boats after he crossed the Hellespont, remember? We can't fight him at sea."

"That works both ways," another man said. "I say we should sit it out. The Macedonians can knock at our gates all they like. We can get plenty of supplies into Halicarnassos by sea, and our walls will never fall! Just so long as no one brings any suspicious wooden horses inside, we'll be all right."

The entire tier dissolved into laughter, making Alexis frown. He knew what they were referring to, of course. Everyone had heard of the story of the siege of Troy by the Greeks who, unable to get through Troy's walls by force, had built a huge wooden horse as a parting gift and hidden their elite troops inside its hollow belly. When the Trojans had hauled the horse into their city, they had also hauled in their enemies – with disastrous results. Troy had lost the war, and the story served as a reminder never to trust an enemy who extended the hand of friendship. But General Alexander was Macedonian, not strictly Greek, and Alexis couldn't believe the Assembly were making jokes at a time like this.

He made his way down the slope, keeping an eye out for Kichesias. What if his friend had encountered a problem getting the body up here? What if some nosy soldier had stopped him and asked awkward questions? The back of Alexis's neck prickled, like it did when Neaera was playing statues so she could spy on him, and he looked over his shoulder with a shiver. But there were so many people in the Theatre it was impossible to tell if anyone was watching him.

Reaching the bottom of the tiers at last, he marched up to the stage.

An official lowered his staff to block his way. "Where do you think you're going, boy?"

Alexis straightened his shoulders. "To speak to the Assembly, of course," he said, trying to look as if he did this every day.

The official who had stopped him laughed. "Go home, boy. The Assembly's got more important things to do than listen to a youngster barely old enough to leave his mother's rooms."

Alexis's cheeks went hot. "I can do better than *him.*"

He pointed to the speaker, whose words were still being ignored. "I thought every citizen had a right to speak to the Assembly? The law says you have to let me speak."

The official frowned. "The law also says you have to be eighteen before you can address the Assembly. How old are you, boy?"

"I'm small for my age," Alexis said, avoiding the question and scanning the hillside for Kichesias. "Please sir, you have to let me speak! It's about my father. He disappeared, and I think my stepmother killed him! I didn't know where else to come."

The official's frown deepened. "You want to accuse your mother of murdering your father? Is this some sort of joke?"

"My stepmother, sir, not my mother. My real mother's dead." Alexis assumed his most innocent expression. "I promise it's not a joke. I know you're very busy with the war and everything, but there's no one else who can help me..."

"Let the boy speak," said a quiet, accented voice behind them.

Both Alexis and the official jumped. A slim Persian of medium height, his black hair styled into ringlets and glistening with oil, was gazing intently at Alexis with his dark eyes. He wore a beaded coat against the chill, and his beard was heavily scented. Alexis had the strangest feeling they had met somewhere before. But before he could chase the elusive memory, the Persian spoke again.

"A murder sounds interesting. It might give us

something to think about other than General Alexander and his wretched Macedonians. To tell you the truth, we're all getting rather bored of this siege." He smiled in an oily fashion at Alexis.

"If you think the Assembly is going to listen to a word anyone else says today, you're crazy, Ishkibar!" the official said, obviously recognizing the Persian. "It's always a complete waste of time when everyone starts arguing like this. I was going to bring things to an end once our friend out there has finished."

"Might as well bring him to an end now, for all the good he's doing," Ishkibar said in an amused tone. "Let the boy have a turn. What harm can it do? If they don't listen to him, no one's going to blame you, are they?"

The official mumbled something about Alexis being underage, and the Persian said he'd take responsibility. While they discussed the matter, Alexis looked anxiously for Kichesias. Without a body, he knew he didn't have a chance of making the Assembly believe him, even if he were allowed to speak.

He flinched as someone touched him on the shoulder. He realized the Persian had asked him a question.

"Sorry," he said. "I didn't hear you, sir."

Ishkibar smiled. "We are rather a noisy lot when we get going, aren't we? What I said was, do you have any evidence?"

The Persian's dark, watchful eyes made Alexis uncomfortable. He couldn't understand why such an obviously rich and powerful citizen was helping him. But

Ishkibar seemed to have some influence with the official, which was too good an opportunity to miss. "Yes," he said firmly. "I do have evidence. My father's body is on its way."

The dark eyes showed a glimmer of surprise. But the Persian concealed his reaction so swiftly, Alexis wondered if he had imagined it.

"Is it, now?" Ishkibar said, frowning down the hillside. "And you claim your stepmother murdered him? How sure are you of that?"

"I know she did it." Alexis set his jaw, expecting the Persian to ask how he could be so sure.

But Ishkibar merely nodded. "A boy often knows his own family better than a stranger," he said cryptically. "Interesting. All right, let's get that wreath off the speaker, and see if we can't make this rabble listen for once."

It was all happening too fast. Already, they were out on the stage, where the current speaker was still passionately waving his arms. He was shouting something about Queen Ada sending presents to General Alexander – though Alexis couldn't work out if he was proposing the Assembly should stop Queen Ada doing this, or that it should take her side against King Orontobates, whom he called the "Persian usurper". With the crowded tiers, the Acropolis rearing over them, and the statue of the war-god Ares standing on its rocky crag against the sky, Alexis suddenly felt very small and insignificant. Why had he ever thought these rich and powerful citizens would listen to *him*?

As if he could read his thoughts, Ishkibar said, "Not to worry, lad. I'll speak for you, if necessary. Now then, let's get our facts straight, shall we? Your father was Diogenes the sculptor, is that right?"

"Yes," Alexis said, too distracted to wonder how the Persian knew. He didn't remember telling the official earlier, when Ishkibar had been listening.

Then he spotted Kichesias at the stage entrance opposite, and his heart began to beat so hard he was afraid he might pass out again. His friend and the black lily-hand carried between them a man-sized burden wrapped in the cloth Alexis had used to cover his project while he'd been working on it. He shivered, unable to look away. The official hurried across the stage and tried to stop them carrying the body through, but the lily-hand raised his branded palm and gave the man a hard stare. The official backed off, giving Ishkibar a helpless look.

"It's all right," Ishkibar said, eyeing the covered body. "I think that's our evidence." He snatched the wreath from the speaker's head, passed it to Alexis, and yelled with surprisingly loud lungs, "Silence, citizens of Halicarnassos! Prepare yourselves to hear a real tragedy!"

Some of the men in the bottom tiers quietened at once, looking curiously at the shrouded body. But the arguments in the top tiers, where Ishkibar's voice hadn't carried so clearly, continued as before.

Alexis stood in the middle of the stage with the myrtle

wreath on his head, letting the noise wash over him as he watched Kichesias and the lily-hand gently lower their burden to the ground. Kichesias raised his head and met Alexis's gaze, something unreadable in his turquoise eyes.

"What are you waiting for?" Ishkibar snapped. "Uncover it, then. Let's see what you've brought for the Assembly to look at."

Kichesias looked questioningly at Alexis.

"It's all right," Alexis said, finding his voice at last. "He's helping us."

The black lily-hand stepped back into the shadows, leaving Kichesias to sweep off the cloth. Gasps of horror rippled through the lower tiers and passed rapidly up the hillside. One by one, the arguments fell silent, replaced by whispers and mutters as people leant forward to see better.

"What's that stuff on his skin?" someone asked in hushed tones. "Is he dead?" ... "Course he's dead! Ever seen anyone alive look like that?" ... "Who's the boy? He looks too young to address the Assembly to me." ... "Shh! Isn't that Ishkibar with him? Let him speak."

Meanwhile, Alexis struggled with an urge to flee and throw up behind the stage. Even though he'd known what to expect, the sight of his father's likeness, brought to life from marble and put so cruelly to death again, made him feel faint. But he made himself stand straight and take deep breaths. Kichesias had done well. The dead man's limbs were covered in dark crystallized statue blood, similar enough at first sight to the body that had been pulled out of the Mausoleum drains, but not so heavily coated that you couldn't see it was a man beneath. As they'd agreed, the face had been left clean of blood so that Diogenes' features would show clearly.

"This is the body of my father!" Alexis said as loudly as he could, pointing to the corpse. He was surprised how his voice rang out around the bowl of the Theatre, echoed by the enclosing rocks until it reached every ear. Any whispering that lingered in the tiers fell silent as the whole Assembly sat up and leant forwards to listen.

Alexis licked his lips. "General Memnon's men found this body in the Mausoleum drains when they were checking security at the start of the siege," he explained. "I think my stepmother, Neaera, put it there."

He was aware of Ishkibar's narrowed stare, flicking between him and the corpse. But the Assembly was listening, which was what mattered. Alexis took another deep breath and launched into his prepared speech.

He told them as much as he dared. How his mother had died giving birth to him, and his father had married Neaera four years later. How Neaera and Diogenes had argued more and more often as Alexis grew up, and how she'd gone after him that terrible night when Alexis lay awake, vainly waiting for his father to come home. It all went fine until he got to the bit about his stepmother coming back from the Mausoleum covered in blood and her telling lies about being attacked so no one would suspect she'd killed Diogenes. Then people started to mutter and shout out questions.

"You expect us to believe a woman killed him?" ... "Impossible! She wouldn't be strong enough!" ... "Someone did, though. That man obviously didn't die of natural causes." ... "Bet it was one of them Macedonians!"

Alexis exchanged a glance with Kichesias, who stood protectively close to the corpse, his unreadable gaze on its calm face. Alexis couldn't resist another look, and his heart fluttered. Had the dead man's finger *moved*?

He shook his head and looked away, angry with himself for imagining things that couldn't be. The arguments in the tiers had started up again, this time over how the Macedonians could have killed Diogenes and smuggled his body into the Mausoleum drains without anyone noticing.

"The Macedonians weren't even here when my father disappeared!" Alexis shouted, unable to believe grown men could be so stupid. "It was five years ago, and I think that's when Neaera killed him. I ask the Assembly for a murder trial!"

At first he thought they hadn't heard. The arguments grew louder. Kichesias bent and pulled the sheet back over the body, beckoning the lily-hand to help him. He glanced again at Alexis and made an urgent motion with his head.

But Ishkibar, still frowning, tweaked the sheet aside again and peered closely at the dead man's face. He picked some dried statue blood off the rigid arm and sniffed it. Kichesias tried to pull the sheet back. But

Ishkibar put a firm hand over his to keep the corpse uncovered and straightened with a sigh.

"This is indeed the body of Diogenes the sculptor!" he called with his powerful lungs. "I recognize him. Five years ago, he made a statue of my dying son for my wife. He was a poor man, but a good man. When my son died, he didn't charge us for his work. If Diogenes was murdered then I, for one, would like to see the murderess brought to justice!"

There were uncomfortable mutters from the tiers, and the men in the lower seats craned forwards for another look. "It's Diogenes the sculptor who studied under Pytheos!" someone exclaimed. "I recognize him, too." Cries of: "So do I!", "Shame!" and "Justice for the sculptor's son!" followed.

Ishkibar finally let Kichesias cover the corpse. "Well done, lad," he said to Alexis with a little smile. "I think you'll get your trial."

Alexis stared at the Persian, his brain racing. No wonder Ishkibar had seemed so familiar! Vaguely, he recalled the rich man from the Hill who had come to the studio, patted him on the head and said how much he reminded him of his own son. "I remember you," he whispered. "That statue of your son was Father's final commission!"

Ishkibar nodded. "And he did a good job. I'd like to see your stepmother brought to trial as much as you would."

"But you must have been the last person to see my

father alive!" Alexis said, excited. "What happened that night? Oh, gods... *did you see Neaera kill him*?"

Ishkibar put a finger to his lips. "Your father came to me that night to tell me he didn't want a fee, and then he left. That's all. This isn't the place to discuss matters that should be for the jury to consider. Go home. The City Guard will arrest your stepmother and take her to the agora when we've set a date for the trial."

"When will that be, sir?" Kichesias asked.

Ishkibar frowned at the interruption. "I'm not sure. The Assembly has a lot of things on its mind just now. The Guard will need to be informed, and the lots drawn for jury duty."

"But Neaera—" Alexis exchanged a desperate glance with his friend.

"I'll do my best to plead your cause," Ishkibar said firmly. He looked down at the body. "I meant what I said. Your father was a good man. He didn't deserve to die like that. Best leave him here. A physician will need to examine the body before the trial, and I can have it taken to an appropriate place."

Kichesias made an urgent noise in his throat. Alexis frowned at his friend. They hadn't anticipated this, but maybe it would be better if the corpse that looked so much like his dead father were kept somewhere he wouldn't be able to see it every day.

He started to nod. But Kichesias said, "No, Alex! Don't you remember? Pasion said he'd arranged somewhere."

This was a lie. But seeing the desperate look in his friend's eyes, Alexis said, "Yes, that's right... The sculptor who looks after us now has prepared somewhere safe for it. We, er, haven't finished the mourning rites yet. But thank you very much, sir. I really appreciate you helping me like this, and I'm sure Father would have appreciated it as well."

The genuine choke in his voice seemed to ease the Persian's suspicions. After another glance at the shrouded body, he smiled and patted Alexis on the head. "I understand. Mourning rites are important. Don't grieve too much, lad. I know it's difficult at first, and you think you can't live without your loved ones. But my people believe their ghosts stay to help you over difficult things. Perhaps your father's ghost was here today, helping to make the Assembly listen – I've never seen them so quiet when someone was speaking as they were with you. You have a rare gift."

Alexis stiffened. But it was an innocent enough remark. Ishkibar was referring to Alexis's storytelling ability, that was all. The Persian couldn't possibly know about his magic.

Chapter 10

TROUBLE

*DIOGENES: With all that marble
pressing down on you, you have a heavier
burden to bear than any of us.*

Kichesias was in such a hurry to get the corpse out of the
Theatre, Alexis didn't have a chance to ask Ishkibar any
more questions about the night of his father's death.
Besides, there were too many people around and the lily-
hand was still with them – tongueless, maybe, but still in
possession of his eyes and ears. It was not until they were
safely back in the old studio with the body of the woken
statue laid carefully on the bench that Kichesias relaxed.

He chewed his lip, staring at Alexis with the same
unreadable expression in his eyes as before.

"What's wrong?" Alexis said, glancing at the lily-hand.

"I'm sorry, Alex! I tried, I really did, but I couldn't do
it. I didn't know a physician would have to examine the

body. I thought it would be all right, at a distance, in the Theatre – and it was! But I failed you. I'm sorry." Kichesias, too, glanced at the lily-hand.

"Couldn't do what?" But Alexis's stomach fluttered as he remembered that brief, half-imagined movement of the dead man's finger.

With a little moan, he snatched the sheet from the "corpse" and stared down into its dark eyes. They were wide open and staring back at him – his father's eyes, yet not his father. He shivered.

"It's all right," Kichesias said to the statue. "You can stop pretending now."

Rather stiffly, the man who looked so uncannily like Diogenes the sculptor sat up. He rubbed the back of his neck and smiled at them with the innocence of a small child. "How did I do?" he said. "Did I do it right?"

Alexis stared from the woken statue to Kichesias and back again. "Oh, gods, Kichesias," he whispered. "What have we done? They're going to send people to examine him! The physician will know at once that he's not dead. The Assembly has agreed to a murder trial. They can't have a trial if the victim is still alive!"

Kichesias hunched his shoulders. "Don't be angry, Alex, please," he said in a little voice. "I thought you'd be glad. It was the only thing I could think of. The sleeping potion didn't work on him, and I couldn't kill him, so I taught him how to play the statue game. He's good, almost as good as Lady Neaera already, and he'll get better at it. Maybe he can fool the physician?"

Alexis thought furiously. The simplest solution would be for his project to die before the examiners came. He'd have to persuade someone else to kill him, though, since Kichesias obviously couldn't. And they'd have to borrow the golden sword from Phoebe again. Maybe the lily-hand? He glanced at the big slave, clenched his fists and looked back at the man with his father's face. What was he thinking of? They couldn't kill him *now*.

His project was following the conversation, frowning slightly and picking at the black statue blood on his skin. For the first time, Alexis wondered whose blood it was. He eyed Kichesias, his heart beating faster, but his friend did not appear to be injured. Alexis studied the woken statue more carefully and noticed a small cut below his ear, where a normal man might have bled to death. Was the wound a result of Kichesias's failed attempt to kill him? Or hadn't his friend tried?

"No," he said, unable to bring himself to ask for details. "No. We have to think of another way." He took a deep breath and turned to the lily-hand. "Princess Phoebe told us to come to the Palace this afternoon. Will you take me there?" Despite his reluctance to get involved in the Princess's schemes, she was the only person he could think of who might be able to help them now.

The lily-hand gave a silent nod.

Alexis took another breath. "First, I need to speak to my friend and, ah... Diogenes alone. Can you wait outside, please, and make sure no one comes in?"

The slave nodded again, moved down the hall, and

took up a position at the street entrance with folded arms. Alexis glanced up the stairs before he shut the studio door. If the old man woke up, it was just too bad. They didn't have any sleeping potion left.

Kichesias started to explain further, but Alexis cut him off. "I know," he said. "It's the statue brotherhood thing, isn't it? I'm sorry I asked you to do it. I knew it would be hard for you. I just hoped that, since Neaera manages to hurt you with her pins, you would be able to... never mind. You didn't kill him, and it was a good idea to have him play dead. I didn't know they would want to examine the body, either."

He considered the man who looked like his father and made himself meet the dark, trusting eyes. "Your name is Diogenes," he said. "You've been ill for a long time, but you're better now. I'm Alexis, and this is my friend Kichesias. We've been looking after you. My stepmother Neaera has accused you of attacking her. That's why you're hiding out here and why you have to pretend to be dead whenever anyone comes. Do you understand?"

His project frowned, but nodded. "I don't remember attacking a woman..."

"That's because you got hit on the head and lost your memory," Alexis said quickly, glancing at Kichesias. His friend nodded. "We don't think you did it, so we're not going to hand you over to the authorities, but you've got to promise not to leave this house, not for anything. It's too dangerous. The Macedonians have laid siege to the city, and we're at war with them."

"I don't remember a war, either," Diogenes said slowly. "But I do remember something... when I was pretending to be dead, you called me your father."

"Yes." Alexis closed his eyes. "That's because my father really is dead. We're trying to prove he was murdered, but we don't have his body, and you look a bit like him so we thought you might be able to help us. Thank you."

"I..." The man still looked confused. He touched the wound below his ear. "I'm not your father, then? Am I Kichesias's father?"

"No!" Alexis looked at his friend. "You're not anyone's father. You're my... uncle. That's why we're looking after you."

"I'm supposed to have attacked my brother's wife?" He looked sad. "And my brother was murdered? I don't remember him at all. What was he called?"

Alexis realized his mistake. He hadn't had enough time to prepare this, and it wasn't easy to make up a story that was so close to the truth, yet keep the vital parts hidden.

"He was called Diogenes, too," he said with a flash of inspiration. "He was your twin. You were both named after a crazy old philosopher who lives in a barrel, because you used to play together in a barrel when you were little."

Kichesias stifled a laugh that emerged as a cough. Alexis supposed it might have been quite funny, if it had been a scene in a play. But he was too close to this particular drama. What he really wanted to do was throw himself into Diogenes' arms and sob: *No, no, I'm lying! You are my father, you really are!*

Diogenes nodded. "Must have been confusing for our mother," he said. "But if your father was my twin, maybe that's why I feel so protective of you. It's almost like you could have been my son."

Alexis bit his lip.

"But I suppose us having the same name at least meant our parents couldn't mix us up," he added with a gentle smile that was so like his father's, Alexis had to turn away to hide the tears that sprang to his eyes.

Diogenes looked more closely at Alexis. "So, you're my nephew – that must be why you seem so familiar. Do I have a wife? Are you sure I don't have any children? It feels like maybe I do."

Alexis shook his head, not trusting himself to speak.

Kichesias rescued him, taking his hand and pulling him to the door. "No, sir. You don't have children. You never married. You used to live in Alexis's house with his family. But I expect your memory will come back soon, and then you'll remember everything. I'm afraid we have to go now. There's an old man who lives upstairs. He hardly ever comes down, so you should be all right if you stay in the studio and keep quiet. Just play dead if anyone comes, and we'll be back as soon as we can."

Before Diogenes could protest, Kichesias dragged Alexis out into the hall and closed the studio door with a thud, putting his back to it and breathing hard. Alexis wanted to rush back in again and beg his father's forgiveness for the lies he'd told him, but Kichesias barred his way with a stubborn expression. The lily-hand watched impassively.

A Macedonian missile landed close to the wall, bringing Alexis to his senses. He swallowed the lump in his throat and sighed. "Do you think he believed us?"

Kichesias nodded gravely. "I think so. I believed everything you told me for ages after you woke me, remember? It was months before I remembered my name, even, and your 'Uncle Diogenes' only just woke up this morning." He smiled. "That bit about them playing in the barrel was brilliant!"

Alexis grimaced. "We can't risk leaving him alone very long."

"I could stay with him," Kichesias offered. "I'll miss seeing Phoebe again, but it would be good to talk to another person who's been a statue. Lady Neaera never answers my questions properly."

Alexis shook his head, reminded of how much trouble they would be in once his stepmother heard about that morning's Assembly. "You'd better go home before Neaera starts searching the Quarter for us. Say I'm... say I'm on an errand for Pasion. I'm sure he'll go along with that, if she asks him."

"What if Pasion comes out here and finds Diogenes?"

Alexis didn't want to think about that too much. "Then Diogenes will pretend to be dead like we told him to, and Pasion will just think he's fallen over and got damaged. There are enough missiles landing around here. Hopefully, the Guard will arrest Neaera before she finds out we're the ones who accused her of murder."

Kichesias bit his lip, and Alexis knew he was thinking of Neaera's gold pins. He felt terrible about sending his friend back to face her alone. On the other hand, his stepmother was unlikely to hurt Kichesias if Alexis wasn't there to see.

"It'll be all right," he said firmly. "I'm going to ask Phoebe if she can get her father to overrule the Assembly so they won't send a physician to examine Diogenes' body. Maybe the King or General Memnon will agree to testify at the trial – they both saw the body from the Mausoleum before its face was damaged. A King's word must be better than a physician's. Phoebe will help us when I explain what happened, I'm sure she will."

And if the Princess proved difficult, he thought he knew how to persuade her.

Kichesias still looked pale. But he nodded. "I'm sorry, Alex. This is all my fault. If I'd done what you said, we wouldn't be in this mess."

Alexis gave his friend a rough hug. "No, it was mine. I should never have asked you to do such a terrible thing. But it came out all right in the end. We got our trial."

His friend sighed. "We still have to make them believe Lady Neaera's guilty. You heard what the Assembly said – they don't believe a woman is strong enough to kill a man. And Lady Neaera will act all innocent at her trial, you can be sure of that. Who was that Persian you were with? Do you think he really will help us?"

Alexis frowned, suddenly uneasy. Why *was* the rich and powerful Ishkibar so keen to see Neaera stand trial? Did he simply feel guilty because he'd been the cause of Diogenes' journey across the city that night? And how likely was it that a nobleman from the Hill should recognize a craftsman's boy he'd last seen five years ago, among the hundreds of people in the Theatre that morning?

He shook his doubts away and said, "Of course he will! He knew my father. And Phoebe will help us, too. Everything will be all right, Kichesias. You'll see."

As Alexis hurried through the streets after the lily-hand, he was glad his escort did not possess a tongue. Quite apart from the fact he needed all his breath to keep up with the big slave, the lack of conversation gave him a chance to organize his thoughts. By the time they reached the Royal Quarter, he was starting to accept that the man he'd sculpted in the image of his father was alive, and he felt a bit more hopeful. The citizens of the Assembly had believed his story. They were going to put Neaera on trial for murder. Once the King had sorted out the physician problem, Diogenes could be kept safely hidden until the trial was over. And afterwards, when Neaera had been found guilty and his father's name had been cleared, maybe Alexis could take Diogenes home and tell everyone he really was his long-lost uncle, come to care for his brother's son.

But as they approached the Palace, his optimistic mood evaporated. The park was alive with soldiers. Everywhere he looked, armed men were searching under bushes, plunging their spears into the undergrowth and running across the lawns. The Royal quays were thick with guards, while yet more soldiers rowed out to the merchant ships in the harbour and boarded them with drawn swords. The garrison rang with shouts as urgent as the night the Macedonians had laid siege to the city. Alexis's heart thumped with anxiety as his escort sprinted to join another lily-hand waiting in the crush at the gates. With a series of quick finger gestures, the two lily-hands proved they didn't need tongues to communicate. Their heads turned, and they glared at Alexis with hostile eyes.

Alexis backed away. Had General Alexander broken through the wall? Maybe he should come back later, when things had calmed down a bit. But already it was too late. As he hesitated, two soldiers ran up to him and pointed their spears at his chest. "Halt!" they ordered. "Identify yourself!"

Alexis gave his name, adding quickly, "Princess Phoebe is expecting me. I'm to help her clean her Collection again."

He had barely got the words out, before the soldiers had him pinned up against a tree with a spear at his throat. They called for backup, and Alexis's legs weakened as he recognized Officer Cleon running across the lawn, his face like thunder.

"*Where is she?*" he yelled, seizing Alexis's shoulders and shaking him, nearly getting speared by his own men in the process. "What have you done with her, you lying little rat?"

"I don't know what you mean!" Alexis gasped. "What's happened?" He eyed the frantic searchers and turned cold all over as he remembered how he'd left Phoebe alone and unguarded in the Temple of Aphrodite. "Oh gods, Phoebe..."

"It's *Princess* Phoebe to you!" shouted Cleon, still shaking him. "I knew you were up to no good when I first set eyes on you! All that rubbish about cleaning ships and statues! We found one of the lily-hands with his throat cut in the street, the priceless Ceremonial Sword of Caria is missing, and the Princess has been spirited away. She's probably in the Macedonian camp by now, if she isn't dead. I'm warning you now, you're in deep trouble, Alexis son of Diogenes! Bring him!" He shoved Alexis towards the soldiers, who caught his arms and dragged him across the lawn towards the Palace.

Alexis did his best to keep up so that they would not dislocate his shoulders, though his head was spinning and ice-cold fear trickled down his spine. *Phoebe gone. The lily-hand who was with her murdered. The sword stolen.* It must have happened while she'd been waiting for her lily-hand to return with the sword, while her second bodyguard had been with him and Kichesias up at the Theatre – a fact witnessed by the entire Assembly of Halicarnassos. He supposed it couldn't look much worse.

He expected the soldiers to drag him straight to the garrison. He was surprised when they hustled him through the main gates of the Palace. They marched him along the marble corridors and into an echoing hall where a group of richly dressed noblemen clustered together before the empty throne, muttering in low voices. Alexis was thrust to his knees on the hard, cold floor and held there by a firm hand on his shoulder. In his confusion, glimpsing palm trees in pots between the columns around the edge of the hall, he thought it was the King's secret harbour where he and Kichesias had come before. But the light was different, and he didn't remember a throne.

He lifted his head slightly and studied the noblemen. Phoebe's father was in the middle of the group. The King's cheeks were pinched and his eyes were red, but his jaw was set in a fierce, tight line. Next to him stood a tall man in armour stained with the grime of battle – General Memnon, whom Alexis had last seen in the Mausoleum back at the start of the siege. The other men were dressed in the Persian style, and Alexis supposed they were the King's advisors. But he didn't have time for a proper look, because his guard chose that moment to push his head roughly back down.

Officer Cleon marched up to the group and saluted the General. "We caught this spy in the park, sir! He's one of the boys who broke into the Palace last month." He gave Alexis a clout on the ear. "Tell the General when you last saw the Princess, spy!"

While General Memnon regarded Alexis over his hooked nose and King Orontobates frowned at him, one of the Persian noblemen detached himself from the group and put a hand on the King's arm. Alexis's world shifted slightly as he caught the scent of the Persian's oiled beard and recognized the man who had commissioned his father's final sculpture and helped him at the Assembly. Hope and fear clashed inside him. Ishkibar must be even more important than he'd realized if he was here in the Palace with the King and General Memnon.

Ishkibar shook his head warningly at Alexis and cleared his throat. "Your Excellency, I'm sorry to interrupt, but this boy isn't a spy. He couldn't have been involved in the Princess's abduction because he was speaking to the Assembly this morning when she disappeared. I don't think the people who took her are still in the city. In my opinion, we should be looking elsewhere."

Alexis breathed a sigh of relief.

The King raised an eyebrow at Memnon, who snapped, "Take the boy away, Cleon! What did you bring him in here for? I'll question him later when we've a better idea of what happened."

Grateful that Ishkibar had stood up for him, Alexis opened his mouth to ask if he could go home. But Ishkibar had already turned back to continue the conversation Officer Cleon had interrupted.

"Sir!" Alexis appealed to the King. "I can explain—"

"Save it for your interrogation, spy!" Cleon growled,

giving him another clout on the ear. He nodded to the soldiers, who hauled Alexis to his feet.

"But I just wanted to say Phoebe was all right when I—"

"I said, save it."

Seeing the anger in the officer's eyes, Alexis braced himself, but Cleon was distracted by a Palace guard who ran into the hall and gasped out, "A messenger from the Acropolis, General sir! Demanding to speak to the King alone!"

"Tell him he'll have to wait," snapped the General. His words ended on a dry cough, reminding Alexis how someone at the Assembly had said Memnon was supposed to be ill. Aside from that one cough, however, the General looked stronger than most people half his age, and his tone was fierce. "The King doesn't have time to listen to spiteful messages from that pretender Ada, and neither do I. We're at war, and the Princess has disappeared. Send the messenger back where he came from."

The guard looked uncomfortable. "Er... it's a woman, sir."

"So? What difference does that make? Send her back immediately and don't bother us again unless it's important." His eyes flashed in anger when he noticed Alexis still kneeling in the middle of the hall. "What is that boy still doing in here? I thought I told you to take him to the cells."

Alexis made a final appeal to Cleon's men as they dragged him towards a dim corridor at the back of the hall, then froze as a woman's voice echoed in the hall behind them. "*Neaera!*" he breathed, dragging his surprised guards behind the potted plants before she could catch sight of him. He should have guessed. Queen Ada's messenger. A woman. Who else?

"Take your hands off me!" Neaera snapped at the guards who had tried to stop her entering the hall. "Tell the Satrap Orontobates that if he wants to see his daughter alive again, he will grant me an audience at once and alone, exactly as Queen Ada requested."

Through the leaves, Alexis watched his stepmother disarm the unfortunate guards as easily as if they were small children. She snapped their spears across her knee, tossed the pieces away, and marched across the marble floor towards the King.

Ignoring the glowering General Memnon, she addressed King Orontobates with an elaborate curtsey. "Your Excellency! I bring greetings from Queen Ada, true and rightful Queen of Caria. She asked me to inform you that Princess Phoebe is alive and unharmed and in a safe place, and will stay that way provided you grant me a private audience so we can work out the details of the surrender of Halicarnassos to General Alexander of Macedon."

For the space of ten heartbeats, no one moved. Even Alexis's guards stopped trying to drag him away and waited to hear the King's reply.

The shocked silence was broken by General Memnon, who growled, "Anything Ada has to say can be said to me as well as to the King. I am responsible for the defence of Halicarnassos in the name of the Great Emperor Darius. Surrender is not an option."

Alexis craned his neck to see Neaera's reaction to this, but his guards had heard enough. They hauled him away and gave him a shove along the corridor. "Get along, you! Whatever's goin' on back there don't concern the likes of us. You're in quite enough trouble as it is."

"But that's my..." Alexis bit the words off. Identifying himself with Queen Ada's messenger didn't seem a very good idea right now. At least Neaera hadn't brought Kichesias with her. He hoped his friend had got home safely.

He heard his stepmother say something that drew a cry of rage from the King. But by this time his guards had turned a corner and he couldn't make out the words. They descended a flight of steps into an underground passage where torches flared on the walls. Alexis considered trying to dodge his guards and run. But these weren't the same tunnels he and Kichesias had taken when they'd found the secret harbour. He might run the wrong way, and this time Kichesias wouldn't be there to help him break down locked gates and doors.

As he dithered, Officer Cleon hurried up behind them carrying a small hydria. "Seems this is your lucky day, boy," he growled. "Apparently, scheming old Queen Ada is behind the Princess's abduction, so you're in the clear. But his Excellency's Chief Advisor still wants to question you when he's finished hearing what the messenger has to say, so we're not letting you go home just yet. In here will do." He opened a door, grasped the neck of Alexis's tunic and pushed him through into a small, dark space. "Chain him to the wall," he ordered, chuckling as Alexis tried to get out again. "Don't want him breaking the door down like he broke the gate last time, do we?"

"But that wasn't me!" Alexis said desperately, shuddering as he glimpsed a set of manacles in the shadows at the back of the cell. "I'm not strong enough to break doors – that was my friend! I want to help you get Phoebe back as much as anyone does. What's Queen Ada done to her? Is she all right...?"

Ignoring his pleas, the guards locked the manacles around his wrists. Officer Cleon motioned them out of the cell, placed the hydria inside, and regarded Alexis from the doorway, frowning a little. "Don't drink it all at once," he warned. "You might be in here a while."

Alexis fought tears. "Please, sir, you can't keep me here! I have to go home. You don't understand! There's someone I have to look after..."

Officer Cleon strode away. The guards shook their heads at Alexis as they closed and barred the door, leaving him alone in the dark with his fears.

Chapter 11

GORDION KNOT

MAUSSOLLOS: Will all that,
then, be of no good to me?

In the darkness, with only an occasional sip from the hydria to break the monotony of his imprisonment, Alexis's imagination ran wild. What was Neaera saying to the King and General Memnon? What had Queen Ada done to poor Phoebe? Was Kichesias all right? He hadn't felt any unexplained pains or discomfort, but then he never did feel his friend's pain when they were apart. This would seem to confirm Phoebe's theory that the bond he shared with a woken statue was all in his mind, which only made him more worried because he had no way of knowing if Kichesias and Diogenes were safe. What if the Assembly sent the physician to examine his father's "corpse" while Alexis wasn't there?

He ran his fingers around his manacles, searching for

the lock mechanism. But he couldn't even see, let alone break them open. He thumped the floor in frustration and accidentally knocked the hydria in the dark. He reached quickly for the jar as it wobbled, but the chain snatched his wrist back. There was a cold shock across his thighs as the precious contents spilled into the dirt of his cell.

"No!" Alexis moaned. He shook the hydria fearfully, remembering Officer Cleon's warning that he could be here a long time. A faint sloshing in the bottom told him there were only a few mouthfuls left. At once he felt thirsty, but dared only wet his lips. He set the hydria carefully in a corner, where he would be unlikely to knock it over again, and wrapped his chained arms around his knees in an attempt to stop himself trembling. The harder he tried to control his body, the more it shivered and shook.

He began to see things. The golden pin piercing Kichesias's hand... Neaera smiling up at his window, when she came back from the Mausoleum covered in blood... the woken statue with his father's face saying, "Who's that boy?" He started to cry, ashamed of the tears but unable to hold them back any longer. "Oh, Father!" he sobbed into the dark. "Why didn't you stop me bringing Neaera to life? Why, *why*?"

Crying only made him thirsty again. He reached for the hydria and took another small swallow, choked, and clutched the handles tightly, afraid of spilling his final few drops of water. Still no one came. Did Neaera know he was here? Was she even now planning her revenge on him for accusing her of murder?

By the time the bar outside scraped and the door swung open, Alexis was huddled against the wall, exhausted, with the empty hydria clasped to his chest. He jerked awake and raised an arm to shield his eyes from the sudden flood of light, shivering as the clank of his chain reminded him where he was. A silhouette in long robes stood over him, carrying something brilliant enough to be the sun and bringing the scent of perfume.

There was a soft curse. Then Ishkibar was kneeling before him in the dirt. He set down the "sun" – only a lamp, after all – and gently extracted the hydria from Alexis's grasp. "It's all right, lad," he said. "No one's going to hurt you now."

While Alexis blinked uncertainly at him, Ishkibar straightened and snapped to the guard who hovered behind, "Get those chains off the boy at once! Whose idea was it to put him in here? No, don't tell me... Officer Cleon 'just doing his job' again, I suppose. You can tell your superior that from now on this boy is under the official protection of Emperor Darius. I'm taking him to my quarters."

The guard obeyed and unlocked the manacles. Alexis scrambled to his feet and wiped his face on his sleeve, embarrassed that the rich Persian who had known his father should see him like this. Silently, Ishkibar handed Alexis a square of soft cloth, embroidered round the edges in gold thread. Then he led the way out of the cell, walking slowly so that Alexis could keep up on his cramped legs. The guard frowned after them, but did not follow.

As they climbed some steps and emerged from the tunnels into the wide marble corridors of the Palace, Alexis reluctantly used a small corner of the embroidered cloth to wipe his nose. Ishkibar kept turning his head to give him encouraging smiles. Before he could make up his mind whether the Persian was a friend or an enemy, they had passed through a pair of tall doors into a well-furnished room lit by lamps with shades of twinkling red and green glass. The floor was covered with a thick carpet, soft and warm beneath Alexis's bare feet. Couches draped in deep, rich colours were drawn up around a three-legged table carved from dark wood. The sight of a bowl of figs and apples in the centre of the table made Alexis's mouth water.

"Help yourself," Ishkibar said, closing the doors and twisting a rope around the handles so that no one could disturb them. "Rationing is not as strict here in the Palace as it is elsewhere in the city."

He lit a burner under a bowl of scented oil to perfume the air, strode to the other side of the room, and folded back an ornate wooden screen to reveal a balcony overlooking a courtyard garden thick with evening shadows. A fountain tinkled somewhere in the dusk, and plants Alexis had never seen before dripped scarlet flowers around the balcony, obviously unaware it was winter. "Mmm," Ishkibar said, stretching out his arms and taking a deep breath. "I'm fond of my mansion on the Hill, but there are advantages to a sheltered spot like this. Wouldn't think a Persian garden could exist out here on the cold shores of the Empire, would you? The King's Palace holds many such secrets." He fixed Alexis with his dark gaze. "But I believe you know that, Alexis son of Diogenes."

Alexis stiffened and glanced at the doors. Could he get that rope off and run before the Persian stopped him?

Ishkibar chuckled. "Don't look at me like that! Relax. Sit down. Eat. Would you like something to drink? I have some good sherbet here – just one of the many advantages of being Chief Advisor to the Satrap of Caria."

Alexis controlled another shiver. Ishkibar was the King's Chief Advisor? Then this must be the interrogation Officer Cleon had threatened him with. Although this room was not the terrifying torture chamber he'd envisaged, the thought chilled him. "I'm very grateful to you for letting me out of that cell, sir," he said, keeping the tremor out of his voice with an effort. "But I really should go home right away. It's nearly dark, and there are a lot of things I have to do."

"Yes, yes, I expect you have." Ishkibar seated himself and waved at the opposite couch. "I have things to do as well. Things for my Emperor. You are, I believe, a little more important to these matters than I previously suspected, so I'd appreciate some of your time, if that's all right with you. Aren't you even going to ask after Queen Ada's messenger?"

"What did you do to her?" Alexis said, shivering again.

His voice must have given him away, for Ishkibar laughed. "She made it easy for us, didn't she? Turning up like that with an ultimatum from old Ada! The King might seem unwarlike and mild-mannered, but Queen Ada made a bad mistake abducting his precious daughter. He didn't need too much persuasion to let Memnon arrest Lady Neaera. She'll be held here in the garrison until her trial. She'll be tried for aiding the enemy as well as for the murder you accused her of this morning. So you should get the sentence you're hoping for, one way or another."

Alexis sat down, more because his legs wouldn't support him any longer than because he wanted to stay.

Ishkibar smiled and poured him the sherbet he'd boasted about, pushing the goblet across the table so Alexis could reach it more easily. "Which means," he continued smoothly, "that you are now without either of your parents and officially in need of a guardian."

"Pasion looks after us," Alexis said, peering curiously into the goblet. He'd never tasted sherbet before.

Ishkibar smiled again. "Sculptor Pasion is a poor man. He can't give you the protection you need now. I've decided that for the time being, you should stay with me."

The sherbet stuck in Alexis's throat. "But I have to be with Kiche—"

Ishkibar held up a hand. "Hear me out. I wouldn't do this for just any boy from the Craftsman's Quarter. But your father and I built up a good relationship while he was working on the statue of my son. We discussed a lot of things, and inevitably we spoke about the loss of loved ones. He told me about your mother. How she died in childbirth, and how she was descended in a direct line from the legendary Kings of Phrygia."

Alexis forgot his thirst and clutched his goblet tightly as Ishkibar continued, "I meant to follow this up before now but, as I'm sure you can imagine, I've been very busy of late. The Emperor wants to know where the sympathies of every person in Halicarnassos lie. He wants to know if his Satrap King Orontobates is doing a good job, what General Memnon is doing with the mercenaries who took the Persian coin, what every member of the Royal Family is up to, and how all this will affect his war with the Macedonians. Information wins wars, Alexis, not heroic deeds. You can send a thousand heroes out to fight, but unless you send them to the right place at the right time, the chances are they will fail. I'm one of the people who tells the Emperor where the right place is, and when it might be the right time."

A few things fell into place in Alexis's head. "You're a spy!" he exclaimed, understanding at last what Ishkibar was doing in the Palace. At the same time, he turned cold. Had Ishkibar been spying on him, too?

His question was soon answered. Ishkibar curled one of his black ringlets around his little finger and gave Alexis an amused look. "I prefer 'undercover security agent'. But you're right. I'm Darius's eyes and ears in

Halicarnassos. There are always threats to his rule. Hundreds of tiny ones like you, Alexis – don't look so surprised! Your ancestry gives you a very minor claim to the Phrygian throne, which is why I've had you on my list for routine surveillance since your father's death. You might have been a threat to the Emperor, had you decided to press that claim, though I admit it seemed unlikely. There are a few bigger ones like Queen Ada, who seeks to make Caria an independent kingdom again. Then there's Alexander of Macedon, who eclipses all others, changes alliances, and brings people like you and me together, drinking sherbet, when normally we would never have cause to meet."

"Officer Cleon doesn't know who you are, does he?" Alexis said.

Ishkibar smiled. "Spies generally don't advertise their real work. Officially, I'm here to advise the Satrap on matters relating to Persia, and I take that duty seriously. At the same time, I report Orontobates' actions back to Darius."

"So not even the King knows who you really are?"

Ishkibar gave him another amused smile. "No."

Alexis started to feel scared. "Then why are you telling *me*?"

"Because I think there's something you're hiding from me, and I think the reason you're keeping it secret is because you don't know who to trust. You're an intelligent boy, Alexis. I want you to understand that I'm above such petty Carian politics as Queen Ada's quarrel with Orontobates, and I want you to realize that the true power in Halicarnassos lies with the Emperor. As his representative, I'm the best person to help you, so you can tell me everything without fear."

He leant back into the cushions and regarded Alexis thoughtfully.

"Let's start with Princess Phoebe, shall we? I understand you met her before she disappeared. She's a wild one, all right. She refused to go to Persia with General Memnon's family, and I hear she was abducted from the streets of the city, when strictly she isn't allowed out of the women's quarters here in the Palace. Some would say she had it coming, and I've no doubt she knows more than a girl of her age should. Did she ask you to do anything for her? To help her father in his quarrel with Queen Ada, perhaps?"

Alexis shook his head. He wanted to laugh because Ishkibar had got things so wrong, but it was too much after all that had happened since he woke up that morning. "Why should I trust you?" he whispered.

Had Ishkibar been watching him while he sculpted Diogenes in the image of his father? Had he been watching four years ago, when Alexis had brought Kichesias to life in the park? All those times when he'd experienced that prickly feeling at the back of his neck and thought Neaera was spying on him... It would explain why Ishkibar had appeared so conveniently at the Theatre when Alexis had asked to speak to the Assembly, and it might explain why he'd helped him... though

Ishkibar had seemed as surprised as anyone when Kichesias had uncovered Diogenes' "corpse". He shook his head again, unable to work it out.

"Purely a routine matter," Ishkibar reminded him. "I send my trainees out on cases like yours. It's good practice for them, and not too consequential if they make a mistake. But since Alexander turned up with his army, the matter has become a little more... urgent. I know, for example, that your stepmother has been helping Queen Ada for some time, and Ada is supporting Alexander, who seeks to become Lord of all Anatolia and who knows what else. I think they intend to use you in some way, but it puzzles me as to how."

He leant forward across the table and took hold of Alexis's hands. The Persian's were soft as a girl's, yet his grip was strong. Alexis stiffened. But Ishkibar merely turned his hands over and examined the palms with their hard knobs of skin and small cuts from the chisel.

"A working boy's hands," he murmured. "But then you're an apprentice sculptor, aren't you? Learning your father's worthy trade. Small fingers, but strong. Are these special hands, I wonder? What else did your father teach you before he died, Alexis?"

"Nothing," Alexis whispered, unable to keep the tremor from his voice.

Ishkibar stared into his eyes so closely that Alexis had trouble focusing on the dark face. "Don't be afraid. I promised your father I'd see no harm came to you, provided you didn't challenge Darius for the rule of

Phrygia. That was the real reason your father came to see me the night he died. He'd discovered I was Darius's man, and he was afraid I might try to remove the threat you represented to Persia, small as it was. He came to beg for your safety."

Again, the fear came. Alexis pulled his hands free. "That's crazy! *Me*, King of Phrygia?" But he thought of the argument between Neaera and Diogenes the night his father had gone to Ishkibar's house, and Neaera's own ambition to rule Caria. Might she have even larger plans than he'd suspected? He drew a shuddering breath. "I don't understand. What do you expect my father to have taught me?"

"It is said that those who are descended from the ancient Kings of Phrygia know the secret of unravelling the Gordion Knot," Ishkibar said. "Is this true, Alexis? Do you know how to untie it?"

Alexis had been eyeing the balcony as Ishkibar spoke. He'd been so certain the spy was working up to ask about the Midas magic, he'd almost made up his mind to jump and chance his luck to the shadows below. The question about the Gordion Knot caught him unawares.

"But that's just a story!" he said, not sure if he was supposed to laugh. He thought of Phoebe, surrounded by her Collection, proudly pointing out the sculpture of King Gordius's cart with its famous Knot. Surely Ishkibar wasn't so gullible?

Ishkibar frowned slightly. "The Knot exists. Phrygia's priests keep it at the Temple of Zeus in the town we now call Gordius. Legend says that only the rightful ruler of Anatolia will be able to undo it, and so far no one has succeeded, not even the Great Emperor Darius, though he did try once – in private, of course, so no one would know if he failed. It's become a test of kingship in these parts. If anyone manages to untie it, they'll be a danger to Darius simply because so many people believe in the legend and will support the successful man. If someone like Alexander of Macedon, who already has an army behind him, manages to untie it, the consequences could be fatal. So you can see why I'm worried. What I want to know is if your father passed on to you the secret of unravelling the Gordion Knot before he died. If he did, then that might explain a few things that have been puzzling me."

Think, Alexis, think.

"But my father wouldn't have known how to untie the Gordion Knot. He wasn't descended from a king like—" He stopped himself just in time. He felt weak and confused. "Please, sir, *please* let me go home. I don't know how to untie it. No one does. It's a joke in the Craftsmen's Quarter! Our masters tease us about 'tying a Gordion' when we get our knots wrong. It just means we've messed up. You've got to believe me." To his shame, tears leaked from his eyes. He turned his face away and wiped them angrily with the embroidered cloth.

When he could see again, Ishkibar was studying him, one arm thrown along the back of the couch. The Persian sighed. "Unfortunately, I do believe you. You're clever with your tongue, but it's one thing to persuade the Assembly to listen to a prepared speech, quite another to resist the powders I slipped into the hydria you were given. And you drank it all, I noticed."

Alexis turned cold. "You put powders in my water?" Then he realized what this meant. "You *knew* I was chained in there! You were just pretending to be concerned!"

Ishkibar raised an eyebrow. "Now, don't get angry with me. I gave you the powders to help us both. I didn't think for a moment anyone would chain a boy in a dark hole like that. I merely told Officer Cleon to keep you somewhere safe until I was ready to talk to you, and to give you time to drink the water, that's all. The powders I gave you are a secret mixture of ingredients Babylonian sorcerers use in their illusion spells. In the right proportions, we've discovered they lower a man's resistance to questioning. They're quite harmless in moderate doses. I often use them when I need information. The alternative is General Memnon's crude methods. I know which method I'd prefer, were our positions reversed."

Alexis kept quiet. Ishkibar didn't seem to realize he'd spilt most of the water in his cell. With such a dirty floor, he obviously hadn't noticed the extra dampness.

"I don't see what the Gordion Knot has to do with me or my father," he said, bowing his head to hide his relief. If he could keep the conversation on the subject of this Knot, it might distract Ishkibar from asking about his real magic. "Why do you think I know how to untie it?"

Ishkibar nodded. "You wouldn't necessarily know the connection. King Gordius was childless, so he passed the secret of untying the Knot down to his adopted son, who was meant to pass it down to his sons, and so on, in case anyone challenged their right to rule. The theory being, I suppose, that they could always go to the Temple and untie the Knot to show everyone they had the right to rule. The boy he adopted was called Midas." He paused, awaiting a reaction.

"You mean my ancestor Midas?" Alexis said, too surprised for caution. "I didn't know he was adopted."

Ishkibar smiled. "People tend to forget that part of the story – it's not as romantic as turning things to gold, is it? I expect the Knot legend is where all the nonsense about Midas's golden touch originated. In this world, as most sensible men soon realize, riches come through power and knowledge, not god-given talents. Gordius's theory was sound enough. The only problem being King Midas didn't have any sons to pass the Knot lore on to. But he did have a daughter, and I'm wondering if he didn't pass the secret on through her. Girls are clever enough with their hands, but not until a son was born to Midas's bloodline would a true challenger to the throne arise... you, Alexis. I checked your ancestry. Your father was telling the truth. It's an unbroken line through the female descent all the way back to the legendary King Midas himself. Since your mother died in childbirth, she obviously couldn't have taught you the secret herself.

But she and your father were very close. It's quite conceivable she should have trusted him with the secret of the Gordion Knot so he could pass it on to you when you were old enough to understand. He might not have told you the reason, considering his wish to protect you, and he might not have even realized the significance himself, but that doesn't mean he didn't show you old Gordius's secret. Think carefully. Did he ever teach you anything about knots?" Ishkibar's eyes were sharp and watchful.

Alexis sipped some more sherbet to give himself time to think. Ishkibar didn't believe in magic, only in secrets! So he'd let him have a secret. He allowed his hands to tremble more than they would have on their own.

"Only how to tie statues into the transport frame so they won't fall out and break," he said as innocently as he could. "But we used our own special knots – all sculptors do." Ishkibar's eyes flashed, and Alexis knew he had swallowed the bait. "I don't know if I can remember them, because Pasion always makes us use his own knots, but if you get me some rope maybe I can show you. Then please can I go home?" He glanced at the balcony again. It was fully dark outside now, with the thick feel of a storm brewing.

"Will this do?" Ishkibar strode eagerly to the door and untwisted the rope from the handles.

Alexis shook his head. "It'll have to be longer than that. Some of the knots Father taught me were very complicated – it really needs to be thicker, too."

Ishkibar's eyes narrowed. But he nodded. "I'll send for some."

Alexis hid his smile of triumph. The effect of the small amount of powders he had drunk must be wearing off. It was getting easier to think. All he had to do now was make sure Ishkibar left him alone with the rope.

"Where did you put Neaera?" he asked. "Are you sure she can't get out and spy on us?"

Ishkibar, who had already pulled open the door to call a slave, frowned. "Women are usually given special cells according to the needs of their sex. But she won't escape, don't worry."

"She's very strong," Alexis warned. "She might be able to break down the door. And she has a special talent. If she does get out and people are looking for her, she can stand so still they'll mistake her for a statue. That's probably why Queen Ada uses her as a messenger. I'd feel safer if I knew you'd checked on her yourself, sir." The dark eyes studied him for so long, Alexis thought he'd gone too far. "She killed my father," he reminded the Persian. "How did she do that, if she wasn't stronger than a normal woman? You have to warn her guards."

Ishkibar frowned again, a thoughtful look in his eye. "You could be right, at that... I saw how she disarmed those men in the hall. I wonder if she has some Amazon blood? Don't worry, I'll see to it. You stay here. Try to eat something. I'll send a slave with the rope so you can practise your knots, and I'll have him bring you some more food and sherbet, too. You look quite pale, and we

163

want to have you in good shape for the trial." He smiled. "You've been most cooperative, Alexis. When this business with the Macedonians is over, I'll see you and your guardian are rewarded."

Alexis relaxed slightly and risked a final plea. "There's one more thing," he said. "My father's body... you said the Assembly was going to send a physician to examine it, but it seems so horrible. He's already dead. Does he have to be prodded and poked by a stranger as well?"

Ishkibar paused at the door, one eyebrow raised. "It's the usual procedure. But in this case, considering recent developments, perhaps the examination can be dispensed with. We haven't really the time now, anyway, and getting a physician out in the middle of the night is never easy."

"When's the trial?" Alexis asked, taken by surprise.

"Tomorrow at dawn in the agora. They're drawing for the jury tonight. I'll send someone to collect your father's body, and you can tell the jury what you told the Assembly. The good citizens of Halicarnassos could do with something to distract them from this siege. I think Lady Neaera will do nicely. Thank you for bringing her to my attention."

Before Alexis had a chance to ask anything else, Ishkibar called a guard to watch the door and hurried out of the room.

Chapter 12

CONSPIRACY

MAUSSOLLOS: Will Maussollos and Diogenes be on an equal footing?

When Ishkibar had gone, Alexis sat very still, suddenly aware of the dangerous game he was playing. A rather hysterical giggle escaped him. Ishkibar believed in a secret knot that could turn a craftsman's son into a king. Yet he didn't believe in King Midas's golden touch. What would he have done, if Alexis really had drunk the tongue-loosening powders and told him the truth?

The click of the door made him jump. But it was only the slave bringing his promised rope and food. He'd been worried Ishkibar might send one of the lily-hands. But this slave was an old woman with grey streaks in her hair. She made a clucking noise when she saw the state of Alexis's tunic, and insisted on serving him a huge pile of delicacies from the tray she carried. She pushed the plate into his hands with instructions to eat up. "Might as well make the most of it, lad," she said. "None of us is sure where our next meal's coming from with this siege goin' on. Whatever the Persian wants you for, take my advice and don't let it ruin your appetite."

Alexis forced down a few mouthfuls to please her, eyeing the coil of thick rope she had shrugged off her shoulder on to the couch opposite. As soon as she'd gone, he pushed his plate away, uncoiled the rope and tested it for strength. He smiled to himself. He would tie knots in Ishkibar's rope, all right – but not the ones the Persian was hoping for.

He secured one end to a convenient column and dropped the other end over the balcony into the dark. It was an easy climb down with the vines curling around him and the scent of the red winter flowers filling his head. The rope ran out before he reached the ground, but Alexis took a deep breath and let go. He crashed through some wet foliage and landed clumsily in the courtyard with a grin of triumph.

He crouched in the shadows to get his bearings. The garden was smaller than he'd thought and completely enclosed by high walls topped with spikes. The fountain he'd heard earlier made a decorative centrepiece. He couldn't see a gate. Lamplight, spilling from the high palace windows, embroidered the leaves with gold. He wondered if it might have been better to use the rope to swing to a neighbouring balcony. Too late now.

As he hesitated, he became aware of men's voices

coming from one of the rooms. He crept towards them using the plants as cover, and his heart lifted as he glimpsed a ground-floor opening where lamplight poured through an archway barred by an ornate metal grille. The shutters had been flung open to catch the night scents of the flowers, giving Alexis a good view of the large, brightly lit room beyond, which was even more richly furnished than Ishkibar's. Inside, King Orontobates was talking to some of his noblemen. The King's words were accompanied by sharp gestures, and he was holding a small jewelled casket, which he waved about as he spoke. He had changed out of his long robes and wore trousers and a tunic in the fashion of the Persian soldiers. A Palace guard knelt on the floor at the King's feet – apparently the cause of his anger.

Alexis crept closer, curious despite the danger. General Memnon didn't seem to be in the room, and neither did Ishkibar. Maybe, if he waited until the King had finished, he could slip through the grille and find a way out of the Palace.

The guard mumbled something to the King and produced a crumpled scroll. Orontobates snatched the scroll, scanned it quickly and flung it aside. He gripped the casket with white knuckles and strode to the grille. For an instant, he seemed to stare straight at Alexis where he crouched in the shadows with banging heart. But the King obviously couldn't see out into the darkness as well as Alexis could see in. The royal eyes were unfocused, and tears of rage glittered in them.

Behind the King, one of the nobles picked up the scroll. "It's probably a hoax, Your Excellency..."

"Read it to me," Orontobates ordered in a tight voice, still staring out into the darkness. "My Greek letters aren't very good. I might be mistaken."

The nobleman looked reluctant, but cleared his throat and read, "*From Queen Ada, Rightful Heiress of Caria...*" He broke off with a little cough. "I apologize, Your Excellency, but that's what it says... er, I'll skip the next bit, shall I?"

"Read exactly what's written," said the King in a dangerous voice. "All of it."

With another cough, the man continued, "Um... *To the Usurper Orontobates: I am most displeased you have imprisoned my messenger Lady Neaera, whom I sent to you in good faith to obtain your personal answer to my request. I can only assume that this petty trial you have ordered for tomorrow morning is an indication of your refusal to consider a peaceful solution to this war. I had hoped that your desire to have your daughter returned unharmed would encourage you to see sense and persuade General Memnon to call off his troops, but I see that further encouragement is required. It has occurred to me that perhaps you do not believe I am holding her. To convince you of this matter, I am returning a small part of the Princess with this message. If you wish to see the rest of her, it is your choice how we proceed. Call off the trial, open the city gates tomorrow morning, surrender Halicarnassos to*

Alexander of Macedon, and your daughter will be returned to you. Otherwise, you will receive another casket like this one every night that this siege continues. The choice is yours, Orontobates."

There was a shocked hush in the room beyond the arch. Alexis's skin prickled, and the small amount of food he'd eaten in Ishkibar's quarters stuck in his throat. *Part of Phoebe?* The sensible thing would be to creep away from the grille and look for another way out, but the horror of what he'd just heard kept him immobile.

The man who had read the message lowered the scroll and frowned at the casket in the King's hands. "Shall I fetch Ishkibar and the General?" he asked.

The King made no answer. He continued to gaze out into the courtyard. Alexis hugged himself, trying to stop his shivers. He stared at the casket, not wanting to see what was inside but unable to look away.

Still the King made no attempt to open it. "Who brought this to the Palace?" he asked the guard.

"W–we don't know, Your Excellency," the guard stammered. "One of the sentries found it in the Royal Park, wedged into the hands of a statue. The scroll was with it, addressed to you personally. We searched, of course, but we found no one in the immediate vicinity. I ordered my men to continue searching and brought the box to you at once."

"No one looked inside?"

"Of course not, Your Excellency!"

The King sighed. "Call off the search," he said.

"Whoever left this in the park will be long gone. You can return to your post."

The guard seemed relieved to escape. The King caressed the casket, and Alexis stiffened as he saw Orontobates' slender fingers move towards the catch. But he glimpsed only a brief glitter of jewels as the lid was raised. The King's expression was stony as he looked inside. The others craned forwards to see. But before they could peer over his shoulder, the King slammed the lid and closed his eyes.

"No," he whispered. He took a deep breath and said in a stronger voice, "General Memnon is not to know about this! I want to see Ishkibar alone in my private quarters at once. This matter is to go no further than this room. Understand?"

There were a few murmurs of disagreement, but the King silenced them with a glare. "This is my city," he said so quietly that Alexis had to strain to hear. "Neither Ada nor Alexander is going to take it from me. There will be no more packages like this one. By tomorrow night, this siege will be over." He tucked the casket under his arm, swept past the muttering nobles, and vanished deeper into his Palace.

Alexis's head spun as arguments broke out in the room beyond the grille. The nobles wanted to storm the Acropolis and rescue Phoebe at once, but were reluctant to defy their King. Alexis only half listened. What did King Orontobates mean, *By tomorrow night, this siege will be over*? Did it have something to do with Neaera's trial? He didn't see how that was going to help Phoebe. Poor Phoebe! It was all his fault for telling her about his magic. If he hadn't involved her in his crazy plan to make a substitute corpse for his father, she would not have been alone in the Temple yesterday.

He started to back away from the arch, but paused as one of the King's men said, "What do you think of this trial? Some boy's supposed to have accused Queen Ada's messenger of murdering his father, isn't he? Seems a strange time to hold a murder trial, don't you think?"

"I expect it's all part of the smokescreen," one of the others said. "I hear Ishkibar was there when the boy spoke to the Assembly. Obviously he put him up to it."

"But even Ishkibar couldn't have known Queen Ada would send the woman to the Palace tonight!"

"I'll bet he did. A body was found. A murderer is required. Why not Queen Ada's messenger? It's juicier than a wishy-washy trial for crimes against the state, you must admit. First rule of combat – distract, then strike! Course, the real murderer will get away with it, but that hardly matters now."

"Ishkibar's a clever one, I'll give him that. I understand he knew the victim? Wasn't it all tangled up with his wife's suicide? I wouldn't put it past him to be killing more than two birds with one stone tomorrow."

The real murderer will get away with it. Alexis held his breath, listening for more. But a louder than normal attack on the city wall and answering shouts from the garrison brought the men towards the grille to peer out.

Alexis quickly stepped backwards – and tripped over an empty pot in the dark.

"Shh! You hear that? Someone's out there!" One of the King's men rattled the gate. "Anyone got a key for this?"

Alexis's heart thudded. He glanced back at the dangling rope. Another rattle as one of the men began to slide open the lock decided him. He raced back to Ishkibar's balcony and jumped as high as he could. But the end of the rope was still too far away. He looked round desperately. Some of the trees in the courtyard were growing in pots like those inside the Palace. Panting with the effort, he managed to twist and pull a sturdy-looking palm closer. Wrapping his arms and legs around the trunk, he wriggled his way up. The palm swayed precariously, but he grabbed the rope and kicked to swing himself higher. He winced as the tree toppled beneath him and crashed into the courtyard below.

The gate under the arch slammed open and the King's men rushed out into the courtyard with drawn daggers.

"Intruders!" one cried, spotting the fallen palm in its broken pot. He looked up and made a jab with his dagger at Alexis's dangling legs. "Quick," he said to the others. "It's a Macedonian assassin! You two go round the other way and up the stairs. We'll wait here and catch him when he falls." He made another ineffectual jab at Alexis's feet. "You're trapped, spy! I don't know how you got in here, but you're not getting out again!"

Alexis hauled himself further up the rope, the muscles

of his arms straining. Two of the men had gone to find the stairs. Five remained below, scowling up at him.

"Bet he was the one who put that casket in the park," growled one.

"Shh, you fool!" said the first. "You heard what the King said! He's probably seen everything, though. We'll have to cut his throat."

Alexis wet his lips in sudden fear. "I'm not a spy!" he called down. "I'm Ishkibar's witness. Ask him!"

"Ha!" said the spokesman. "Expect us to fall for that? It just proves you were listening. Send us all running off in search of Ishkibar so you can escape, is that the idea? We're not that stupid."

"I'm practising my knots," Alexis said desperately. "Ishkibar told me to. I was just... er... testing them to see if they held my weight." He wriggled further up, hoping he might get back into Ishkibar's quarters before the others found the stairs. But the rope twitched in his hands, and with sinking heart he saw the two men who had gone up the easy way peering over the balcony, along with the sentry Ishkibar had left to guard his door.

"Shake him off!" one of them hissed.

"No, cut him loose!"

"All right! I'm coming down!" Alexis called.

The five men in the courtyard stiffened, and Alexis eyed their daggers uncertainly. He didn't have any choice, though, because the rope suddenly went slack as it was cut from above. He half fell, half jumped into the circle of blades below. The spokesman seized his hair, dragged his head back, and put his dagger across Alexis's throat. But before he could carry out his threat to silence him, Ishkibar hurried out of the archway.

"Stop!" he called in a commanding tone, frowning at Alexis. "What's going on here?"

The noblemen excitedly explained they'd caught a Macedonian spy.

"He's not a Macedonian," Ishkibar said wearily. "Let him go." His gaze took in the fallen coils of rope. He shook his head. "I'm disappointed in you, Alexis son of Diogenes. Anyone would think you were trying to leave without saying goodbye. The night's half gone, and I'm sure you don't want to miss the start of the trial. You really ought to get some sleep, or you'll be no good at all as a witness tomorrow morning."

The man holding Alexis seemed disappointed to discover his captive had been telling the truth. With obvious reluctance, he released him into Ishkibar's custody.

The Persian's long fingers tightened on the back of Alexis's neck as they left the courtyard. "That was really stupid," he said softly. "Where did you think you were going? Everyone's jumpy with this siege, and the Palace Guard is on maximum alert tonight. You could have got hurt. Then where would we be? We'll look pretty silly if we're unable to produce our star witness tomorrow. If I'd known you only wanted the rope so you could climb out of my room, I would have sent up a longer one – you could have broken your neck! Thank you for your tip, by the way. We caught Lady Neaera on her way out of her cell. She's been adequately restrained, and I've doubled her guard. We'd look pretty silly without a defendant tomorrow, as well." His smile was cold.

Alexis said nothing, still thinking of what he'd overheard outside the King's room. Ishkibar had already admitted Diogenes went to see him the night he died to plead for Alexis's safety because he'd found out who Ishkibar really was. It was all starting to make a chilling kind of sense.

Ishkibar frowned. "What's wrong? You needn't be afraid of me, Alexis. If you really don't know the secret of the Gordion Knot, I won't hold it against you. It was a bit far-fetched, I must admit, but it was a possible reason why Queen Ada might be in league with your stepmother, and right now I can't think of another one."

"You're a murderer!" Alexis hissed, his skin crawling where the Persian was touching him. "I heard the King's men talking about the trial. They said the real murderer would get away with it, and that you were killing more than two birds with one stone... *You* killed my father, not Neaera! I'm going to tell everyone the truth tomorrow!"

Ishkibar let go of his neck and stared at him in surprise. He laughed softly. "Oh, I see. You think I silenced your father because he'd found out I was Darius's man, don't you?" He shook his head sadly. "Do you really think I'd kill the man who had sculpted such a sensitive image of my dying son and asked for no fee?"

Alexis didn't know what to think. If Ishkibar had killed his father, then that would make Neaera innocent, which he didn't want to believe. "You might have ordered someone else to do it."

The Persian sighed. "Come now. Would I be protecting you and helping you bring Lady Neaera to trial, if I had killed your father?"

"You might. You might want her to get the blame so no one suspects you."

Ishkibar shook his head. "In that case, why am I letting you speak as my star witness?"

Alexis had no answer to that. He felt lost and frightened. Their footsteps echoed across a vast, shadowy hall. "I want to go home tonight," he whispered. "I don't want to stay here."

Ishkibar sighed again. "I'm afraid that's not possible. I need to make sure you turn up in one piece and able to testify at Lady Neaera's trial. Since you insisted on using my rope for purposes that I never intended, you've seen something you shouldn't have. After tomorrow it won't matter, but right now we can't risk rumours about the Princess's health running riot through the city."

Alexis's heart gave an extra thud. Momentarily, he forgot his distrust of the Persian as he recalled the expression on the King's face when he'd peered into the jewelled casket Queen Ada had sent him.

"What was in the box?" he whispered.

Ishkibar shook his head. "That's not for you to

know. I advised Orontobates to send his daughter to Persia with General Memnon's family precisely because I feared something like this would happen. Unfortunately for the Princess, he didn't insist she obey him. When a man is ruled by the women in his family, there's always trouble. But the gods work in mysterious ways. We needed something to break the stalemate of this siege, and it seems Queen Ada's little gift has worked the miracle Memnon and I were unable to bring about with words alone. Orontobates has finally started to act like a real king." He smiled, as if this was worth any amount of fear and pain on Phoebe's part.

Alexis was starting to suspect the trial was not the only thing planned for tomorrow morning. But already they were at the top of the stairs, and Ishkibar was guiding him with a gentle pressure on his elbow past the sentry and into his quarters, where the food the slave had brought waited half-eaten on the table exactly where Alexis had left it. The sticky, congealed delicacies turned his stomach. He eyed the sherbet suspiciously, remembering the powders Ishkibar had put in his water.

Ishkibar pressed his lips together. "I know you don't trust me, Alexis. I can't say I blame you. But you'll have your chance to speak tomorrow, and the jury will decide Lady Neaera's guilt or innocence. We're very democratic here in Halicarnassos. Just remember that you'll clear your father's name if you tell them what you told the Assembly. They'll already hate Lady Neaera for acting as Queen Ada's messenger, so it shouldn't take too much effort on your part to persuade them she's a murderess. No one is going to put *me* on trial for murder, whatever you might persuade them to believe. Think about it."

Chapter 13

TRIAL

DIOGENES: No, indeed, your Excellency;
we shan't be on an equal footing.

Ishkibar took Alexis to the agora in the darkest time just
before dawn. They travelled on foot, accompanied by a
detachment of Palace guards. To Alexis's relief there was
no sign of Neaera. When he asked where she was,
Ishkibar informed him she would be brought from her
cell when the jury had chosen their judge for the day.

Alexis shivered as he tried to keep up with the
Persian's quick stride. Clouds hung over the city,
obscuring the fading stars. Not a sound came from
outside the walls, where the Macedonians had yet to
start their daily barrage. It reminded him of the morning
he'd woken Diogenes, except that today the streets of
Halicarnassos were host to citizens hurrying furtively
through the shadows. Ishkibar had explained that there

would be 201 jurors at Neaera's trial – the odd number ensuring they couldn't have a split vote. Alexis supposed the rest were coming to watch. Soldiers moved openly through the crowd, a few of them heading for the agora to keep order, others for the walls. Soldiers were a normal sight in the streets since the siege began, so Alexis didn't take much notice of them. But he soon realized more of the people abroad this morning were armed than he'd first thought. As the morning breeze strengthened, lifting the corners of their cloaks, he glimpsed the glitter of blades and breastplates hidden beneath. Some of the men carried bows with tar-wrapped arrows, reminding Alexis of the King's words. *By tomorrow night, this siege will be over.* He shook his head and hurried to catch up with Ishkibar. Whatever the soldiers were up to, it didn't concern him. He had quite enough to think about today.

The agora was empty of market stalls. In their place, benches had been positioned for the jury, a few of them already occupied by excited jurors. A chair for the judge waited at the top of the steps in front of one of the public buildings. Next to the judge's chair, two men were setting up a pair of large urns with taps – the water clock that would time the speakers. In the centre of the area defined by the benches and the judge's seat, a wooden platform had been erected, fenced with a little gate and a ladder for access. Two armed guards waited at the bottom of the ladder. Alexis shivered again. That was where Neaera would stand while she was tried. More soldiers formed a wall of spears around the benches, keeping the audience back from the court.

The sky was growing lighter with a hint of pink over the hills to the east. Ishkibar pointed to a short bench positioned at the foot of the steps. Alexis slowly walked over to it, thinking about what he'd learnt last night. After tossing and turning on the couch in Ishkibar's quarters, he still hadn't made up his mind who was guilty of killing his father. But even if Neaera hadn't done it, she must have been involved because of the statue blood. He couldn't stop the trial now, even if he'd wanted to.

Two people were already sitting on the witness bench, huddled into their cloaks. Alexis's heart lifted when he saw that the nearest was a girl. But it wasn't Phoebe. He had an impression of long red hair, cheap bangles and grubby legs. Then the second figure looked up.

"Kichesias!" he exclaimed with a surge of joy and relief.

His friend leapt to his feet. Oblivious of the strange girl, they embraced.

"Alex!" Kichesias cried. "I was so worried! No one would tell me anything! They just said I had to come here today and speak as a witness at Lady Neaera's trial. I thought that meant you couldn't be here... I thought something horrible had happened to you!"

Alexis thought of the cell and the powders Ishkibar had put in his water. He forced a smile. "Ishkibar thought it best I stay with him last night. He was concerned for my safety. Star witness, aren't I?"

Kichesias sighed as they sat down. "That's all right, then. But Alex, listen! I think something serious is happening at the Myndos Gate. I saw soldiers swarming all over the towers on my way here. And I think Phoebe's in danger! I was up in the Acropolis yesterday afternoon – Lady Neaera left a message with Pasion saying I had to go there as soon as I turned up – and I overheard her and Queen Ada talking. Lady Neaera said she had an idea how they could use Phoebe to make the King do what they wanted if he proved difficult. When I heard that, I hid so she wouldn't see me, and then she went off on one of Queen Ada's secret errands. Oh, Alex... what if they're planning to kidnap the Princess?"

"It's worse than that," Alexis said heavily. Quickly, he explained what he'd seen in the King's courtyard.

Kichesias paled. "I didn't know she was already a prisoner! I bet they're keeping her up in the Acropolis! Why didn't I investigate when I had the chance? I thought she was safe in the Palace because she'd asked you to go there and see her, and all I could think of was getting out of the Acropolis so I could come and warn you. We've got to rescue her right away, Alex!" He leapt to his feet again.

"Sit down," Alexis hissed, seeing Ishkibar glance their way. "Neaera will be here in a moment. We're witnesses, remember? We can't go anywhere until the trial's over."

"But Phoebe—" Kichesias blinked rapidly.

Alexis touched his friend's arm. He was worried about the Princess, too. But whatever horrible thing Queen Ada had done to her in order to send the King that casket could not be undone now, and they were about to learn the truth about his father's death.

"We'll get her out afterwards," he said gently. "She'll be fine until tonight. The scroll said Queen Ada wouldn't send another casket to the King until then." Hoping this was true, he peered anxiously round the agora. "Have you seen Diogenes? Ishkibar's supposed to have sent someone to collect the body. I hope he remembers to play dead."

Kichesias drew a deep breath. "You needn't worry about Diogenes. I went back to check on him after I got out of the Acropolis, and he was fine. I took him something to eat, taught him how to chew and swallow properly, and then I went home to warn you about what Queen Ada had said. You weren't there, of course. But it was getting late, and Pasion said we'd better wait until morning before we started looking for you, because of the curfew. The City Guard came in the night and hauled me here to the agora for the trial... They wouldn't tell me *anything*, Alex! When you weren't here, I thought the worst. And now the Queen's got poor Phoebe. She must be so frightened..." He blinked up the hill, where the Acropolis glowed like fire in the first flare of sun. "What do you think was in the casket?"

Alexis shook his head helplessly. "I don't know. Hair? One of Phoebe's bracelets, maybe? It wasn't big enough to hold much more. I thought the worst when I saw it, too. But her Great Aunt wouldn't really hurt her, would she? She's probably just trying to frighten the King."

Kichesias gripped the edge of the bench and a dangerous stillness came over him. "If she's so much as *touched* Phoebe..."

"It was probably hair," Alexis said quickly. "That would be enough to prove they were holding the Princess prisoner."

"It was a finger," came a faint whisper.

They had forgotten the third witness, the girl. A chill rippled down Alexis's spine, and Kichesias stared at her in horror. "Phoebe's *finger*?" he moaned. "No... oh *no.*"

"Who are you?" Alexis demanded. "How do you know?"

The girl drew her cloak closer and cast a furtive look around the court. Although she looked younger than them, she had rouge on her lips and kohl smudged clumsily around her eyes. Her bright hair was confined in two messy braids. "I know 'cause I saw it," she said, her thick accent making her words difficult to follow. "That's why I'm here. I have to tell the jury what I saw, or the soldiers who caught me said they'd put me in prison, and I couldn't bear that."

"You saw Phoebe?" Kichesias said. "Where? How? Are you one of Queen Ada's slaves?"

The girl shook her head. "My name's Anteia. I'm one of the women who follow General Alexander's army." She gave a nervous giggle as they stared at her. "I know what you're thinkin', but I'm not *that* kind of camp follower. I came with my mother to help with the cooking and stuff. Armies have to eat, you know, and they're always too busy fightin' to think about preparing food properly. They're always getting hurt, too, so I do a bit of stitchin' up their wounds as well." She looked up as an ox-cart drew up at the edge of the agora and a knot of soldiers gathered round it. "Is that the woman who's on trial? Yes... I definitely seen her in the camp."

Alexis stiffened as one of the men helped Neaera down from the cart and the others formed up to escort her to the defendant's enclosure. When she was marched past the witness bench, Neaera looked his way and their gazes met. His stepmother's eyes contained anger – he'd expected that – but a strange sadness too, almost as if she pitied him.

"Neaera's been to the *Macedonian camp*?" Alexis whispered as her guards hustled her up the ladder into the defendant's enclosure.

By this time, all the jurors had arrived and the benches were growing noisy. The audience packed the colonnade and filled the streets as far back as Alexis could see. At last, he spotted two Persian soldiers escorting a handbarrow pulled by slaves along the quay. In the barrow lay Diogenes, still covered in dried statue blood, as rigid and motionless as yesterday morning when he'd played dead for the Assembly. Alexis watched the woken statue carefully as the slaves manoeuvred the barrow into the court, but it was impossible to tell if he was pretending or not. Neaera hesitated when she saw the "corpse" and darted another glance at Alexis, a flicker of uncertainty in her dark eyes. The jurors on the front bench leant forwards with gruesome interest, and one of them got up and prodded the crystal coating on Diogenes' arm. Alexis held his breath. But the man in the barrow did not move, and after a moment the juror sat down again and muttered to his neighbour.

That man is not my father, Alexis reminded himself firmly. *If he's dead, then it's only what I planned to do to him.*

When he returned his attention to Neaera, she had been successfully installed in the enclosure. The gate was shut, and the guards had tied her wrists to the rail. She could have broken the ropes with one quick tug, of course. But she stood like a queen with her head held high, staring directly at the jury and ignoring the body in the barrow. She held the rail gently as if she had simply chosen to rest her hands there. The men on the front benches shifted uncomfortably under her gaze. Alexis could imagine her beauty shining over them. Even dishevelled after a night in prison, and with streaks of silver in her mussed hair, Neaera still had that power.

Kichesias was questioning Anteia in hushed tones, asking if she knew where Phoebe was being kept. Alexis didn't hear the girl's answer. The sun, which had been working its way rapidly down the hill, bathed the roof of the colonnade and cast long shadows across the tense crowd in the agora. The judge took his seat. The man in charge of the water clock opened the tap. And Ishkibar, who seemed to have taken on the role of court usher, clapped his hands for order and called in his ringing tones for Alexis, son of Diogenes the sculptor, to speak.

"That's you!" Kichesias whispered, nudging him. "Hurry up, then we can go and rescue Phoebe!"

Alexis stood up, avoiding Ishkibar's dark gaze. His legs did not seem to belong to him as he walked across the agora to stand before the jury. He deliberately didn't look at Neaera, but he felt her eyes on him as he told his story, exactly as he had told it to the Assembly yesterday.

The reaction was much the same. After some sympathetic noises for Alexis's loss, cries of: "Impossible!" and "A woman could never overpower a healthy man!" came from the benches, and the juror who had prodded Diogenes called out, "How is she supposed to have done it? Stuck him with her peplos pin?"

Laughter broke out, but Alexis winced at the comment and made the mistake of glancing at Neaera again. She was smiling faintly. He lost his thread of thought as he imagined her breaking the ropes and reaching for the golden pins in her pocket. But surely the guards would have confiscated them before they imprisoned her?

The jury was getting noisier, and the water level in the top urn was falling. Ishkibar had told Alexis the jurors weren't supposed to interrupt, but they weren't paying attention any more. He could feel his one chance to clear his father's name slipping away.

"I think she had help!" he shouted desperately. "From a man my father went to see that night, who lives up on the Hill." Out of the corner of his eye, he saw Ishkibar stiffen and whisper something to the man controlling the clock.

Mutters of "A man from the Hill?" ... "Who?" ... "What's the boy talking about?" passed round the benches. But the jury quietened. They were listening again, and – although it seemed to be flowing faster than before – his water had still not run out.

"My father's final commission was a sculpture for Ishkibar, Chief Advisor to the King," Alexis said, pointing to the Persian. "My father went to see Ishkibar that night. On his way home, he was murdered."

The agora was completely silent now. The jurors leant forwards, and some of them cast suspicious glances at Ishkibar. In the hush, shouts and the clash of blades carried across the city from the direction of the Myndos Gate, and a great plume of smoke rose into the early morning air out of the hills where General Alexander had made his camp. The people in the agora took little notice. The fighting outside the walls had been going on for so long they'd become bored with it. The human drama unfolding in the agora was much more interesting. Their attention fixed on Alexis as he told them all about Diogenes' final commission.

Before he could get as far as accusing Ishkibar of sending assassins to murder his father, the man watching the clock clapped his hands to indicate the water was gone, and Ishkibar strode forward with a look like thunder.

"Time's up!" he said, glowering at Alexis. "Since I have been implicated in this crime, I will speak to the jury myself."

Frustrated, Alexis had little choice but to return to the witness bench. He could feel Neaera's gaze on his back all the way. Kichesias shifted closer, his eyes wide. "What are you *doing*, Alex? What was all that rubbish about Ishkibar? Lady Neaera will get off free at this rate."

Alexis shook his head. "They won't believe Neaera's strong enough to have killed my father, and after what I heard last night I don't know any more if she *did* kill him. Ishkibar had as good a reason to murder my father as she did, perhaps more."

"But Ishkibar's *helping* us!"

Alexis shook his head again. That had been running round his mind all night, too. "I think he just wants someone else to take the blame so no one will suspect him. The King's men said Ishkibar's wife committed suicide from grief after their son died. Perhaps he blames my father for not making a good enough statue of the boy to stop her?"

Kichesias sighed and hunched his shoulders. "Lady Neaera's watching us. She's not innocent, Alex. Don't forget the statue blood and her gold pins."

"Don't look at her. She can't do anything to us here."

"They've only used rope to restrain her."

"I know. But she's hardly going to demonstrate her superior strength to the jury after what they just said, is she? She'd be convicting herself. Right now they think she's a helpless, weak woman incapable of overpowering a man."

"Tell them the truth," Kichesias said quietly. "They'll believe you then."

Alexis stared at his friend in horror. "I can't do that!"

"Why not? You don't have to tell them I was a statue too, do you? Just tell them about Lady Neaera. Then they'll sentence her and restrain her properly with golden chains because they'll understand, and we can all go. This trial will drag on and on otherwise, and we have to find Phoebe before tonight! Look, the man on the clock is blocking the flow so Ishkibar gets longer, the cheat!"

This was true. The urns had been reversed, and this time the man in charge had opened the tap so just a tiny drip came out, not the wild flow Alexis had been given at the end of his speech. Ishkibar was using the extra time to spin a long-winded, emotional story about his dying son and his excellent relationship with Diogenes the sculptor. He spoke very softly and persuasively, and when he told them how his grieving wife had taken poison shortly after her boy died, several of the jury dabbed at their eyes. Alexis clenched his fists, but there was nothing he could do. Ishkibar had obviously bribed the man to fix the clock. He'd probably bribed all two hundred and one jurors, too.

"If you don't tell them, I will," Kichesias said.

"No, Kichesias!" Alexis hissed, grabbing his sleeve. "Please don't."

"Do you want them to let Lady Neaera go? Can you imagine what she'll do to us once she gets us home and we're alone with her?"

"No..." Alexis glanced at Neaera again, visions of her golden pin piercing his friend's hand. "I mean, yes, I know she'll be angry. But everything's such a mess, Kichesias! I don't know if Neaera killed my father. I don't know if Ishkibar's lying. I don't even know if Diogenes is still alive! Is he playing dead like before, or did those soldiers kill him for real? The surviving lily-hand who came with Phoebe knew about the golden sword and the trick we played on the Assembly. He might have told Ishkibar about it."

Kichesias frowned at the barrow where Diogenes lay. "Don't be silly. The lily-hands can't talk, remember? Diogenes was good at the statue game before, and he'll have got better with practice. You told him to play dead if anyone came – they wouldn't have been expecting to find him alive."

"Lily-hands communicate with their fingers. I've seen them do it."

Kichesias chewed his lip. "I bet they don't communicate with people who aren't lily-hands. It sounds like a secret language to me."

Anteia, who had been biting her nails as she waited her turn to speak, was listening with interest. "You mean that man's not really dead?" she asked.

"Shh!" said Alexis and Kichesias together.

"I can believe it," she said. "I seen men like that after battles. They die for a bit, and then we wake 'em up again by blowing into their mouths and thumping on their chests. You have to be quick, though. If you leave them too long, they won't wake for nothin'."

"This is different, believe me," Alexis said stiffly.

Anteia shook her head. "I always wonder where their spirits go. They say some weird stuff sometimes, when they wake up. Mother says it's just fever-talk, but I think it must be very confusing to think you've died and then find you're suddenly alive again." She eyed the smoke in the hills. "I hope this trial don't go on much longer. There'll be a lot of wounded today with all this fighting. They'll be missin' me up at the camp."

Alexis exchanged a glance with Kichesias. He doubted the girl would be allowed back to the enemy camp after the trial, even if she did what Ishkibar wanted and the Macedonians survived the battle that was obviously in progress up in the hills. He didn't say anything, though. Anteia didn't seem to realize she was a prisoner of war, and he didn't want to worry the girl unnecessarily.

The fighting seemed to be moving closer to the city, and the smoke was now so thick that it was drifting across the sun. A sudden outcry from the direction of the Myndos Gate finally made the jurors look round. Ishkibar glanced that way as well and made a cutting motion with his hand. The man watching the clock opened the tap fully, and the water ran out.

The urns were reversed, and Ishkibar called for Kichesias to speak.

Alexis watched his friend anxiously. But Kichesias didn't say anything about the reverse Midas touch. He didn't say very much at all, in fact. As he approached the jury, he made the same mistake Alexis had and looked up at Neaera. After that, he hunched his shoulders and chewed his lip and stammered his way through an account of where she'd taken him and who she'd spoken to while she'd been acting as Queen Ada's messenger. The jury muttered a bit, and someone shouted out, "Don't call her Queen! Old Ada's not our Queen any more! Long live King Orontobates!"

When Kichesias returned to the bench, he hadn't even used his allotted time on the clock. He chewed his lip and cradled the hand Neaera had pierced with her pin, avoiding Alexis's gaze. Ishkibar scowled and tapped his foot impatiently as the court waited for the rest of Kichesias's water to run out.

During the delay, more sounds of fighting came from the west side of the city, and a large troop of mounted soldiers galloped through the agora towards the Myndos Gate, distracting the jury. The audience under the colonnades started to break up. Some people ran after the horses, cheering and shouting encouragement.

Finally, the top urn was empty, and Ishkibar ordered the clock reversed again. "Anteia the Macedonian!" he called.

As the jurors' heads turned to look at her, Anteia shrank into her cloak. She cast a nervous look at Ishkibar.

"Go on," Kichesias said. "Or your water will run out before you even start!"

The girl ventured into the space beside the enclosure and darted a quick look at the frowning Neaera. "Neaera's worried," Alexis whispered. "I don't think she knows why Anteia's here." He returned his attention to the girl, curious in spite of himself to hear what she would say.

Anteia, however, had yet to speak a word. She clung to her filthy cloak as if it were her only friend, twisting its folds nervously and casting glances towards the distant battle. The jurors grew restless. "Isn't that one of Alexander's camp followers?" one of the men shouted out, and the others laughed as Anteia reddened. "More likely she's one of Alexander's brats!" another called, grinning. "What's your mother do, girl? Who's your father? Do you know?"

"This is awful," Alexis said, gripping the edge of the bench. "I wish I'd never asked for a trial, now. They're treating it as some kind of sick joke."

But Ishkibar clapped his hands and said, "Quiet in court!" At the same time Anteia, who had been peering curiously at Diogenes, hooked her braids behind her ears and frowned at the man who had insulted her mother.

"My mother's a healer," she said in her terrible accent. "She ain't clever, and she can't speak your tongue as well as me. But she brings people back to life, and I help her." She glanced at Alexis, and his heart gave an extra thump. Had she seen that Diogenes wasn't really dead? Would she give them away?

The smoke from the battle cleared slightly, and the jury settled down. Anteia glanced at Ishkibar. "I'm here to tell you about that woman," she said, pointing to Neaera. "She often comes to our camp in the hills. She brings presents for General Alexander from your Carian

Queen Ada. General Alexander calls her his mother, even though everyone knows she ain't really, 'cause we left his real mother safe back home in Pella. None of his men were allowed to bring their wives, and the General leads by example..."

"Get on with it!" someone shouted, and the same man as before said, "Don't call Ada Queen!" But Ishkibar shushed them and indicated that Anteia should continue.

"Any rate," she said, licking her lips. "I was up at the camp last night, helping in our special tent for the wounded, when suddenly there's this great fuss outside. It was a Carian on horseback. Our sentry challenges him, but he says Queen Ada's asked for a special present from her adopted son and he's come to fetch it 'cause her usual messenger is indisposed. I see him go off with some soldiers into one of the tents where we're not allowed, and there's this terrible scream. When they come out, the Carian's got somethin' in his hand. We can't see what it is, but he grins and says it'll make the Usurper Orontobates listen all right. Then he puts whatever it is into his satchel, jumps on his horse and rides off. I think he was goin' back to the city, but it was very dark last night and his horse stumbled on the hillside. The Carian fell off and got knocked out. There was lots of blood, so they brought him back to our tent and asked Mother to stitch up his head. I got given his satchel to look after. I know I shouldn't have, but I couldn't resist lookin' inside. It had a finger in it. A small one, like a girl's."

She paused. The jury was listening now, all right, but

the clock was nearly out of water, despite the man slowing the flow to the tiniest drip.

"I knew it was somethin' I shouldn't have seen, so I didn't tell anyone I'd looked inside," Anteia went on. "But I remembered the scream. So as soon as the Carian had been bandaged up and ridden off with his satchel, I slipped over to the tent they'd got the finger from. It was heavily guarded, so I couldn't get very close. But I heard someone inside sobbin' like their heart would break. It was that awful, I broke Mother's rule and went to talk to the women who go into the men's tents at night. They get to hear a lot of secrets that way, and one of them told me about a hostage Queen Ada had sent to General Alexander just yesterday – a girl my age, who was supposed to be the King's daughter. She said that woman brought her to the camp, same as she brought all his other presents." She pointed to Neaera again, and the jury whispered among themselves. Anteia set her sharp little jaw. "It did my head in to think of the poor girl hurtin' like that, even if she's supposed to be our enemy. So I crept out of the camp and came to your city to tell someone."

As if it had been fixed to do so, which it no doubt had, the water ran out exactly on her final word, leaving the jury eyeing Neaera with hatred. "Those Macedonian devils have got Princess Phoebe!" they muttered. "They've cut off her poor finger!" One of them got up and spat into Neaera's face. "Traitor!"

Neaera stepped backwards, and Alexis saw her tug for

the first time at the ropes that bound her. She didn't break them, though. By the time Ishkibar had ordered the urns reversed once more, she was calm again, smiling serenely despite the juror's spittle running down her cheek.

Alexis frowned at Anteia as she sat down. "Was that true?" he whispered. "You weren't just saying it because Ishkibar told you to?"

"Course not!" Anteia scowled. "Would I make somethin' like that up? Why would I risk my life comin' down here and get myself arrested, if it weren't?"

"Seems a big thing to do for someone you haven't even met."

"They chopped off her finger!" Anteia said fiercely. "No one deserves that. It's horrible."

"I believe her," Kichesias said, turning paler than ever. "It's worse than I thought, Alex! Phoebe's in the Macedonian camp! We'll never get her out of there without help."

"Maybe the King's already rescued her," Alexis said, though the groans and screams outside the city walls didn't sound promising. "Maybe that's what the fighting's all about. Shh! It's Neaera's turn."

"Lady Neaera, widow of Diogenes the sculptor, will now have an opportunity to answer the charges!" Ishkibar called, and the jurors fixed their attention on the accused.

This time, Ishkibar let the man watching the clock open the tap fully from the start and did nothing to keep the jurors in order when they whistled and jeered. It took

Neaera a good third of her allotted time to make herself heard above all the noise – not helped by the sounds of the battle, which seemed to have spilled through the Gate into the city streets. Alexis's stomach tightened. He wondered what would happen if the Macedonians reached the agora before the trial was over.

"I am accused of terrible things," Neaera began, indicating the witness bench. "But ask yourselves who speaks against me. A boy whose father disappeared five years ago and who obviously resents me because I'm not his real mother, a slave who dislikes discipline, and a Macedonian *camp follower*." She let the sneer in her voice say what she thought of Anteia. "Surely some of you good sirs have rebellious children and slaves of your own? I expect there have been times when they hated you after you disciplined them?" There were a few wry chuckles among the benches, and Neaera smiled. "I'm sure you can understand why they might do this to me. Yet I have never beaten either my slave or my stepson. You can examine their backs for proof of that. You'll find not a single scar. As for the little camp follower, I've never set eyes on her before in my life. I doubt they even understand the charges, yet these three underage *children* accuse me of murder and Macedonian sympathies – it's quite obvious they're being used in a political game." She allowed her gaze to rest briefly on Ishkibar. "I do not deny I support Queen Ada's cause. Go up to the Acropolis, and you will find a good number of your own friends and colleagues who also support her.

Halicarnassos is a Carian city. The Persians stole this land. I merely wish to preserve for my children and my children's children the wonderful things King Maussollos built. Am I to be punished for such thoughts?"

She paused, while the jury nodded and muttered. Neaera turned her brilliant smile upon the ones who had agreed most enthusiastically and jerked her head in the direction of the Myndos Gate.

"You can see the smoke and hear the fighting in our streets! Are we going to sit here in the agora, wrangling among ourselves, while the Macedonians and Persians between them destroy King Maussollos's fine tomb and his beautiful Palace by the sea? Are we going to let them burn everything that is handsome and proud in Caria? I might be guilty of disciplining my family when they disobey me, and I might be guilty of supporting Queen Ada's cause. But I am *not* guilty of murdering this man you see before you, nor of crimes against my homeland! If you still doubt me, ask yourselves how I am supposed to have done this terrible deed. With my bare hands?" She wriggled her bound wrists, and some of the jurors chuckled. "Examine the body. You will find no wound. Yes, it is true I went to the Mausoleum the night Diogenes the sculptor disappeared. But I was attacked from behind. When I turned round, my husband was there. I didn't see anyone else. He pretended to be concerned and took me into his arms, but I was terrified. I struggled free and I ran home. Perhaps I was wrong. It was dark. Perhaps my attacker was someone else, who killed Diogenes after I'd gone and hid his body in the drains? All I know is that my husband was the only person I saw at the Mausoleum that night, and we'd been arguing earlier. Men sometimes get violent in such situations. Do you blame me for thinking what I did?" The water in the clock ran out at this point, but Neaera got in her final word. "Since my husband cannot rise up from the dead and speak in my defence, I plead innocent of all the charges!"

The jurors muttered some more. Some seemed to believe that Neaera might have been attacked by a ruffian who had ambushed Diogenes hoping to steal the fee he was supposed to have collected from Ishkibar. When Diogenes couldn't produce the money, they said, the ruffian might well have panicked and killed him. But they weren't willing to let Neaera walk free yet.

"What about the Princess?" a man called out. "Did you give her to the Macedonians, like the girl said?"

Neaera looked at Anteia and raised an eyebrow. "The little camp follower was arrested entering the city, wasn't she? You can't blame the girl for telling lies to save her own skin."

Ishkibar clapped his hands angrily and indicated the clock. "Time's up!" he repeated. "Alexis son of Diogenes, have you anything to add before the jury consider their verdict?"

Alexis frowned. Neaera had as good as admitted to the court that Diogenes might not have attacked her that night. His father's name was clear, whether or not they found her guilty of murder.

As he hesitated, Kichesias hissed, "Say no, Alex! We have to hurry if we're going to find someone to help us rescue Phoebe. I think the Macedonians are inside the city!"

Alexis stood on shaky legs. The jurors were no longer looking at Neaera with hatred, but with grudging pity. Two of them approached the barrow for a closer look at the "corpse". Neaera smiled at them, turning on the charm with all her considerable skill. More smoke drifted across the sun, momentarily obscuring Alexis's view of the defendant's enclosure. He saw Neaera's hand move sharply, and had a sudden vision of her getting free and doing something horrible to him and Kichesias before anyone could stop her. But when he approached the benches, she was still safely in her enclosure gripping the rail, gazing at him with the same mixture of anger and sorrow as before.

He thought of the statue blood on his father's body and the way Neaera hurt Kichesias with her peplos pins. If he couldn't decide, then he'd let the jury work out· if she were guilty. As Ishkibar had said, it was their job. But first they needed to hear all the facts.

"I know Lady Neaera had something to do with my father's death," he began quietly. "I don't know if she had help, but the reason I know she was involved is because that black stuff you see on his body is her blood, and it's poisonous to humans. I think that's what killed my father. My stepmother is fooling you. She's not human. She's a statue."

He told them everything. How he'd inherited the reverse Midas touch; how he'd brought Neaera to life to be his mother eight years ago; how she was strong and cruel and wanted power; even how she kept taking him to wash in the river on Mount Tmolus, hoping for his magic to be reversed so he could turn things to gold and make her rich.

Absolute silence followed his words. The approaching battle was forgotten as everyone stared at him – some in disbelief, others in wonderment, others clearly stunned by his story. Neaera's eyes were narrow with fury. Kichesias was madly chewing his lip. Anteia stared at him with her mouth open. Ishkibar was the only person in the agora who didn't seem surprised by what he'd said. A slow smile of understanding spread across the spy's dark face, and he nodded to himself as if he should have guessed about the magic all along.

It was Neaera who broke the spell. She threw back her head and laughed. "Don't children tell such fantastic tales?" she said, still laughing. "Perhaps we should ask my stepson to wake the statue of Ares to settle this war, or bring the chariot on top of the Mausoleum to life so old King Maussollos himself can lead the Carian army to victory?"

Some of the jurors laughed with her, and others shouted out angrily that they hadn't come to waste their time listening to children's tales. Others seized on the poison idea, though, pointing out that the black crystal covering the corpse was strange, and that they could easily prove if the boy was telling the truth by giving him something gold to touch.

The benches erupted with arguments. It took a lot of clapping and shouting on Ishkibar's part to calm the court. "Don't forget poison is a woman's weapon!" he said when he had everyone's attention. "You've heard the evidence. We haven't time for demonstrations now. It's time to vote. Holes for guilty, solids for not guilty, as usual. Put your discarded token in the second urn. Quickly, please."

A man went round the benches handing out the tokens, which the jurors, still arguing, dropped into the urns while Neaera watched. She appeared quite calm. Strangely, considering the trial had gone as he wished, Ishkibar was the one who seemed most nervous. He kept glancing in the direction of the Myndos Gate and then back at Alexis, frowning.

Alexis returned to the witness bench, shaking with reaction and renewed tension. What had he *done*? Whatever had possessed him to tell half Halicarnassos about his magic? He only hoped that most of the people in the agora had not believed him.

Four men hurried to collect the urns and tipped out the votes to begin the count. But they'd hardly started, when a horseman galloped into the agora. He stared round wildly, spotted Ishkibar standing behind the judge's chair, and urged his foam-covered mount up the steps. Blood flowed down his arm and his eyes were wild.

"The King's wounded!" he gasped out. "They were expecting us up at the camp... Some fool panicked and closed the gates too early... the bridge collapsed! We lost a thousand men, at least, and some of the Macedonians still got through. We burnt some of their siege engines, but we didn't get them all. It was a massacre..."

Ishkibar turned pale. He grasped the soldier's elbow, dragged him off to one side and questioned him in a low tone. The man lowered his voice and replied too softly for Alexis to hear. But the damage had been done.

"The King's dead!" shouted the over-excited jurors, only hearing half the message. "The Macedonians have captured the city! We're all going to die!"

The panic spread rapidly, not helped by another cloud of smoke blowing across the agora. The people trapped under the colonnade began to push and scream. The soldiers guarding the court tried to keep order, but were swept along in the crush.

"Quick!" Kichesias said, seizing Alexis with one hand and Anteia with the other and dragging them through the crowd. "If the Macedonians have won, they won't need Phoebe as a hostage any more – they'll kill her!"

Anteia pulled back. Alexis dug in his heels as well. "No, Kichesias, wait! Neaera... the verdict..."

But the defendant's enclosure was empty. Two frayed pieces of rope dangled from the rail. The men who had been guarding Neaera lay senseless on the ground nearby. The judge had abandoned his seat, and the horse's churning hooves had scattered the tokens, which had become hopelessly mixed with the discarded ones from the second urn, overturned in the crush.

Alexis almost laughed. Then he spotted Neaera, and the laughter died in his throat. She was bending over the barrow where Diogenes was playing dead. Even though he'd once planned to kill the woken statue himself, Alexis broke into a cold sweat. "Neaera's doing something to Diogenes!" he gasped. "Kichesias, quick!"

His friend saw the danger, too, and changed direction, still dragging the terrified Anteia after them. Alexis screamed at people to get out of the way. But fighting their way across the agora was like trying to run through an earthquake. People fell over the benches and sprawled at their feet, sobbing that the Macedonians were coming to murder them all.

In the confusion, Neaera raised her head and met Alexis's gaze. She gave him an amused smile. Very deliberately, she bent and kissed Diogenes on the lips. Then she threw a bench at some guards who were trying to cut her off, and vanished into the crowd.

Chapter 14

CHIMAERA

*DIOGENES: Maussollos will groan when
he remembers the things on earth above, which he
thought brought him happiness.*

Alexis's stomach twisted as they fought their way across
the agora towards Diogenes. Everything was spinning
out of control. He might have cleared his father's name,
but Ishkibar knew about his magic, the Macedonians
were about to capture the city, Phoebe's life was in
danger, and Neaera had escaped. It was obvious that
Kichesias needed all his strength to keep them from being
separated and carried in different directions by the
panicking crowd. Before they reached the barrow, it was
overturned in the crush, tipping Diogenes out with a
thud.

Fearing the worst, Alexis fell to his knees beside the
motionless body and touched the dried statue blood. He

couldn't see any further signs of injury, but he didn't trust Neaera. "Uncle Diogenes!" he said. "Wake up! You can stop pretending now. The trial's over."

The rigid body relaxed. Alexis breathed a sigh of relief as Diogenes sat up and blinked at all the fleeing people and the smoke. He touched his lips. "Someone kissed me," he said. "It felt... very strange."

"Forget the kiss," Kichesias said. "We've got to find some soldiers to help us rescue Phoebe! We'll need horses to get her away from the camp. Anteia can show us the tent she's being kept in—" He winced as the girl tried to free her hand by biting his fingers. "Ow! Stop that!"

"Let me go!" Anteia sobbed. "I'm not goin' nowhere with that *sorcerer*!" She made a sign against evil at Alexis.

Alexis couldn't blame the girl for not wanting to have anything to do with them. Kichesias's plan was hopeless, of course. It was crazy to think they would succeed in rescuing the Princess, when half the Carian army had failed. Yet, for Phoebe's sake, he knew they had to try. "Can you show us the way to the camp?" he asked.

Anteia shook her head wildly. "It won't do you no good! The Princess said—"

"Phoebe said *what*?" Kichesias caught her other wrist and dragged her closer. His turquoise eyes were fierce. "You told us you never saw the Princess! Little liar!"

"I never lied," Anteia sniffed. "I just didn't tell it all. The Princess said it'd be dangerous for me if I told. Don't hurt me, please!" She was still staring at Alexis as if he were some kind of monster.

"What did Phoebe say?" Kichesias hissed, shaking her.

Anteia started to cry. "It didn't make no sense!"

"Did you see her hands? Which finger did they chop off?"

"I don't know! I never saw her! I *swear*!" Anteia's words ended on a shriek when Alexis put his hand on her arm.

"Let her go," he told Kichesias.

"But she'll only run off, and we need her to show us where Phoebe is."

Alexis sighed. "Anteia," he said. "Anteia, look at me! I'm not a sorcerer. I'm just a boy with a backwards curse. I can't hurt you. It only works on statues and things made of gold."

It was no good. The girl went limp in Kichesias's grasp, her eyes squeezed shut in terror. The agora was getting noisier as people fled the streets of the Craftsmen's Quarter, where the Macedonians had evidently breached part of the city wall. More soldiers from the garrison galloped through in the opposite direction, knocking people over and adding to the panic. Not a juror remained in the court. The judge's chair was smashed, the benches overturned. The barrow that had been used to carry Diogenes splintered as a horse kicked it. Some people had even jumped into the harbour and were desperately trying to swim out to the ships. Alexis hated to think what Ishkibar and Neaera might be up to, and still Anteia refused to listen. He stared at her helplessly, not knowing what to do.

Diogenes stood up and brushed himself off. "What's the matter, child?" he said, wiping the tears from Anteia's cheeks and drawing her gently away from Kichesias into his arms. "What's all this fuss? My nephew's not going to hurt you, silly."

The girl looked up into the man's kind eyes, gave a shudder, and buried her face against his chest with a sob. After another sob, she looked up at him again. "I knew you weren't really dead," she sniffed. "I knew it."

"So why are you afraid of my nephew?" Diogenes asked.

Alexis shivered. Diogenes might have called him *nephew*, yet the way he was holding Anteia was exactly the way Alexis's father used to hold him when he was afraid, all those years ago.

"He said he brought that woman who was on trial to life," Anteia insisted. "He *said*!"

"And you told the jury your mother brought people to life by thumping on their chests and blowing into their mouths," Diogenes reminded her. "What's the difference?"

"We bring them *back* to life!" the girl said with a stubborn jut of her jaw. "Not make life out of... out of... stone!"

"I don't make life," Alexis said slowly, glancing at Diogenes. "Not exactly, anyway. It's more like I catch a spirit, maybe one that's lonely or wants to live again, and it goes into the statue I'm trying to wake, and then— "

"We haven't time for this!" Kichesias interrupted, staring round at the fleeing people. "We have to get Phoebe out of the Macedonian camp before they decide she's no longer any use to them!"

Diogenes remained calm amidst all the noise and smoke and panic, his strong arms encircling Anteia. "What did the Princess say to you, child?" he asked gently. "Try to remember. It might be important."

Anteia frowned. "I don't remember it all... something about waking a great hero to save your city. Wake the shimmera? Kimmera? Somethin' like that. She kept sayin' it was the only way to win against General Alexander." She pulled a face. "You're wastin' your time, though. The women up at the camp say no one will ever beat General Alexander in a fight – he's got magic of his own that stops him being killed."

Diogenes raised his eyebrows.

Alexis looked at Kichesias. "Wake the Chimaera?" he whispered.

"That's it!" Anteia stared at them uncertainly.

Kichesias frowned. "Wasn't that one of Phoebe's monsters?"

Alexis nodded and curled his hand. "The big white one with the three heads. Remember how she pointed to it first, when she asked me to prove I could make statues live? She told me she'd painted its claws gold, so the magic should work on it all right."

Kichesias's eyes brightened. "And she said it's supposed to defend Caria from her enemies! If you wake the Chimaera, Alex, we won't need an army to get into the camp! Can you really do it?"

Diogenes frowned, one black-encrusted arm still around Anteia. "The Chimaera was always an unpredictable creature," he warned. "Wasn't that why the King of Lycia ordered Bellerophon to kill her in the first place?"

Alexis was too distracted to notice this hint that Diogenes' memory was coming back. He stared up the hill through the drifting smoke, weighing up their choices. He thought of Phoebe, captive in the Macedonian camp, waiting for someone to come and chop off another of her fingers – or worse. The trial had gone on well into the afternoon, and already the sun was sinking into an angry copper haze over the western wall, where the fighting continued. They didn't have a lot of time. Even if they could find some soldiers willing to help them, they were unlikely to persuade them to try another raid on Alexander's camp so soon, especially with the King wounded. On the other hand, the Chimaera, if he managed to wake it, should be bound by the same statue magic as Kichesias, Diogenes and Neaera. He ought to be able to control it a little, and the monster would certainly be a distraction while they sneaked into the camp.

"Let's try it," he said.

It was easier getting into the Palace than Alexis had anticipated. Most of the guards were occupied, loading the ships in the Royal Harbour with baggage and supplies so that King Orontobates' court could evacuate the city. In the confusion, Diogenes managed to steal a small, leaky boat from a merchant who had laden it with too many spice jars and was having trouble pushing off from the quayside. Kichesias threw the jars into the harbour, while Diogenes did the same for the merchant. The man spluttered curses as he splashed to safety, while Anteia watched with her hands over her mouth. But the girl must have decided she was safer with them than on her own, because she didn't try to run off.

They rowed the leaky boat as quietly as they could into the shadow of the Palace wall. There was little need for stealth. The guards were intent on their tasks and ignored the many boatloads of confused, frightened families trying to escape before the Macedonians came. The entrance to the underground canal had already been opened to allow the royal fleet to emerge from the secret harbour. They waited for their opportunity and quietly paddled into the tunnel.

Torches burned inside, sending golden ripples around the walls and making Alexis cough. Anteia stared around her, wide-eyed. The water in the bottom of the boat had reached their knees by the time plops and creaks around the bend ahead warned them of an approaching ship. As its enormous shadow rushed up the walls, they scrambled out on to the towpath and flattened themselves against the side of the tunnel, leaving their little boat to splinter beneath the ship's bows.

"It would have sunk, anyway," Kichesias said as they

hurried up a flight of dark stairs towards the upper levels of the Palace. "We did that merchant a favour."

Alexis was silent, trying to remember the way to the women's quarters. The thought of meeting Ishkibar in one of the corridors sent a chill down his spine. But all the rooms they passed had been abandoned. Tables of half-eaten food were left for the flies, and wine dripped from overturned amphorae on to the expensive couches.

Alexis hoped the women's quarters might be deserted, too. But two big lily-hands guarded the door with crossed spears, exactly as before. When they saw him, their expressions turned ugly. Neither of them was the black slave who had helped carry Diogenes up to the Theatre and escorted Alexis back to the Palace the day Phoebe had been kidnapped, but they obviously knew the whole story.

Alexis tried to explain. "I know you probably blame me for what happened to the Princess," he began. "But we're here to help her. There's... ah... something in the Princess's Monster Collection that Queen Ada wants. If we take it to her, she'll persuade General Alexander to let Phoebe go."

The lily-hands' eyes narrowed. One of them jerked his spear along the corridor, obviously indicating that they should leave.

Kichesias exchanged a glance with Diogenes, who nodded and readied himself for a fight. But before the two woken statues could test their strength against the lily-hands, Anteia pushed past them and marched fearlessly up to the two big slaves.

"I'm the Princess's friend," she said in her terrible accent, opening her cloak a little at the neck. "I've spoken to her, and she said to let these boys in. I know you got to do what I say, because you're lily-hands and I'm a woman!"

There was a pause as the lily-hands studied Anteia's kohl-lined eyes, rouged lips and obvious youth. The two big men exchanged a flurry of hand gestures, and the spears slowly raised. Alexis breathed a little easier.

One of the lily-hands opened the door and indicated that they could pass. But when Diogenes tried to follow, the spears came down again.

"He's too old to enter the women's quarters," Kichesias said. "He'll have to wait here. You wait with him, Anteia!" Before the lily-hands could change their minds, he seized Alexis's hand and pulled him through the doors.

The women's quarters appeared as deserted as the rest of the Palace, yet the room containing the Princess's Collection was still locked. Kichesias didn't hesitate. He efficiently broke down the door, and they hurried inside. Phoebe's statues of monsters were still there, but to Alexis's relief she seemed to have been telling the truth about getting rid of the dead things. The hall smelled better than he remembered. The bench in the centre was empty.

In the light from the corridor, the big three-headed statue of the Chimaera reared pale and ghostly above all the rest. Its lion's jaws were open in a snarl, the goat's horns that sprouted from its back were wickedly spiralled, and the snake's head at the end of its tail curled over its back. Its eyes were still red but, as Phoebe had promised, its enormous claws glinted gold. Alexis stared up at the monster with a shiver of doubt.

"Even if I do manage to wake it, the bond's different with an animal," he whispered to Kichesias. "It might not understand what we want it to do."

"We'll have to take that chance," Kichesias whispered back. "Phoebe said it'll kill Caria's enemies, and that means the Macedonians."

"But they weren't always Caria's enemies. What if it tries to kill us first?"

"It won't. The magic will stop it. You know that."

Alexis closed his eyes, not sure he knew anything any more. When he opened them again, the lily-hand who had escorted them to the Collection was peering in at them, obviously waiting for them to pick up one of the smaller monsters and come out again.

"Do it, Alex!" Kichesias hissed. "Quick."

Alexis placed his palms against the Chimaera's nearest leg. Thrusting his doubts behind him, he reached for the magic.

Think of it as capturing a spirit... Do chimaeras have spirits? Yes, there was one once, a long time ago, killed by a man riding a winged horse who forced a lump of lead into her mouth, which melted and seared her insides. The pain must have been awful, cooking the poor creature from the inside out... Remember that pain, Spirit of the Chimaera, and return to this body a sculptor has made for you. It might not be your own body, but it's almost as good, and you will have three heads again and four good clawed feet, and be able to breathe fire over Caria's enemies! When you wake, go to the hills where the Macedonians are camped and burn their tents – but don't kill any Persians, and don't burn the tent the Princess is in. Persia isn't Caria's enemy, not any more. Macedonia is. Come, Spirit of the Chimaera, come!

It was alarmingly easy, much easier than it had been with Diogenes. He felt the Chimaera's spirit enter the monster's leg in a fierce rush, and snatched his hands back with a cry. The whole hall lit up with white light, showing the other sculptures frozen in their positions. The lily-hand backed away from the door with a look of terror, and Kichesias gazed upwards in awe with one hand raised to shield his eyes.

"It's white," he whispered. "All shining white like the moon..." As the Chimaera began to move, he gripped Alexis's elbow and dragged him backwards against the wall. "Look out! It's coming!"

The lily-hand turned and ran, his hands fluttering uselessly in an attempt to warn his comrade, whom he'd left at the entrance to the women's quarters watching Diogenes and Anteia.

The Chimaera reared up, crashing her goat's horns into the ceiling and bringing down plaster. She lashed her snake-tail and snapped a column, lashed again and toppled three smaller monsters, which crumbled like sand. Her lion's head swung round, and her three pairs of red eyes fixed upon the statue of the winged horse, Pegasus. She roared her anger and leapt. With a great cracking and crunching, the horse's delicate marble wings splintered, and Pegasus was crushed beneath the Chimaera's golden claws. Not many of Phoebe's creatures survived. Maybe one or two of the smaller ones – there wasn't time to check. The Chimaera leapt towards the door and caught the fleeing lily-hand in her lion's jaws, lifting him high into the air.

"No, Chimaera!" Alexis cried, finding his voice at last and rushing out into the corridor after the creature. "Put him down! He's a friend!" The Chimaera lashed her tail again, eyeing Alexis with her snake's head. Hissing in frustration, she spat out the lily-hand and crashed through the double doors. A terrified scream came from the other side.

"Anteia – oh gods, I forgot, she's a Macedonian! I told the Chimaera they were the enemy!" Alexis raced after the monster, his legs trembling so much he didn't know how he kept on his feet, let alone was able to run.

Behind him, Kichesias paused to check the lily-hand, who had survived his ordeal with only a broken arm. The second lily-hand lay outside the doors, stunned but alive. A trail of cracked columns and crumbling plaster showed the way the Chimaera had gone.

Alexis stared around wildly and spotted Diogenes crouched in an alcove with his wide, strong shoulders turned towards the corridor and his head down, motionless again.

"Fath— Uncle Diogenes?" Alexis whispered, his teeth chattering in sudden fear.

"Where's Anteia?" Kichesias said urgently, leaving the lily-hand to tend his groaning comrade. "We need her to show us where Phoebe is being kept! She's not...?"

For a horrible moment, as in the agora, Diogenes did not move. Then his shoulders shuddered, and he turned to face them. "Has the monster gone?" he whispered. "Thank the gods she doesn't seem to remember how to breathe fire! If she could, I think we'd all be dead."

Anteia crawled out of his arms, unharmed. "Was that... was that the Princess's Chimaera?" she stammered.

Kichesias nodded. He chewed his lip as he stared at the wounded lily-hands and the destruction in the corridor.

Anteia blinked. "And is it goin' to attack General Alexander's camp?"

Alexis nodded. "I think so. That's where I told her to go when I called her spirit. It's a she-monster, you see..." His words trailed off. He'd told the Chimaera to burn the tents, hoping that would drive the Macedonians out of the camp and create enough confusion for them to rescue Phoebe. But if the monster couldn't breathe fire, she might try to harm her enemies another way. He, too, looked at the lily-hands. He felt a bit sick.

"Then please hurry," Anteia said, very pale. "My mother's up there." And she burst into tears.

Chapter 15

MACEDONIAN CAMP

*DIOGENES: Diogenes will
be able to laugh at him.*

No one tried to stop Alexis and his companions as they
followed the trail of destruction left by the Chimaera. The
few stragglers they met in the corridors were too intent
upon looting the unguarded royal treasure to take any
notice of them. By the time they emerged from the Palace,
the sun was setting, the smoke over the hills had thinned,
and the noise of the fighting was dying down. But the
quayside was still crowded with people trying to leave by
sea before the Macedonian army entered the city, while
battle-weary Carian officers on horseback did their best to
calm the population. "Return to your homes!" they called.
"There's no cause for alarm. Everything's under control.
The gates are shut. Our walls are still standing. Stay calm!
We will protect you from the Macedonians!"

But the people were no longer listening. They wailed that the King and General Memnon had abandoned them, and the women sobbed that General Alexander had sent a three-headed monster to eat their children.

Diogenes raised an eyebrow when he heard this. "The Chimaera must have come this way. If we hurry, we might be able to get through the Old Gate while the guards are still distracted."

But by the time they reached the top of the hill, there was a log jam of refugees around the old foot gate, which was firmly closed and barred.

"Too late," Anteia said, eyeing the guards warily.

Kichesias scowled. "I can break it down easy enough, if we can get those people out of the way. Hurry!"

As Alexis eyed the crowd doubtfully, Anteia tugged at Diogenes' hand. "We don't have to use the gate," she said. "This way! There's a hole in the wall at the corner, where I climbed through before. Two of General Alexander's men made it as a dare after they got drunk one night. Your soldiers built a new tower behind, but there's a way round the edge. It's a bit tight, but it ain't guarded."

Kichesias's scowl deepened. "How do you know it isn't guarded? If this is a trick, and those Macedonian butchers cut off any more of Phoebe's fingers, I'll hand you back to Ishkibar!"

Diogenes calmly placed himself between Kichesias and the girl. "Anteia wants to get to the camp as quickly as we do," he reminded them. "It's a good idea. The

Chimaera will be long gone by the time we get through this crowd, and the guards are hardly going to sit there and watch us break it down. Do you think I'll fit through the gap, child?"

Anteia sucked her lip. "I don't know... maybe. Kichesias might not, though." She pulled a face at the boy, which Kichesias didn't see because he was already hurrying through the rich district of the Hill towards the city wall.

In the lengthening shadows, no one noticed them creeping through the gardens of the mansions. When they reached the wall, the guards manning the defence towers had their backs to them. They were peering into the darkness of the hills, arguing excitedly about the Chimaera, which must have already gone over the wall. Like the people in the streets, some of the guards seemed to believe that the monster had been sent by the Macedonians. Others said it had come to save Caria; whereas the ones who obviously hadn't got a proper view of the creature scoffed that the rest of them had been drinking too much unwatered wine, and should be keeping a lookout for the real enemy. Alexis just wished he knew who the real enemy was.

It was much quieter on the Hill than down at the harbour. Lights glowing between the trees showed that, despite the evacuation of the Palace, many of the richer citizens had chosen to stay and defend their homes. They even heard music and laughter from someone's symposium party.

"How can they have a party at a time like this?" Kichesias said, still scowling. "Don't they realize their city's about to be captured?"

"Maybe they're the ones who support Queen Ada?" Alexis suggested.

"They were havin' parties just the same, the night General Alexander's two drunks got through your wall," Anteia said with a scornful look. "We almost took your Gate with just two men! I wish we had, then you'd never have gone and woken that monster."

Kichesias's expression darkened, but Diogenes studied the wall with his calm brown eyes. "Where's the gap, child?" he asked softly.

Anteia let go of his hand, scrambled over a rock and disappeared into a small hole under the rubble. Alexis glanced up to check the guards weren't looking and followed her. It was a tight squeeze, and very dark and rough. He felt his way around the edges of the stones, following Anteia's noises. Someone started to squeeze through after him, bringing down small avalanches. There was a glimmer of starlight ahead, a final twist of the tunnel, and then he was out in the clear air on the other side of the hill gazing down into a valley scattered with rocks and shadows. Far up the slope beyond, camp fires flickered in the darkness. He shivered, imagining the panic the Chimaera would cause once she reached the Macedonian tents.

"Anteia?" he whispered, looking round for the girl.

In answer, an arrow thudded into the earth beside his

foot. Alexis flattened himself against the wall, his heart thudding. A bowman was standing on the battlements, silhouetted against the first stars, peering down. There was a scrape in the shadows nearby, and Anteia broke cover and raced down the hillside, her cloak and braids flying. The bowman straightened, put another arrow to his bow and took aim.

"Anteia!" Alexis shouted, abandoning caution. "Look out!"

It was pointless trying to be quiet any more. Whoever was behind him in the tunnel was making enough noise to wake the dead. Rubble exploded from the hole, and Kichesias's golden curls appeared, covered in dust. His friend grinned in triumph. Then he saw Anteia running away, let out a curse and raced after her.

Alexis's heart twisted in fear for his friend as the second arrow left the guard's bow. It arced downwards and struck Kichesias in the back of the knee as he ran between the weapon and its intended target. The boy sprawled on the hillside with a grunt of surprise. Anteia whirled, her hands over her mouth and her eyes wide.

"Run, you idiot!" Alexis shouted, feeling the pain of that arrow echoed in his own leg. "Keep running!"

For a horrible moment, he thought she was going to panic and run the wrong way. But when the guard on the wall raised his bow again, she raced out of range and ducked behind a large boulder. A third arrow clattered after her, wide of the mark. Kichesias seized the chance to scramble to his feet and limp to safety as well. The arrow that had hit him had snapped on impact with his statue body, but it had obviously hurt. Reinforcements pounded along the top of the wall, calling out questions that the bowman answered in an excited tone, jabbing his finger at the rock where Anteia and Kichesias crouched.

Diogenes arrived in a second explosion of stones, took in the situation with a single glance, and placed himself between Alexis and the guards' weapons. "Go," he said. "Arrows can't hurt me, can they? Just like they can't hurt your friend Kichesias."

"Uncle Diogenes..." Alexis began awkwardly, aware the woken statue had heard every word spoken at Neaera's trial. He must know by now that he wasn't really Alexis's uncle. Did he realize the whole truth? Alexis looked sideways at the kindly face that was so like his father's and shivered.

Diogenes gave him a gentle push towards the track. "No time now. Stay in front of me. I'll shield you."

Alexis fixed his eyes on the rock where Kichesias and Anteia had taken refuge and ran faster than he ever had in his life. His back prickled all the way. At any moment, he expected to hear Diogenes, who was running so close behind him that he could feel the woken statue's breath on his neck, cry out. He braced himself for the echo of the pain. But although several arrows whistled past their ears, they reached the rock unscathed and threw themselves flat behind it. The soldiers on the wall lowered their bows and shook their heads.

"Bloody refugees! Let 'em go. If they want to take

their chances out there with the Macedonians, good luck to 'em!"

As they caught their breath, Alexis frowned at his friend. Kichesias was clutching his knee, shock and pain twisting his handsome features. "It hurts, Alex!" he whispered. "More than Lady Neaera's peplos pins! What's happening to me?"

Alexis shook his head, feeling helpless. Immediately after the arrow had struck his friend, his own pain had faded, but Kichesias was obviously still suffering. "I don't know. Maybe the arrowhead had a trace of gold in it?"

He saw sweat break out on his friend's forehead as Kichesias tore a strip off the hem of his tunic. Refusing Anteia's help, the boy bandaged his own leg. He gritted his teeth as he tested his weight on it. "I'm all right. We've got to hurry!"

Diogenes helped the injured boy negotiate the dark track, while Anteia and Alexis followed in silence.

"I don't know how he's walkin' so fast," Anteia said, frowning at Kichesias's back. "I'm sure that arrow pierced him. He should have let me help. That bandage ain't tight enough to do any good."

"Kichesias is stronger than normal people. He'll be fine, don't worry."

Anteia's frown deepened. "Arrow wounds are nasty. Even if the head broke off, he might get an infection... oh!" She stopped in the middle of the track and stared at Alexis in dawning horror. "He's one of them, too, isn't he? He was a statue, and you made him live, just like you did to your stepmother and that monster in the Palace! You *are* a sorcerer!"

Alexis sighed. "I told you, I'm not a sorcerer. I've inherited my ancestor's curse, that's all, the same way people inherit... blue eyes, or blond hair. Kichesias shouldn't have been hurt at all by that arrow – it wasn't gold. I can't understand it." Uneasy, he remembered the tears in his friend's eyes when he'd told him about the casket Queen Ada had sent to the King. Until that moment, he hadn't known statues could cry, either. "Show us the way past the sentries and where the Princess is being kept, and I promise I won't let the Chimaera hurt you," he said, thrusting his worry aside. "Or your mother, either," he added as he remembered Anteia's main concern.

"Can you really control it, then?" she asked in a small voice. "Like a real sorcerer?"

"Diogenes and Kichesias do what I say, don't they? The Chimaera will obey me as well. It's part of the statue magic."

Anteia gave him a quick smile, and Alexis felt terrible for lying to her. He didn't have the first idea how he was going to stop the monster from hurting the girl's family.

They lost their view of the camp as they descended into the valley, and the smell of smoke reached them before the tents came into sight again, making Alexis's heart beat faster. But the blackened area they found at the lower edge of the campsite was not recent enough to be the Chimaera's work, and the skeletons of tents poking out of the ash must have been abandoned before the fire, because there were no bones. Alexis remembered the smoke they'd seen at dawn during the Persian raid to rescue Phoebe. If this was the result, then the King and his troops had not penetrated far into the Macedonian camp. On the other side of the burnt area, General Alexander's cooking fires and tents made a sea of orange and black that covered half the hillside. A sheer rock face rose at the eastern edge where the horse lines had been set up. Frightened neighs from that direction indicated where the Chimaera had gone. Men were racing across the camp to rescue their horses, strapping on weapons as they went.

"She must be looking for a lair," Diogenes whispered as they crouched behind one of the burnt-out tents to let the Macedonians run past. "Poor thing. I think she's as frightened as we are."

"At least she's causing a distraction." Kichesias said, looking round for Anteia. "Where are they keeping the Princess...? Hey, come back here!"

Taking advantage of the confusion, Anteia had suddenly sprinted for one of the brightly lit tents at the edge of the camp. They didn't need the smell of strong herbs and muffled groans coming from inside to identify it as the Macedonian blood tent. Kichesias gave chase and, despite his limp, caught the girl before she cleared the burnt area, dragging her back with one hand clamped over her mouth. Anteia struggled briefly, then seemed to remember he was an enchanted statue and went limp in his grasp. She stared at the tent flap, tears in her eyes.

"If you try that again..." Kichesias hissed.

Diogenes put a warning hand on the boy's arm. "Your mother will be fine, Anteia," he said. "The Chimaera's just looking for a place to hide. She doesn't seem able to breathe fire, and I don't think she'll hurt anyone if they don't try to hurt her first. She was very frightened and confused when my s— when my nephew woke her in the Palace, and I expect that's why she attacked the lily-hands. As soon as the Princess is safe, we'll take the Chimaera back with us, won't we, Alex?"

Alexis shook himself, too distracted to notice Diogenes' slip of the tongue. "Yes... yes, of course."

Anteia blinked at the blood tent, where another groaning Macedonian soldier was being carried inside on a stretcher. "There's so many hurt," she whispered. "Why do men make war? It's so stupid."

"General Memnon's troops came off worst," Alexis reminded her, forcing himself to concentrate on why they'd come. "Where's Phoebe being kept? Do you want her to be hurt, too? Kichesias is right. General Alexander will probably order her killed when she's no longer any use to him as a hostage."

Anteia did not argue after that. Silently, keeping to the shadows, she led them deeper into the camp. Using Kichesias's and Diogenes' skill of freezing like statues, they got past the sentries without being spotted. Finally, they came to a small tent pitched on its own at the foot of the cliff. An argument was going on outside the flap.

Alexis's heart thumped as they crept closer. He half expected to see Neaera there. But two sentries armed with spears were blocking the way of two more Macedonians, one of whom held the bridle of a fidgety horse that had obviously caught the Chimaera's scent. They spoke the Macedonain dialect very fast in their rough soldiers' accents, making their words impossible to follow.

"What are they saying?" Kichesias demanded.

Anteia frowned. "They've orders to fetch another finger. But it's weird. They say a real one this time, and they can't agree. The young one says they should use another like last time, because who's goin' to know? The one holding the horse says King Orontobates obviously knew it wasn't really his daughter's finger, or he'd have surrendered the city by now. The sentries are saying wait, the night's only just begun, give the Satrap a chance. The older man don't like it. He says the Persian fleet has left the bay, and General Memnon's up to something. He thinks Memnon sent the white lion... I think he means the Chimaera... to cause a distraction in the camp while the Persians plan another attack. The young one seems sorry for the Princess. But I don't understand." She frowned again. "I saw the finger they took last time. It was definitely real."

Alexis couldn't think straight. He eyed the Macedonians, wondering if Diogenes and Kichesias could overpower all four of them before they raised the alarm.

But Kichesias had clenched his fists at the mention of Phoebe's finger. Before anyone could stop him, he rushed towards the men with a terrible cry. Diogenes sighed and followed. There were two thumps as the sentries fell senseless. The horse reared in alarm, and the man holding its reins was dragged off balance. Diogenes knocked him out before he had a chance to see what had hit him. The youngest soldier managed to draw his sword, but didn't attack. His blade wavered between man and boy as he took in Kichesias's bandage and the fact they were both unarmed.

Alexis seized the opportunity to pull Anteia out of the shadows. "We've come for the Princess!" he declared with as much confidence as he could manage. "Halicarnassos has surrendered, so you don't have to keep her here any more."

The young soldier frowned and said slowly in their own tongue, "Who are you? Where are you taking her? Our orders said nothing about this."

"Your orders have been cancelled," Alexis said. "Go and check."

The soldier hesitated, looking uncertainly at Anteia, who nodded. Diogenes waited until the young Macedonian glanced across the camp, and calmly snatched the sword out of his hand. The soldier leapt back, clutching his wrist and staring in terror at the man who held his sword by the blade with not so much as a drop of blood. "Y–you nearly broke my fingers!" he stammered.

"That's nothing to what you did to our Princess!" Kichesias said through gritted teeth.

"But that's the whole point! We didn't—"

Kichesias pushed him aside and disappeared through the tent flap. Alexis and Anteia hurried after him, leaving Diogenes to watch the prisoner.

It was dark inside the tent. A huddle on the floor under a rough blanket showed that the Princess was sleeping. She did not move when they came in, and they rushed anxiously across. As Kichesias dropped to his knees and pulled back the blanket, there was a cry behind them and a wild-eyed apparition leapt out of the shadows and brought a hydria down on top of Kichesias's head.

"No, Phoebe!" Alexis shouted. "It's us!"

Too late. He winced as the hydria shattered with a blow hard enough to have felled a grown man and its water poured out.

Kichesias blinked, shaking shards of pottery from his curls. He raised a hand to his head. "That hurt," he said. But he was smiling at Phoebe through his dripping fringe, a soft gleam in his eyes.

"Kichesias...?" Phoebe whispered. "Alex?"

She sank to her knees on the blanket with a little moan. There was a rattle as she did so, and they saw she had been chained by the ankle to a stake hammered into an exposed slab of rock at the centre of the tent. Her wrists were joined by a short length of chain as well. She was still wearing the trousers and glittery waistcoat she'd worn the day Alexis had woken Diogenes. But her captors had taken her cloak, her cheeks were smudged with dirt, and her ringlets were frizzy. They realized she was shivering.

"We've come to get you out," Alexis explained, and she gave a huge shudder and closed her eyes.

"I thought you were the Macedonians!" she whispered. "They told me if I didn't behave, they were going to chop off my finger for real next time! It was so horrible, Alex! They blindfolded me and put chains on me, and when I could see again I was in this tent. I didn't even know where I was at first, and I couldn't understand their accents. I was so frightened! But then a man all wrapped up in a cloak came in, and he spoke Persian. I never saw his face, but he explained that I was in General Alexander's camp. He said they were going to send the finger to Daddy... Please say they didn't send it to him, please..."

"I'm afraid they did, Phoebe," Alexis said, frowning at the Princess's hands. It was too dark inside the tent to see properly, but she didn't seem to be hurt.

Anteia darted past them and seized Phoebe's chained wrists, examining her hands. "You're all right!" she said. "It weren't yours, after all! Oh, I'm so glad! You were cryin' so hard, I was sure they'd cut it off you! Why did they bring it in here? Whose was it?"

Phoebe peered at Anteia. "You're the girl who spoke to me before, aren't you? They told me the finger was from a woman who'd been killed in a Persian raid on the camp. They just wanted to measure it, I think. They brought several, all different sizes, and laid them out in a row. I'd been asleep, so those fingers were the first things I saw when I opened my eyes, and the shock made me scream..." She shuddered at the memory. "Were you the one who told Kichesias and Alex where I was? Thank you."

"Don't thank her!" Kichesias muttered. "She was going to run off and leave us in the middle of the enemy camp."

"We've got to get Phoebe out of here," Alexis said, before Anteia and his friend could start another argument. "Someone might come to see what's happened to those men."

At once, Kichesias was serious. He frowned at Phoebe's chains, took hold of the stake, eased his wounded leg into a more comfortable position and braced himself. A stillness came over him and sweat broke out on his brow. For a moment nothing seemed to happen. Then the rock cracked, and the stake came sliding out. He handed it to Phoebe. "Here – you'll have to hold this. I can't risk trying to break open the manacles, in case I hurt you. We'll have to go back to the city and get them removed properly. Diogenes will carry you if you can't run. He's waiting outside."

"Diogenes?" Phoebe said, with a confused look at Alexis. "But I thought—"

"Kichesias didn't kill him," Alexis said quickly. "There's no time to explain now. Come on!"

They crept to the flap, Phoebe clinking slightly. Anteia stopped them at the entrance and silently undid her cloak. Without it, she seemed even smaller and skinnier than before. "I know it's dirtier than you're used to," she said to Phoebe. "But you'd better take my cloak. You can't go out there dressed like that. The sentries'll spot you at once."

Kichesias gave Anteia a suspicious look. But Phoebe drew the stiff, dark material about her with a smile. She didn't seem to mind the smell. "Thank you, Macedonian girl. I shan't forget this."

Anteia shrugged. "Just go! I won't be able to do anythin' if you get caught. I've got to go and help Mother with the wounded—" She broke off as they emerged into the night, and her hands flew to her mouth. "Oh, what's happenin' *now*?"

They ducked back under cover as a troop of Macedonian soldiers galloped past. Men raced out of the nearby tents, shouting to one another. Officers barked orders in the Macedonian tongue, and more horses were bridled and mounted. Alexis looked anxiously for the Chimaera. But the Macedonians were heading away from the camp, towards the city. At the bottom of the hill, an orange glow lit the sky, reflected in the bay beyond. By its light, they could see the massed ships of the Persian fleet, fleeing east.

"Halicarnassos is on fire!" Phoebe cried. "General Alexander's burning the city! Daddy's down there! And all those poor people are trapped inside!"

"They're not trapped. Someone must have opened the gates." Diogenes pointed to the hillside, where refugees were running up the hill towards the camp. The sentries let them past, and the frightened citizens were allowed to gather around the Macedonian campfires, sobbing that their homes were burning, while the camp-women heated soup to feed the extra mouths. Their snatches of conversation soon made it clear what had happened.

"Your Satrap set fire to your city!" spat the young soldier, who was sitting outside the tent with his hands on his head while Diogenes stood over him with his own sword. "He's watching it burn, while he runs away by sea! What sort of man does that to his own people?" He spat on the ground. "Persian scum!"

"Daddy would never run away and leave me!" Phoebe said fiercely, her small fists clenched as she stared after the ships.

Alexis frowned. The ships in the bay, coupled with the evacuation of the Palace they'd witnessed, and now the fire below, seemed to make the Macedonian's accusations all too true. Some of the refugees, though, were talking excitedly about a monster with three heads, and a sick feeling lodged itself in his belly.

"What if it's the Chimaera?" he whispered. "What if she's learned to breathe fire? I told her to seek out Caria's enemies. I meant the Macedonians, but what if she thinks all enemies of Persia are Caria's enemies and has gone looking for Queen Ada? Neaera has the statue magic. She might try to turn the Chimaera against us."

"My Chimaera?" Phoebe's eyes lit up. "So you *did* wake her! I bet she's beautiful!"

"She's a monster," Anteia said firmly. "You'd better not let your Carian Queen send her back up here. Go after it – *hurry*!"

"Don't worry," Kichesias said, for once in full agreement with the girl. "We're going."

They left Anteia at the entrance to the blood tent. As they hurried down the hill, Kichesias helping Phoebe with her chains, Diogenes said quietly to Alexis, "That went better than I expected. A rescued princess, the Macedonian girl reunited with her mother, and no one dead. Now we just have to find the Chimaera and Lady Neaera and finish this thing. Where do you think my wife is hiding, Goldenhands?"

Alexis stopped dead and stared at the woken statue, a little shiver going down his spine. Diogenes' eyes twinkled, exactly like his father's used to when they'd played "Greeks and Persians", back when Alexis had been young enough to believe that fighting was just a game and that people who died got up again afterwards ready to play again.

"The Acropolis," he said, pushing his questions firmly aside for later. "Queen Ada's stronghold. That's where she'll be."

Chapter 16

ACROPOLIS

*DIOGENES: Diogenes has no idea
whether he even has a tomb for his body,
for he didn't care about that.*

From the top of the hill, the drama in the city below was like a play in a gigantic theatre. Flames were rising from the defence towers and from several places within the walls. It looked as though the arsenals where General Memnon stored his spare weapons had been set alight to stop the weapons falling into Macedonian hands. Although this meant the Chimaera probably hadn't been responsible for them, the fires were being spread by the strong westerly wind, and already the houses nearest the wall in the Craftsmen's Quarter were alight. Out in the bay, lit by that terrible reflection of red and orange, the last of the Persian fleet was sailing away into the night.

"I hope Pasion managed to get his old master out,"

Alexis said, looking for clues as to where the Chimaera might have gone.

The others were silent as they surveyed the scene. Macedonian soldiers from the camp galloped through the streets, adding to the panic. But General Alexander must have given orders that the city should be saved, because his men seemed to be fighting the fire, and they had forced open the old foot gate so that the refugees could flee to safety. Through its arch, Alexis saw a Macedonian horseman snatch a torch from a lone soldier who was trying to set fire to one of the lookout towers, and mercilessly cut the Persian's throat.

Phoebe gave a choked cry. "They're killing everyone! I've got to find Daddy!"

Before anyone could stop her, she gathered up her chain, stumbled towards the gate and disappeared into the flow of refugees.

"No, Phoebe!" Kichesias yelled, limping after her. "Wait! It's too dangerous!"

Diogenes shoved people, mules and hand-barrows out of the way with his strong arms, but the Princess had a head start and knew the back ways of the city better than they did. With her borrowed cloak she blended into the crowds, and they lost her in the dark alleys off the main street. They found themselves in a courtyard near the Temple of Ares, surrounded by refugees making for the Acropolis. Kichesias stared around helplessly, still calling for Phoebe.

"She'll be all right, Kichesias!" Alexis had to seize his

friend's shoulders and shake him to make him listen. "She'll have gone back to the Palace. You know how good Phoebe is at creeping around. I'll bet she knows all the secret ways in."

"But no one's there, only looters! The King was on one of those ships!"

"We don't know that."

"The lily-hands haven't left," Diogenes pointed out. "They'll look after her."

Kichesias didn't look convinced. But he must have seen the futility of fighting their way across the chaotic city after a Princess who didn't want to be followed. When Alexis reminded him they had to find Neaera before she and Queen Ada could turn the confusion to their advantage, he sighed and nodded reluctantly.

They gazed up at the Acropolis, perched on the crags above them with its tiled roofs and temples. The main courtyard had been opened to admit the refugees, but Queen Ada's soldiers were checking everyone at the gates before letting them in. The fortress itself rose from the cliff, steep and unscalable. In the base of the cliff were rock tombs, little more than rough caves, which might have provided shelter from the fires. But the tombs were supposed to be haunted, and even at a time like this people shunned them.

"General Alexander will have to sit out another siege if Queen Ada decides to defy him," Diogenes observed, studying the defences. "Any ideas how we're going to get inside?"

Alexis frowned at the tomb openings, wondering if the Chimaera might have taken refuge in them – they looked as if they would make a good lair. If so, the creature should be safe enough down there until they'd dealt with Neaera. He straightened his shoulders and pointed up the winding path to the gates of the Acropolis. "Easy," he said. "We pretend to be refugees."

Kichesias and Diogenes glanced at each other, but did not argue. They closed protectively on each side of Alexis as they approached the narrow tunnel through the rock with its crush of refugees and alert guards. Queen Ada's men wore tabards over their armour, emblazoned with the Carian Royal Lion like those of the guards they'd seen in the Palace, but the Queen had added her own touch in the form of scarlet plumes on their helmets. The refugees were made to wait in line while the guards searched everyone, even the smallest children, confiscating anything that could be used as a weapon and writing down their names before letting them through.

Kichesias chewed his lip as their turn drew nearer. "This might not be such a good idea, Alex," he whispered. "Remember what happened when we tried to get into the Palace the official way?"

Alexis forced a grin. "We got in, though, didn't we? This is the quickest way to find my stepmother."

It was too late to back out now. They were already in the tunnel with armed guards behind them as well as in front. One of Queen Ada's men snatched the sword Diogenes had taken from the young Macedonian soldier in the camp, and pushed him roughly against the wall. "What's this?" he demanded. "Who are you trying to kill?"

"Just defending my family," Diogenes said calmly, careful not to resist. "People are going crazy out there. No one's keeping order."

The guard's eyes narrowed. "Name?"

"Diogenes…" He glanced at Alexis. "The sculptor."

Alexis stiffened. But the guard wrote this down without comment. "And your name?" he snapped at Kichesias, who was undergoing a similar search for weapons.

"Kichesias, slave of Lady Neaer–*ah*!" Kichesias's words ended on a gasp of pain as the man searching him prodded his bandaged knee.

The guard looked closer at him and whispered something to his comrade. A message was passed up to the watchtower, and an officer stamped down and peered at Kichesias. Obviously recognizing him, he cursed under his breath. "That's all we need!" he muttered. "Take the slave to the dungeons."

Alexis's heart missed a beat. He darted forwards and grabbed the officer's arm. Two guards immediately dragged him back, but he had the officer's attention. "Sir, I'm Alexis, son of Diogenes the sculptor, and stepson of Lady Neaera! We have to see her at once. It's very important. We've come from the Macedonian camp."

The officer laughed. "Is that so? Then I'm afraid you have to go to the dungeons, boy, because that's where she is."

The guards hauled them away without further explanation. Alexis's thoughts whirled as they were hustled through a small door and along a dark corridor into the depths of the fortress. Dungeons? Had Neaera been arrested? Had Queen Ada discovered how dangerous she was?

The men escorted them down a spiral of uneven steps and dragged open a door to reveal an underground chamber with walls of rough, bare rock lit by a single smoky torch. Chains swung from the ceiling, casting sinister shadows over chilling items of furniture – a chair with leather straps attached to the arms and legs; a bench with strange holes in it; and a bed frame with manacles glinting at its head and foot. Alexis's heart beat faster. The modified chair was occupied by a man wearing a torn and bloodied Persian robe, slumped in his bonds. A woman crouched over the chair, doing something to the prisoner with a long pin that glittered gold in the torchlight. It was Neaera.

Diogenes stared at her with an unreadable look in his eye. Kichesias let out a little moan and curled his hand in sympathy.

Without pausing in her work, Neaera hissed, "What do you want? I told you I wasn't to be disturbed!" Then she looked up and saw Alexis.

She smiled very slowly. Her gaze took in Kichesias and Diogenes, and her smile broadened. She wiped the blood off her peplos pin and tucked it carefully into a fold of her sleeve. The prisoner sank lower in his bonds, his head flopping forwards on to his chest and his filthy, blood-encrusted ringlets hanging round his face. Mercifully, he seemed to have slipped into unconsciousness.

"At last!" Neaera murmured with an amused smile. "My disobedient family has decided to return." She flicked a finger at the guards. "Leave us."

Queen Ada's men hesitated. "It might be best if we stayed, my lady," one of them ventured, indicating Diogenes. "This man was caught at the gates with a Macedonian sword."

"I told you to go!" Neaera snapped, but she frowned at Diogenes. "On second thoughts, manacle my dear husband to the bed before you leave. And tell Queen Ada I want to be informed as soon as General Alexander gets here."

"Did the Persian talk, my lady?" The guards glanced curiously at the prisoner as they manhandled Diogenes on to the bed, where they locked the manacles about his wrists and ankles. Diogenes played along, letting them think he was human. "Did he tell you where General Memnon's headed?"

"That information is for Queen Ada's and General Alexander's ears alone!" Neaera snapped. "Now leave us. I can control a couple of boys, don't worry." She frowned at Kichesias's bandage then smiled again with that cruel twist of her lips Alexis remembered so well.

Diogenes was testing the manacles. He looked at Alexis, a question in his eyes. Alexis shook his head slightly. The woken statue could break free any time he wanted, but any show of strength would only encourage the guards to remain.

At last, the guards saluted and left, closing the door behind them. Neaera fingered her peplos pin as she considered Alexis. Alexis clenched his fists, wishing he dared leap across the cell and snatch it from her. All the things he'd been meaning to say had deserted him. He felt like a little boy again.

His stepmother chuckled. "I knew you'd come back eventually. The magic won't let you leave me, will it? And despite your brave accusations at my trial, seeing me hurt would hurt you just as much. I wonder what would have happened if we hadn't been so conveniently interrupted by the fighting, and the jury had found me guilty? Would you have let them give me poison?" She smiled again. "But poison wouldn't have worked on me, anyway, would it? Nothing can kill a statue apart from a golden weapon, and they didn't believe that part, did they?" She shook her head. "Did you honestly think they would? You're such a child sometimes, Alex."

"Why did you do it?" Alexis demanded. "Why did you kill my father?"

"You mean you still don't know?" Neaera abandoned her unconscious prisoner to approach Kichesias and touch his cheek. The boy jerked his head away, making her laugh. "I underestimated you, Alex. I was sure you'd guessed the truth, and that was what gave you the courage to stand up and accuse me of murder before all

Halicarnassos. But you really don't know, do you?" She stepped past Kichesias and lifted Alexis's hand, stroking his trembling palm with her cold fingertips. "You have such strong magic, yet you don't understand it at all!"

Alexis stiffened. He could not take his eyes off that golden pin, glittering in her sleeve. *Touch it.*

"Leave Alex alone!" Kichesias said, pushing her away.

She laughed again. "So loyal, aren't you, Kichesias? Do you think I would damage Alex's magic hand? The gold pin is your particular demon, remember? You seem to be in some pain already, though. What happened? Someone kick you with a golden slipper? I didn't know a statue could suffer pain like humans do. That's fascinating. But let's get to the point, shall we? Alex, I need you to work your magic for me one last time. I've done as much as I can in this woman's shell. I want you to transfer me to a more suitable body."

Alexis stared at his stepmother, bewildered. "But I thought you wanted me to wash in the river at Mount Tmolus so I could turn things to gold and make you rich?"

Neaera shook her head impatiently. "That was before I understood how things are. I thought I was stuck with this body until it died. But then you made a statue of your father and you put his spirit into it. You did the same for the Chimaera you so foolishly loosed upon the city. Admittedly, with the monster, there was really only one spirit that would have fit in that particular body shape. But Diogenes was different. You *chose* him, Alex.

From all the available ghosts of men haunting Halicarnassos at the time, you found your father's and you called him back. I didn't know you could do that. I wish I'd known years ago – it would have saved us all a lot of trouble. But since you didn't try to bring him back before, I assume it's something you've only just learnt to do."

A shiver went down Alexis's spine. "But Diogenes can't really be my father," he whispered, staring at the man locked in the manacles, who was lying quietly and listening to every word. "He just looks like him. I only made him so I'd have a body with my father's face to show the Assembly..."

Diogenes gazed at him with his kind brown eyes, and Alexis's stomach leapt with hope. He remembered the way the woken statue had called Neaera his wife and how he'd used Alexis's old pet name during their escape from the Macedonian camp.

"He *can't* be my father," he whispered. "He didn't recognize me when he woke up!"

"Of course he didn't," Neaera snapped. "The last time he saw you, you were seven years old. You've grown up since then, and memory takes time to return to us. I'm surprised you didn't realize that."

Alexis staggered, grabbed for Kichesias's arm, remembered his friend was having difficulty standing himself, and clutched at the nearest support. This happened to be the chair holding the prisoner. A lingering perfume rose from the Persian's beard, mixing sickeningly with the odour of stale sweat. The perfume niggled at Alexis's memory, but all he could think was: *It's true! Diogenes really is my father!* He'd been telling himself for so long that the woken statue couldn't be his father, he hadn't seen the obvious. Statues were confused when they woke up. Kichesias had been, and so had Neaera. It made sense that Diogenes would have been confused, too. And he *had* been thinking of his father's spirit when he'd touched the statue he'd made...

"*Father!*" he choked out, staggering across to the bed and gazing down into the lined face. "I'm sorry, I'm so sorry!"

Diogenes' brown eyes looked back up at him, calm and slightly amused. Alexis wondered how long he'd known who he really was. "Get up!" he shouted, pulling at his arm. "Break the chains! Now!"

"Don't waste your strength, Diogenes," Neaera warned. "I had them lined with gold – which, as I'm certain your son must have explained to you, is the only substance in this world that can take away our strength. I thought I might need them for Kichesias, but I don't think my young slave is as strong as he once was. Seems he's getting his wish to be human, though perhaps not in exactly the way he'd hoped. Fell in love with the little Princess, did you, Kichesias? It seems to have weakened you. A mistake I'll be careful not to make." She laughed a little. "When I'm in my new body and have married Queen Ada, who will be Queen of all Caria as soon as General Alexander reinstates her on the throne, I might be generous and release you. Alexander thinks Ada's no threat to him, being older than his mother and sending him all those presents. Of course, it might be a different matter when he realizes exactly who she's marrying. But by then our ambitious Alexander and his army will be heading into Persia to challenge Darius and his barbarian hordes. I doubt he'll be back this way to bother us again."

"You're crazy!" Alexis said, looking in anguish at the manacles that restrained his father. He could just make out the gold strips, hidden cleverly on the inner surfaces between two bands of iron, impossible to reach while the manacles remained locked. Helpless tears sprang to his eyes. Neaera had tricked them yet again. Then he realized what his stepmother had said. "Marry Queen Ada?" he whispered in confusion. "But you can't! You're a woman."

"I'm a woman? Really? Did you check? You were so young, Alex. You grabbed the first spirit available in the Mausoleum, didn't you? Oh, I know you hadn't a clue what you were doing, so I'll forgive you – provided you work the magic again and transfer me into my new body so I can rule my country and my fine city of Halicarnassos as it is meant to be ruled, by one of the ancient Carian blood, a man strong enough to resist the Persian yoke and restore Caria to her former glory!"

Alexis stared at her. *My country. My city. The first spirit available in the Mausoleum.* "Oh gods," he whispered, finally understanding the terrible thing he'd done that day when his father had lifted him on his shoulders to better see the statues. "You're... you're the old King, aren't you? I put King Maussollos's spirit into your statue!"

Neaera smiled at their stunned expressions. "Not so loud. Our Persian friend is still alive, I think. He might be listening." She grabbed the prisoner's hair and lifted his head to check.

"Alex!" Kichesias exclaimed, staring at the unconscious prisoner. "Isn't that...?"

"Ishkibar!" Alexis said, more bewildered than ever as he saw the tiny bloody holes Neaera's peplos pin had made in the Persian's face and neck. "What's he doing here? I thought he helped you murder my father... I didn't trust him."

"I know you didn't." Neaera was still smiling. "It was all rather amusing, really."

On the bed, Diogenes cleared his throat. "I think it's time you knew what really happened that night at the Mausoleum, Alex," he said quietly. "The trial helped bring things back for me. I was going to tell you later, when you'd accepted who I was, but considering the circumstances I think you need to hear it now."

Neaera narrowed her eyes at Diogenes. She started to shake her head then seemed to change her mind. She seated herself on the bench and rested one ankle on her opposite knee in a most unladylike fashion. "Why not?" she said with a chuckle. "Let's hear it. I only know half the story, after all, and the Persian has been frustratingly stubborn so far. Maybe you can cast some light on things, my dear?"

Diogenes ignored her sarcasm, shifted slightly in his chains, and fixed his gaze on the rocky ceiling. "What you said at the trial was quite right, Alex. I went to Ishkibar's mansion that night to beg for your life. I'd discovered who he really was from his wife, who was so grateful for the sculpture I'd made of her dying son that she told me something she shouldn't have in order to save your life. She warned me Emperor Darius did not allow possible threats to his Empire to live, and told me about Ishkibar being his agent in Halicarnassos and how he was investigating your ancestry. She advised me to leave the city and take you across the Aegean Sea, where you'd be safe. But Halicarnassos was... is our home. I didn't want you to spend the rest of your life looking over your shoulder, and I thought your new mother was happy in the Craftsmen's Quarter."

He kept his eyes on the ceiling, so he was spared seeing Neaera's scornful expression.

"So I got down on my knees and begged. I said I wouldn't take a fee for the statue, if Ishkibar would only leave you alone. I wouldn't tell anyone who he was. And I promised I would make sure you never went anywhere near the Gordion Knot, or otherwise tried to challenge the Emperor. Ishkibar seemed happy enough with my promise. But he had me followed. I called at the Mausoleum on my way home to check my suspicions, and two men followed me in. It was dark. I knew the

Mausoleum well. They didn't. I dodged around a bit and got them separated, chasing their own shadows. I jumped the first one, meaning to disarm him and demand he tell me what his orders were concerning you. That was when I saw Neaera, standing up on the first tier of the Mausoleum as if she were a statue again. Before I could warn her to stay where she was, she jumped down, and the assassin I was grappling with struggled free and stabbed her in the confusion. He had a curved Persian dagger with spells glittering on the blade. They must have been written in gold, because she started bleeding that black statue blood."

He paused. Neaera fiddled with her peplos pin, but didn't interrupt.

"I caught her in my arms," Diogenes went on. "I thought she was dying. But, of course, it was the other way around and her statue blood poisoned me. I felt weak and dizzy. I remember my jaw locked up so I could barely speak, and it was all I could do to warn her there was a second assassin. By then both men had fled, but Neaera stayed. Before her wound scabbed over, she dragged off my cloak and smeared her blood all over me to finish the job. The last thing I heard was her running away. I never knew if the assassins returned, or if they'd intended to kill me. I didn't know if they'd found and killed you, Alex. I had no idea if my death had been any use – not until you called me back yesterday morning, and I began slowly to remember."

He turned his head and looked at Neaera. "Until that

night, I never knew how much you hated me. It makes more sense now. I can imagine the anger of a spirit who was once a great king, imprisoned in a woman's body and married to a poor craftsman, forced to look after his son because the boy is the only person in the world who might make him powerful again."

Alexis's mind was churning too much for words. But Kichesias scowled at Neaera. "Then Alex was right all along! You *did* murder his father. You poisoned him with your blood."

"I was attacked first," Neaera said. "I didn't lie about that."

"By a Persian assassin! Alex's father never hurt you. He tried to warn you!"

"But that night," Alexis whispered. "When you came back to the house, you had real blood on you. Human blood."

"Didn't think I'd let Ishkibar's assassins live to tell the tale, did you?" Neaera said with a sneer. "It was easy enough to catch them. They thought me wounded and weak, a mere woman. I slit their throats and left the bodies nearby. I had to hide Diogenes' body in the drains because of the statue blood, so I told everyone he'd attacked me and disappeared. I thought he'd get blamed for killing the assassins, only Ishkibar must have cleaned up after himself because as far as I know no one ever found their bodies. Thank you, dear. That explains a few things. But enough delay!" She sprang to her feet, seized Kichesias's wrist and placed her pin over his hand. "You two will come with me. Diogenes can stay here and keep the Persian company."

"But – but – *why*?" Alexis said, still fighting tears. "And what were you doing in the Mausoleum that night, anyway?"

Neaera made an impatient sound. "Why? Do you still have to ask why? I wanted to be free, of course! Free of male rule! It was too good an opportunity to miss. And as for what I was doing in the Mausoleum..." Her expression softened. "I used to go there at night, when no one else was around. It's my tomb, after all."

"How did you catch Ishkibar?" Alexis said desperately, to delay Neaera further while he thought of a way to free his father. *Change*, he willed, trying to force a finger between his father's wrists and the tight iron bands. *Change!* But he couldn't reach the treacherous gold lining. The tears he'd been struggling to hold back dripped on to his father's chains.

Neaera pressed her lips together and dragged Kichesias through the door, her pin glittering in the torchlight. "Come away from there!" she snapped. "Wipe your eyes. You'll have time for fond farewells later."

Left with little choice, Alexis obeyed. He cast a final anguished look at his father as Neaera slammed and barred the door. Diogenes gazed back at him, his expression unreadable.

Neaera seized a torch from the wall and took them deeper into the foundations of the fortress. The stonework gave way to rocky tunnels, and they heard noises up ahead – roars, bleats and an angry hissing. Alexis paused in sudden hope, realizing where they must be.

Neaera smiled at his reaction. "Yes, it's the Chimaera. Thank you for waking her. I've decided to keep her for a while in case I need her help to persuade the good people of Halicarnassos that I'm their rightful King. The poor creature was quite bewildered when I found her. She killed quite a few of Ada's men, but I was able to catch her easily enough. Did you send her into the tunnels after me? You should have realized the statue magic wouldn't let her hurt me. I've found her a nice golden chain to keep her quiet. I plan to feed her on Ada's Persian prisoners, once they've told us everything they know. Ishkibar can have the honour of being her first meal, and the little Princess can be next now she's outlived her usefulness." She chuckled at Kichesias's moan. "Love makes us weak, remember? I'll be doing you a favour. Ah, here we are!"

She hustled them along a side tunnel into a cave, where a giant twice the height of a normal man stood motionless in the shadows, draped in a white cloth. She thrust Kichesias to the back of the cave where he couldn't escape, and swept off the cloth. The gigantic figure was a statue, obviously new since some of its paintwork was still wet. The face was strong-featured with a full beard and moustache and a slight frown between the eyes. The giant's limbs were straight and strong. The work was good.

"Isn't he lovely?" Neaera said, running her hand over the gilded marble robes. "I had Pasion oversee the work, while you must have been busy making a new body for your father. Ironic, really, though this one took rather more manpower. Pasion and his team thought they were working on a commission for the Queen, of course – I could hardly tell him the truth. It's a copy of the statue of Maussollos that stands on top of the Mausoleum. I did consider using that one, but getting it down would have been difficult with the Persians swarming all over the place. Besides, I'm pleased with the way my tomb turned out. It'd be a shame to destroy the decor."

Alexis stared at the gigantic statue, numb.

"So work your magic, Alex," Neaera said softly. "Transfer my spirit into this fine male body, and I'll see your friend gets proper treatment for his knee and your father is kept safe from harm."

Alexis glanced at Kichesias. His friend was crouched against the rock in the back of the alcove, sweating. "You can't feed Princess Phoebe to the Chimaera," Kichesias whispered. "We rescued her from the camp."

Neaera frowned at him. "Quiet, you! What's wrong, Alex? Need some more persuasion?" She advanced on Kichesias with her peplos pin.

"I can't," Alexis said.

Neaera frowned again. "I had Pasion use plenty of Ada's gold paint on it, so don't give me that excuse. I'm warning you, I can hurt your friend and your father badly. But if you help me, you'll be treated well. I'll even save the life of the little Princess, since you seem to care about her so much. The Satrap will have to die, of course, but his daughter's no threat to me. I can easily marry her off to someone who'll teach her who's in charge and make sure she's locked up in the house, as all decent girls should be. She's nearly old enough."

Kichesias's face twisted in anger. But Alexis straightened his shoulders and took a deep breath. He poured all his skills of persuasion into his voice. "You don't understand. I'm not refusing to do it. I *can't* do it. I know more about the magic now, and it's true what you said before. I have to capture spirits in order to bring statues to life, but I can't capture a spirit unless it's already lost its body... unless it's free."

Neaera frowned as what he was saying sank in. She caressed the statue and said in a dangerous tone. "If you're lying—"

"I'm not!" Alexis said, his heart beating faster. "You have to leave your old body first. Otherwise, when I try to wake your new body, another spirit will get into it first. One of the people who was buried down here, I expect. This is part of the tomb complex, isn't it? There must be loads of old ghosts down here anxious to live again in such a fine, strong body."

Neaera thought about this. "You mean I have to die?"

Alexis met her gaze. He was gambling everything on Phoebe's theory that the pain he shared with a woken statue was in his mind and not physical. "If you want your new body, yes."

He made himself breathe normally while Neaera stared into his eyes, searching for the slightest sign that he was lying. In the back of the cave, Kichesias was very still, watching them.

"Then so be it," Neaera said. "There'll have to be a few precautions, though." She smiled slowly. "I know you too well, Alex. You're a sly one. You might be thinking that once I'm gone, you'll be free to do what you like. But I think I know how to make sure you bring me back."

Chapter 17

SURRENDER

*DIOGENES: But he has left for the best
of those who come after the report that he has
lived the life of a man.*

Neaera left four guards to watch Alexis and Kichesias while she disappeared into the fortress to make the preparations for her own death. Worried by how readily she had agreed, Alexis thought about trying to get past the guards. He might be able to use his magic to release the Chimaera before she came back. But if they ran now, Neaera would know he had tricked her. So he crouched with Kichesias in the cave at the feet of the gigantic statue of King Maussollos, and made himself wait.

"Was that true?" Kichesias whispered. "What you told her about having to die?"

Alexis sighed. "I don't know. But if she falls for it, there's no way I'm bringing her back again. She – *he* – can haunt me all my life, but that spirit's not getting into another body. I'm never waking another statue again, Kichesias, no matter what. I swear it."

His friend chewed his lip. "But what about the magic? If she dies, you'll feel it... you might die, too!"

"Phoebe thinks it's all in my mind," Alexis said as confidently as he could. "When Neaera uses her gold pins on you, I don't get a hole in my hand, do I?"

Kichesias still didn't look happy. "Do you think Lady Neaera really is the spirit of King Maussollos?"

Alexis frowned. "It's possible, I suppose. And it would explain why she's so keen to rule, to have power."

"I can't believe a king would be so cruel. Wasn't King Maussollos supposed to be powerful and good? He built this city, didn't he? How can anyone so cruel build something so beautiful?"

"I don't know. Maybe spirits change after they've been out of their bodies for a long time, or maybe being trapped in Neaera's body twisted it somehow?"

Kichesias gave him a quick look. "If she really dies, we'll be free."

"Yes."

They fell silent, keeping their worries to themselves.

When Neaera returned she was carrying the golden Ceremonial Sword of Caria, which Phoebe had smuggled out of the Palace for Kichesias to use on Diogenes. Alexis was startled, before he remembered how the sword had been stolen the day Phoebe was kidnapped. Its scarlet tassels were dusty, but the blade shimmered in the shadows like a slice of the sun. Neaera held the golden weapon casually in one hand as if it were no heavier than a dagger, beckoned the guards out into the tunnel one by one, and whispered something to each man. Their expressions turned serious, and they glanced back at the two boys with looks that turned Alexis cold.

Two of them disappeared briefly and returned carrying a small water clock, which they set up at the entrance to the tunnel. The other two seized Kichesias's arms and marched him back towards the dungeons. Alexis tried to follow, but Neaera gripped his wrist and held him in the cave.

"Merely part of my precautions," she said. "They won't hurt him unless you try to trick me."

When Kichesias had gone, Neaera passed Alexis into the custody of the remaining two guards and tested the edge of the golden sword with her thumb. "I had it sharpened," she explained, showing him a line of black blood. "I thought it might come in useful, though I admit I didn't anticipate using it on myself."

She smiled at his anxious glance along the tunnel. "You're wondering what I ordered them to do to Kichesias, aren't you? Listen very carefully, Alex. The lives of those you love depend upon you understanding this. I've given each guard a different password, known only to them and myself. As soon as I've finished with the sword, they are to take it out of the cave and leave you here alone. They'll watch the entrance, of course, so don't get any ideas about leaving before you've brought me back. Unless a giant looking exactly like this statue returns before dawn and tells all four guards the correct passwords, they are to use the golden sword to kill Diogenes and Kichesias. Even if three of the passwords are correct and one is wrong, they are to kill them. And if anyone tries to harm any of the guards before dawn, the others will kill Diogenes and Kichesias immediately. The four of them will remain on high alert and watch each other's backs until then. They've been trained to do this. Until I return in my new body to give them the passwords, Kichesias, Diogenes and yourself will be restrained in the dungeon. You have until the water in the clock runs out before they come for you. That should give you ample time to put my spirit in my new body. I have told them that if things go wrong, and no one returns to give them the passwords, they are to let you watch the executions, then sell you to the Athenian silver mines as a slave so that you can think about how you betrayed your friend and your father while you work out the rest of your miserable little human life chained in darkness and despair." She smiled as the horror of her words dawned on his face. "So no tricks, Alex! If you lose my spirit, you lose everything you care for. Take him further back – I don't want him poisoned by my blood."

"But what if you don't remember the passwords...?" Alexis said desperately as the guards dragged him to the back of the cave and held him fast.

Before he'd even finished the question, Neaera had reversed the golden sword against the wall. She held the lion-hilt steady with both hands and set her throat against the sharpened point. With a sigh that almost sounded like pleasure, she closed her eyes and stepped forwards.

Alexis couldn't help crying out. Yet even as his scream echoed along the tunnel, he readied himself. When the guards took the sword away, they would have to release him. If he could dart after them and touch the golden weapon before they realized what he was doing, he might be able to change it into something that wouldn't harm his father and friend... He hadn't reckoned with the terrible strength of the statue bond. As the sword clattered to the ground and Neaera collapsed beside it, Alexis's ears roared and the cave filled with shadows. When he could see again, he was kneeling on the rock beside his stepmother's body. Black statue blood was crystallising around her, and the guards and the sword had gone.

Fighting off his dizziness, he approached Neaera cautiously, expecting a trick. But the spirit that had animated her was absent. She was a statue again, like the one he'd touched at the Mausoleum, only eight years older. He looked down the tunnel after the guards, then up at the huge marble face of Maussollos.

He clenched his jaw. "Never again," he whispered. "No matter what."

He told himself that Kichesias and Diogenes had already served their time in this world. Bringing them back to live again in their statue bodies had been selfish – his desire, not theirs. The golden sword would free their spirits, if it came to the worst. But meanwhile, the water in the clock was still running. He had a little time yet before the guards came for him.

He tore a piece off the cloth that had covered the statue of Maussollos and carefully used it to scoop up some crystals of Neaera's blood that had not quite dried. Keeping close to the wall, Alexis made his way slowly down the tunnel to the junction. He held the poisonous blood ready like a weapon and paused to listen. The guards were very quiet. Hope glimmered. Perhaps they'd decided Neaera was crazy after seeing her kill herself, and gone back to their posts?

He took a tentative step round the bend – and a foot kicked the blood-soaked cloth out of his hand. Before he could recover, the guard had slammed him against the wall.

"Going somewhere, boy?" His captor peered into the top urn, while his comrade kept watch on the golden sword, which was propped safely in an alcove out of Alexis's reach. "Time's almost up – better get back in there and finish whatever it is you have to do."

With an effort, Alexis calmed his heart. He tried to think of something that might persuade the guards to let him close enough to the sword to touch it, but his mind was blank.

"Better give Daddy's sword back and let my friend go!" called a haughty female voice from the darkness behind them.

The guards whirled. Alexis peered up the tunnel,

hardly daring to hope. "Phoebe...?" he whispered.

"It's the Satrap's daughter!" the second guard exclaimed. "She must have escaped from the camp." He started down the tunnel towards the Princess, but hesitated as torchlight flickered behind her casting a monstrous shadow up the walls. Alexis tensed. The shadow had the jaws of a lion, the horns of a goat, and an enormous snake's tongue that flickered across the ceiling. "She's got some sort of monster down there!" screamed the guard, racing back.

The Chimaera came after him in a rush of animal stink, a rattle of claws, roars, hisses and bleats. A gold collar glinted around her neck, dangling the broken links of Neaera's gold chain. The other guard released Alexis and snatched out his sword in terror. The Chimaera bit his arm off at the elbow, spat it out, and smashed the second man against the rock with a single swipe of her tail. She avoided the golden sword with mincing steps and lowered her lion's head to examine Alexis. Then she spotted Neaera's statue body lying at the feet of the huge image of Maussollos. She roared again and leapt past Alexis, knocking over the water clock on her way. From the cave came a great noise of stone cracking and crunching. A cloud of white dust billowed out.

Phoebe arrived, breathless. "Isn't she beautiful?" she shouted above the noise the Chimaera was making. "We got in the secret way through the tombs – found her chained down there, the poor thing! The lily-hands wanted to leave her tethered, but I ordered them to set her free. I know what it feels like to be chained." She rubbed her wrists, and Alexis saw red marks around them where her manacles had been removed.

Phoebe gave a shudder and glanced over her shoulder. "It's nearly light outside. General Alexander's arrived, and Daddy's gone up to see him and Great-aunt Ada – I told you he wouldn't run away and leave me, didn't I? The lily-hands are down here somewhere. We heard you yell, so we made a diversion. Where's Kichesias?" She looked into the cave, saw the unrecognisable heaps of marble beneath the Chimaera's feet, and paled. "He's not...?"

Alexis wiped the dust from his eyes. "No – that's the remains of Neaera's new body. But Kichesias is still in danger, and so is my father!" Quickly, he explained how Neaera had died, and what precautions she had taken to ensure he brought her spirit back.

Phoebe clapped her hands in relief and delight. "Lady Neaera killed herself? Really? She must be stupid!"

"She's not stupid. Two of the guards are dead, but that still leaves two of them to kill Kichesias and Diogenes. I'm sorry, Phoebe, but I've got to try to change your father's sword into something other than gold. I don't know if I can choose, but I'll try to make it as valuable as I can. Maybe silver."

Phoebe tore her gaze from the Chimaera and stared at him. "What are you talking about, Alex? Daddy will never forgive me if I let you use your magic on the Ceremonial Sword of Caria! Get away from there. The lily-hands are coming."

"I have to change it! It's the only thing I can think of."
Alexis hopped with impatience as the lily-hands ran up
with torches and blocked his way. It had been one thing
to convince himself that Kichesias's and Diogenes' spirits
would be better off free when there had been no way out
other than to wake the statue of King Maussollos. But to
lose them now...

"Relax, Alex." Phoebe heaved the ceremonial sword
from the alcove, and her lips twitched into a smile. "Not
many of these around. Daddy says they're far too heavy,
too expensive, and not much use as a regular weapon
because gold's too soft against iron. We've got this one
back now, so what are the guards going to use?"

Alexis stared at the sword, finally realizing the flaw in
Neaera's carefully crafted plan. Four guards. One
weapon. When Phoebe laughed, he laughed too.

The Chimaera seemed happy enough in the cave,
grinding Neaera's old and new bodies to dust. Hoping
the creature would not decide to follow them in search of
more "enemies", Alexis led the way back to the torture
chamber. There was the sound of a scuffle along the
tunnel, and more lily-hands ran to join them, fingers
flickering in their secret sign language. One of them took
charge of the golden sword. The others formed up
around their Princess.

The door of the torture chamber was slightly open.
All was silent and dark inside, and Alexis's stomach
fluttered in renewed anxiety for his father and friend. The
lily-hands indicated that he and the Princess should wait

outside, while two of them ventured in holding their torches high.

Their caution was justified. A figure leapt out of the shadows behind the door and knocked the first lily-hand flat, sending his torch flying. As the other whirled, his spear raised, a second figure whispered up behind him with something small and sharp in its hand. The other lily-hands rushed inside, but Alexis recognized their two assailants and ducked between them. "Stop! Father! Ishkibar! It's us!"

Diogenes' face brightened in relief. He climbed off the fallen lily-hand and helped the big slave to his feet. Ishkibar slipped a little dart back inside his robe and gave Alexis a level stare. "So you got away from her," he said. "What happened?"

"Alex!" Kichesias cried, limping out of the shadows where he had been hiding. "Where's Lady Neaera?"

"Dead," he said tightly, noticing Neaera's final two guards lying motionless near the far wall.

"They're dead, too," Kichesias said. "Ishkibar came round while we were gone, and he and Diogenes freed each other. Ishkibar had that poisoned dart hidden in his robes all the time Lady Neaera was torturing him, but he didn't try to use it on her because he knew it would do no good after what you'd said at the trial about her being a statue. He used it on one of the guards when they brought me in, and I disarmed the other one in the confusion. I didn't mean to kill him. I must have hit him too hard." He looked sadly at the bodies by the wall.

"They were going to kill you and Father," Alexis said in a hard voice.

"Only because Lady Neaera ordered them to. How did she die? How did you get away?"

While Alexis explained for the benefit of his friend and his father, Phoebe and Ishkibar spoke rapid Persian together. Alexis couldn't tell what they were saying, but he saw the wary look in Ishkibar's eyes as he addressed the Princess and wondered at it. Finally, Ishkibar grunted, picked up one of the dead guards' weapons and headed out of the dungeon, taking one of the lily-hands with him to carry the golden sword. The atmosphere immediately lightened.

"I told him where Daddy was and what he hopes to do," Phoebe said. "Don't worry, Ishkibar will advise him so everything goes all right for us. Come on, let's follow them. I want to see Great-aunt Ada surrender."

Alexis glanced back down the tunnel, where the Chimaera's hisses and roars still echoed. "We ought to secure the Chimaera first. I told her the Persians were Caria's friends. I think she attacked Neaera's statue because she thinks the enemies of Persia are Caria's enemies. She'll probably go for Queen Ada next."

Phoebe shook her head. "She'll be fine till we get back. Besides, Ishkibar says, 'The enemy of my friend is my enemy, and the enemy of my enemy is my friend'. So if Great-aunt Ada is surrendering the city to General Alexander, and Daddy is helping her, then that makes Great -aunt Ada a friend... sort of." She frowned, as if she'd confused herself. "Anyway, there are lots of torches burning up in the fortress, and the Chimaera's scared of fire. Maybe she remembers the last time she died and doesn't want to repeat the experience – if she doesn't breathe fire no one can melt lead in her stomach, can they? Thank you for waking her, Alex. I'm going to keep her for ever."

"I didn't wake her to be your pet—" Alexis broke off as his father rested a warning hand on his shoulder. If the Princess wanted to keep a monster as a pet, who was he to stop her?

"How did you get free?" he asked, suddenly noticing the broken bed frame. "I thought the gold stole your strength?"

"Oh, that." Diogenes smiled. "Your tears did the trick, Goldenhands. They ran down the inside of the manacles and turned the gold to iron. It took me a bit of time to catch on, but luckily Ishkibar had some theories of his own about your magic, and when he came round he encouraged me to try breaking them. As he pointed out, it was the saliva in King Midas's mouth that changed his food and drink to gold, not his hands, and clearly the magic is just as powerful in you. One of the few occasions I can think of when changing gold to common metal is useful." He gave Alexis a boyish grin.

Phoebe led the way to the upper levels of the fortress with her head high and her ringlets tumbling freely around her dirt-streaked cheeks. She'd thrown back Anteia's cloak so the guards would recognize her. They avoided her eye and some of them whispered, "Sorry, Princess," as she passed. The story of the finger sent to the King was obviously well known.

The courtyard was packed with people and lit by a huge crimson sun rising through the smoke that lingered over the city. The lily-hands forced a path through the crowd until they emerged near the fortress steps, where two thrones had been placed side by side facing the gates. Phoebe let her borrowed cloak fall back to cover her clothes, betraying sudden nerves, and Kichesias put a protective arm around her. Alexis stood close to Diogenes, half wishing his father would put his arm around him in a similar manner – although he knew Diogenes was deliberately holding back from such a show of affection because he didn't want to embarrass Alexis in public.

Carian guards in full lion regalia lined the edge of the courtyard, and more of Queen Ada's men stood on the steps. One throne was occupied by an old woman with silver hair, dressed in glittering robes of gold and orange. The Queen sat erect, her withered hands resting on her knees, staring straight ahead with a fixed expression. Beside her, on the second throne, sat King Orontobates, also richly robed but in the Persian style. He looked pale, and a thick bandage around his ribs showed where he had been wounded in the unsuccessful raid on the Macedonian camp. Yet he, too, sat erect, and his beard had been freshly curled and oiled. Across his knees lay the golden Ceremonial Sword of Caria, more or less clean of Neaera's bloodstains. His fingers played with the tassels, exactly as they had done the night Alexis and Kichesias had surprised him in his secret harbour. Like a dark shadow, Ishkibar leant on the back of the Satrap's throne, sweating a little, a fresh robe thrown over his filthy clothes and his eyes darting warily from side to side.

A horn sounded outside, and the gates at the far end of the courtyard were thrown open to admit a river of red light down which the Macedonian soldiers, still in their stained armour and smelling of smoke after the night spent fire fighting, marched towards the thrones. In their midst pranced a great horse the colour of copper. The beast's neck was arched, and as it snorted at the crowds Alexis noticed an unusual mark in the shape of an ox's horns between its eyes. Its rider was not very tall and looked startlingly young with his head bare. But he wore on his breastplate the gorgon's head surrounded by writhing snakes, and his gaze fastened upon the two thrones with a look of determination that left no one with any doubts as to who he was.

"General Alexander of Macedon!" announced one of his escort. "King of Macedonia, Conqueror of Anatolia, Emperor of the World!"

Ishkibar gave a little cough. Alexis supposed this last claim did seem a bit premature, but no one noticed. All eyes were on the young King Alexander as he expertly controlled his dancing horse.

"He's going to ride right up the steps!" Kichesias whispered.

"Shh!" Phoebe hissed. "I want to hear what Great-aunt Ada says. Daddy might still end up in prison."

People averted their eyes from the gorgon's head as the conqueror passed, but to Alexis's relief no one seemed to turn to stone. Alexander reined in his horse before the thrones so that it stood with its forelegs on the top step and its hind legs two steps further down. He bowed his head slightly to Queen Ada. "My dear adopted mother," he said clearly in Greek. "Do you have a final present for me?"

The Queen frowned at a whispered order from Ishkibar. Stiffly, she rose to her feet and knelt before Orontobates. "I ask the Satrap's permission to surrender," she mumbled.

"Louder!" Ishkibar said.

Queen Ada shot him an icy glare and said more clearly, "I ask the Satrap's permission to surrender the city of Halicarnassos to King Alexander of Macedon."

Ishkibar smiled faintly. Orontobates made the kneeling Queen wait, as if giving her time to remember what she'd done, while the watching crowds muttered and whispered. Then he nodded and, with considerable effort because of his wound, passed the golden sword into her hands. Queen Ada turned with a look of triumph and presented it to Alexander. The Queen needed the aid of two of her guards to lift it high enough for Alexander to take, but not one person laughed.

Alexander accepted the Ceremonial Sword of Caria with a reverence that befitted the occasion. He turned his horse to face the crowds, lifted the sword high above his head so that it burned in the sunlight, and called out in a strong voice, "Halicarnassos is from this day forward part of the New Macedonian Empire! I crown my adopted mother, Ada, Queen of Caria to rule in my absence. Since he has surrendered peacefully, I will permit the former Satrap Orontobates and his family to live quietly in the city, provided he moves out of the Palace and makes no attempt to reclaim the throne or recall the Persian troops to Halicarnassos. To ensure his obedience, and to help Queen Ada restore order, I will leave 3,000 of my men stationed here in the Acropolis."

Phoebe let out her breath as General Alexander lowered the sword and rested it across his horse's withers. His gaze roved around the hall, pausing here and there as if marking possible troublemakers. He noted Queen Ada's look of unease at the mention of the troops, marked Ishkibar's narrowed eyes, and saw the way Orontobates pressed a hand to his wounded ribs and sought out his daughter in the crowd. Following the Satrap's gaze, he spotted Phoebe, jumped his horse down the steps and rode towards her.

The lily-hands moved protectively closer to their Princess, and Kichesias clasped her trembling hand. Diogenes stepped in front of them. Alexis eyed the golden sword resting across the horse's withers. He edged closer so he could work his magic on it if need be, but General Alexander did not threaten the Princess. Instead, he leant down and softly asked her a question in Persian.

Phoebe, who had tensed at his approach, looked surprised and answered in the same tongue. General Alexander smiled and straightened in his saddle. His gaze passed over Diogenes and Kichesias and came to rest on Alexis.

"I'm told you've lost your stepmother," he said. "War claims many casualties, but I'm always sorry to see a woman killed before her time, particularly one who has been as helpful to my cause as the Lady Neaera." He paused, and his lips twisted a little as if he knew very well Neaera was not who she had appeared to be. "I understand you're descended from King Midas and have an unusual gift. I don't need any statues brought to life, since I've more than enough men willing to fight for me, and I prefer to keep my gold as gold. But I wonder if, by any chance, you know the secret of unravelling the Phrygians' infamous Gordion Knot?"

The relief was so great, Alexis almost laughed. He exchanged a glance with Kichesias. Diogenes went very still. At the top of the steps, Ishkibar was watching them intently with his dark eyes.

He shook his head. "I'm afraid not, sir."

Alexander sighed. "A pity, but no matter. The Knot will doubtless be easier to conquer than Halicarnassos proved to be. I am, nevertheless, in your debt for removing one who would have opposed me. If there is anything you need, Alexis son of Diogenes, just speak to one of my officers."

He passed the golden sword safely into the hands of Queen Ada's guard, gave Orontobates a brief salute, and wheeled his horse. Whistling happily like a boy who has just won a game, the conqueror trotted out of the courtyard towards the rising sun.

Chapter 18

MOUNT TMOLUS

DIOGENES: A life, most servile of Carians, that towers above your memorial and is built on surer foundations.

That was the happiest winter of Alexis's life. His father moved back into his old home in the Craftsmen's Quarter and shared the sculpting work with Pasion, giving Pasion more time to look after his old master, whose house beside the wall had miraculously survived both the fire and the Macedonian missiles. Diogenes lost no time in freeing Kichesias from his slave status, and, although it was clear Orontobates would not be content to live as a commoner for long, Phoebe made the most of her new freedom by visiting the studio daily to tease the apprentices. Barefoot and with her hair in tangles, she looked more like a craftsman's daughter than a princess. Yet Kichesias was as besotted with her as ever, and the three of them spent many happy hours together roaming the city and the hills where part of the Macedonian army was still camped.

There seemed little Alexander of Macedon's men could do to make Alexis's life more perfect. But as Halicarnassos slowly settled into its new status under Macedonian rule – not much different from Persian rule, once everyone became used to the different uniforms of the soldiers patrolling the streets – Alexis remembered the promise he'd made to Kichesias as they crouched at the feet of King Maussollos's giant statue. *Never again*. The Macedonians eventually broke camp at the end of the winter. Anteia told them the baggage train was travelling back to Sardis to pick up the road to Gordium, where they'd been ordered to rejoin General Alexander for the start of the spring campaign. Alexis then knew he had to visit Mount Tmolus one last time.

The pilgrimage turned into quite an expedition. Kichesias and Diogenes insisted upon coming, of course, and so did Phoebe, chaperoned by a small bodyguard of lily-hands who had stayed on to serve the former Satrap's family out of loyalty to their princess. Orontobates, despite rumours that he was already seeking a political alliance with Queen Ada, came too, claiming that he wanted to see the countryside he'd once ruled. Phoebe wouldn't hear of leaving her new pet behind, so the Chimaera was dragged along as well, hissing and bleating at the end of her golden chain.

Finally there was Anteia, whose curiosity overcame her fear of the creature.

They travelled as far as Sardis with the baggage train, where they left the Macedonians and took to the hills in high spirits. They found the place on the slopes of Mount Tmolus where Neaera had made Alexis wash in previous years easily enough. The sun was setting behind the peaks when they arrived. There had been rain earlier in the day and the glen smelled of green, growing things. The river tumbled noisily in full spring flow, its sands sparkling with the gold that was supposed to have been washed from the hands of Alexis's ancestor, King Midas.

Phoebe exclaimed in delight, and she and Anteia at once rushed off to see if they could find any large nuggets, watched by a thoughtful Orontobates. Diogenes and the lily-hands quietly began to unpack their camping things from Pan's back, while the mule laid back his long ears and bared his teeth at the Chimaera.

Kichesias came to stand beside Alexis and looked at the water. "Do you want to camp here and try in the morning?" he asked.

Alexis shook his head. "I'll try it now. Get it over with."

He knew he'd never be able to sleep in this place. Too many memories haunted this glen – memories of Neaera standing on the bank with her peplos pin glittering against Kichesias's hand so that Alexis would obey her.

She's gone, he told himself firmly. *She can't hurt us any more.*

Seized by a sudden urge to be alone, he made his way upstream. The shadows lengthened as he entered a narrow gorge between steep cliffs. Here, the noise of the river was louder, filling his head. The laughter and chatter of the others faded behind him.

When he could hear nothing but the voice of the river, he knelt on the bank and plunged his hands into the rushing, glittering water. He closed his eyes. "God of the river," he whispered. "I need your help." He told the river god he was worried about the spirits of his father and friend, whom he'd brought back from death to live again in unnatural statue bodies for selfish reasons. He told the god he was worried about the Chimaera, too, even though he'd only woken the creature because he'd wanted to help Phoebe. He prayed for his curse to be washed away, *really* wanting it, willing the god to hear him with all his heart, as he had never done when Neaera stood on the bank, watching. "I don't want the golden touch like King Midas had," he whispered. "I only want the spirits I called back to be free again."

He held his breath as his hands slowly turned to ice, but there was no answer from the god. When he opened his eyes, he saw only the water, tumbling down through the gorge, darker than before.

With a sigh, he pushed his hands under his armpits to warm them. He made his way slowly back to the camp, his teeth chattering.

The sight of Kichesias, waiting for him at the mouth of the gorge motionless as a statue, made his heart miss a beat. He quickened his pace. But as he scrambled over the wet rocks, his friend's face broke into a relieved smile. "I suppose the god didn't come, as usual?" he said.

Alexis shook his head.

"Just as well! Your father sent me to find you. Guess who turned up while you were praying? That snake, Ishkibar!"

"What's *he* doing here?" Alexis said, his heart fluttering with anxiety as it had not done since Neaera died.

Shortly after the surrender of the city, Ishkibar had vanished. No one had missed the spy, and Phoebe said he would probably be arrested if he returned to Caria. But Alexis couldn't help remembering the look in Ishkibar's eyes at the trial, when he'd told the jury about his magic. He began to have a very bad feeling about this.

Kichesias shrugged. "I think he's in trouble."

In Alexis's absence, the lily-hands had pitched their tents and lit a campfire. Pan was grazing near the river on a long tether, one wary ear cocked towards a grove of olive trees at the far side of the glen, where Phoebe had secured the Chimaera. The monster was quiet for once, crouched in the shadows at the end of her golden chain. Orontobates and Diogenes stood side by side in the clearing, flanked by the lily-hands. Ishkibar knelt at their feet, his ringlets bedraggled and his head bowed. He was offering his sword, hilt uppermost, to the former Satrap.

A horse waited nearby, its head hanging and sweat steaming from its back.

"I've failed," Ishkibar was saying. "Alexander has conquered the Gordion Knot, and all Anatolia recognizes him as King. He didn't even bother trying to unravel it – he just sliced it in two with his sword! My life is not worth a grain of sand. I bribed one of Alexander's companions to assassinate him, but his men found out about it. The Emperor thinks I've gone over to the Macedonians, and the Macedonians are seeking me as Darius's spy. Everyone from here to Babylon wants my head. I throw myself on your mercy, Your Excellency! I've nowhere else to go. I beg you to end my miserable life – and I beg you, Diogenes, to sculpt me a new body with a different face so your son can bring me back in a form that will enable me to hide from my enemies."

Orontobates started to shake his head. But Diogenes took the offered sword and held its point at Ishkibar's throat. The Persian stiffened. Diogenes glanced at Alexis, and his face was hard as stone. "My son wants to ask you something first," he said.

Ishkibar nodded. "Ask anything you like. But for the gods' sakes, be quick! They're after me, and they've got dogs to smell my trail. The sooner I'm in a new body, the safer it'll be for all of us."

Alexis approached the kneeling Persian. He knew exactly what question his father had in mind. "Did you send those two men to kill my father, that night at the Mausoleum?" he asked.

Ishkibar began to laugh. But when Diogenes' expression tightened and the sword pressed harder, he stopped laughing and sighed. "It's such a small part in the greater scheme of things, but I suppose there's no harm you knowing now."

He closed his eyes, as if trying to remember the details. "I sent them to follow your father and see where he went and who he spoke to. They were only to kill him if he tried to tell anyone I was Darius's man. Most people in the Palace at the time wouldn't have been surprised, but it would have compromised my position with Queen Ada, who thought I supported her claim to the throne – a carefully crafted deception, since I was officially there, of course, to see her dear brother Pixodarus removed from power to make room for Orontobates. When I found my men's throats cut and heard Diogenes had disappeared, I admit I was worried. But he'd left you behind, so I knew he'd be back. Then his body turned up in the Mausoleum." He chuckled. "That's about the only thing we can thank Alexander for, making Memnon search those drains. So will you help me? I know you can do it. You have strong magic."

Alexis stared in disbelief at the man who had been responsible for his father's death. "You were working for *Queen Ada*?" he repeated, finally realizing what had been bothering him about Ishkibar's part in the siege. Ishkibar admitted he'd been in Halicarnassos longer than Orontobates had been Satrap. He claimed to be Darius's man, but five years ago, when Diogenes had been murdered, Queen Ada's younger brother Pixodarus had been on the throne and Alexander of Macedon was only just beginning to plan his campaign.

"You're a double agent, aren't you?" he whispered, seeing the truth at last. "You were working for General Alexander as well as for Emperor Darius! I bet you told Queen Ada where to find Phoebe the day she was snatched. You were helping the Macedonians, all along!"

"That's true!" Anteia said fiercely. "I seen him up at the camp."

There was a cry of rage from the trees, and Phoebe rushed across the clearing. "Anteia's right, Daddy!" she said, pointing to Ishkibar. "He was the Persian who came to my tent in the Macedonian camp. He was all wrapped up in a cloak so I wouldn't recognize him, but it was him all right. I *thought* I recognized his voice!"

Orontobates froze and said in a dangerous tone, "Is this true, Ishkibar? Did you arrange my daughter's kidnapping?"

"Of course." Ishkibar smiled, as if he were proud of the fact. "The whole bluff with the finger was my idea. But I did it for your sake, Your Excellency, to force your hand so you'd attack Alexander's camp. It nearly worked... but Alexander's forces were just too strong."

"So you went over to the other side," Orontobates said in disgust. "To save your skin."

Ishkibar shook his head. "No, I told you. I only pretended to be Queen Ada's man and to help General

Alexander. My loyalty was – is – to you alone, Your Excellency. I swear it."

The former Satrap shook his head. "I trusted you with my life, and you lied to me and put my daughter in danger! Your word is not worth the air it displaces. I should never have trusted a man who poisoned his own wife – oh, I know very well how you punished her for warning Diogenes about you, and told everyone she'd committed suicide! But it's over, Ishkibar. This time you'll pay the penalty you deserve."

Orontobates spat on the Persian's dark curls. Without another word, he put an arm around Phoebe's shoulders and guided her away.

For the first time, Ishkibar's dark eyes showed a flicker of uncertainty. "Diogenes!" he appealed. "Surely you can appreciate why I did what I had to do? Alexis, I helped you bring your stepmother to trial! Now it's your turn to help me. Please, I beg of you, put me in a new body! I don't care how handsome or tall it is."

"No," Alexis said, realizing he was no longer afraid of the Persian. It didn't surprise him to learn that Ishkibar had murdered his own wife and claimed it was suicide. "You didn't help me. You used me. You used all of us. Anyway, I can't do it. The river god came and washed away my gift."

Kichesias glanced sharply at him. Ishkibar frowned, as if he knew Alexis was lying but couldn't work out how to prove it.

Diogenes smiled and passed the sword to one of the

lily-hands. He wrapped his cloak around Alexis's shivering shoulders and guided him after Orontobates and Phoebe. Alexis didn't see what the lily-hands did to Ishkibar, but whatever it was, they were swift and silent. From the corner of his eye, he glimpsed Ishkibar's horse galloping off with a limp body tied across its back. The Persian might have been alive, or he might have been dead. He supposed there wasn't much difference, now that everyone was hunting him. The dogs on his trail would find him eventually, and his career as a spy was over. Ishkibar had been responsible for his father's murder, yet he hadn't actually done the deed. Neaera had poisoned Diogenes with her blood, and that had been Alexis's fault for waking her statue in the first place with the spirit of a dead king before he had understood the magic.

None of it seemed to matter any more. All he could think of was how warm his father's arm felt, not statue-like at all.

A little gasp from Phoebe interrupted his thoughts. He saw she'd untied the end of the Chimaera's golden chain, perhaps intending to let the creature join the chase after Ishkibar, but her pet hadn't moved. Phoebe was staring into the shadows under the trees with tears in her eyes. The monster remained in a crouch, dappled by moonlight, motionless and quiet. Too quiet.

"The Chimaera's turned back into a statue, hasn't she?" Alexis whispered, realizing with a slightly sick feeling that what he'd told Ishkibar must have been the truth, after all. "The river god really did answer my prayer! Her spirit's free."

"Don't be sad, Phoebe," Kichesias said, slipping his arm around the girl. "I bet the Chimaera's happier now. She never much liked being on the end of that chain, did she?"

"But—" Phoebe looked at Kichesias, and then at Diogenes. She gave a muffled sob and voiced all their fears. "That means... you're not going to change back to stone as well... are you?"

Orontobates stared at Kichesias and Diogenes in horror as he realized what his daughter meant. The lily-hands exchanged finger flickers in the shadows. Alexis clenched his fists and closed his eyes in an effort to control the bubble of loss and pain that was swelling inside him. It had been the right thing to do, the only thing. His father and friend were merely returning to wherever he'd called their spirits from. He'd had no more right to bring them back than he'd had to bring back the spirit of King Maussollos to be his stepmother.

Kichesias's voice made his eyes snap open again. "I think we're all free now, Alex," he said in a wondering tone. "I *thought* I felt something while you were in the gorge praying to the river god. It was like when that arrow hit me... painful, yet good as well. I can feel things again, Alex! Properly, like I used to. I'd almost forgotten what it was like."

Diogenes nodded, his eyes twinkling. "Just because something is set free doesn't mean it has to leave, does it?"

Alexis's heart leapt in sudden understanding. The river god had done more than answer his prayer. Much more.

"Father and Kichesias chose to stay and be human!" He buried his face in his father's chest to hide his tears of joy and gratitude. "That's why they're so warm, Phoebe! They're not just magic any more. They're really, truly alive!"

GUIDE TO ALEXIS'S WORLD

Alexis and his friends lived in the Carian capital of Halicarnassos (modern Bodrum in Turkey) in 334BC at the time of the siege of the city by Alexander the Great, when Caria was a distant part of the Persian Empire.

The quotes in the chapter headings are taken from Lucian's *Dialogues of the Dead* translated by M. D. Macleod and reprinted by kind permission of Harvard University Press. This particular dialogue is a fictional conversation between the spirits of King Maussollos and a philosopher called Diogenes the Cynic – if you read the chapter headings in order, you should be able to follow their ghostly conversation. King Maussollos was buried in the Mausoleum at Halicarnassos, and Alexis's father was named after Diogenes the Cynic, who shunned riches and lived in a barrel.

The following guide might help.

Acropolis	An easily defensible fortress, usually built on a hill inside the city walls, where citizens take refuge in times of attack.
agora	Market place.
amphora	A jug for storing oil or wine.
Aphrodite	The Greek goddess of love. She was very beautiful.
Ares	The Greek god of war. His statue stood on the rocks above Halicarnassos.
Assembly	A large group of citizens responsible for their particular city's laws and general policy. They met regularly throughout the year, and more often in emergencies.
centaur	A creature of Greek myth with a horse's body and the torso and head of a man.
Chimaera	Fire-breathing, three-headed, female monster (part-lion, part-goat and part-snake) that used to terrorize Caria's neighbour, Lycia. She was killed by Bellerophon, riding the winged horse Pegasus, who thrust a lump of lead into

her mouth, which melted in her stomach and killed her.

In this story, the resurrected Chimaera cannot breathe fire.

chiton   A style of Greek women's dress, fastened with brooches and ties rather than pins.

Cynic   A follower of the Greek philosophy that claimed it was only possible to be good if you turn your back on the comforts of life, including your family and friends. The most famous Cynic was a Corinthian named Diogenes, who took this philosophy so literally that he left his house and made his home in an old barrel.

Gordion Knot   A complicated knot used by King Gordius of Phrygia to tie the shaft to his ox-cart. He dedicated the Knot to the Temple of Zeus in Gordion, and legend claimed that whoever managed to untie it would be Lord of all Asia. In 333BC, Alexander the Great cut it with his sword.

Gorgon   A woman of Greek myth who had snakes instead of hair. Her stare was supposed to turn people to stone.

harpy	An ugly creature of Greek myth, half-bird and half-woman with a scolding tongue.
hydria	A water jar.
lily-hands	Slaves who serve in the women's quarters of the Palace in Halicarnassos. They have their tongues removed so that they cannot talk about what they see there. Lily-flower designs branded into their palms show that they can be trusted to look after the royal women.
Mausoleum	The magnificently decorated tomb of King Maussollos of Caria. One of the Seven Wonders of the Ancient World, it stood at the crossroads in the centre of the Carian capital Halicarnassos. Later, all tombs of the same style were named mausoleums.
mercenary	A soldier who fights for money, rather than for his country. Halicarnassos was defended by a mixture of Persian troops answering to the Satrap Orontobates and Carian mercenaries led by General Memnon (who was considered one of the best of the Persian Emperor's generals, even though he was himself a mercenary).

Midas	Alexis's distant ancestor – a legendary King of Phrygia whose touch could turn things to gold. Midas grew tired of his gift when he accidentally turned his own daughter to gold, and was "cured" when he washed in the river on Mount Tmolus. Alexis therefore inherited his gift, but in reverse – his touch can change gold to other things and bring gold-painted statues to life (see *statue magic*).
Mount Tmolus	Mountain near Sardis, where King Midas went to wash in the river Pactolus and lost his golden touch. This is where Neaera takes Alexis on annual pilgrimages to ask the river god to reverse his magic.
mummi-fication	A technique of preserving the dead, usually by wrapping the corpse in bandages, which originated in Ancient Egypt.
myrtle wreath	A crown of myrtle leaves, worn by whoever is speaking to the Assembly.
Pan	A minor Greek god, half-goat and half-man, who had a reputation for wild behaviour – hence our word "panic".

Pegasus A winged horse, the legendary mount of the hero Bellerophon who killed the Chimaera.

peplos pin A long, decorative pin used to fasten the shoulders of an old-fashioned style of Greek women's dress called a "peplos".

Poseidon The Greek god of the sea, also of horses. He sent earthquakes.

Satrap A Persian ruler put on the throne of outlying countries such as Caria to rule in the name of the Emperor. Phoebe's father Orontobates married a Carian princess, making him both Satrap and King of Caria.

siren A beautiful sea-creature. Sirens were supposed to sing sailors to sleep so that their ships were wrecked on the rocks.

statue magic When Alexis brings a statue to life, there is a magical bond between them that means that they cannot hurt or leave each other. The woken statues feel cold and smooth, have the gift of standing statue-still, are very strong, have black crystalline blood that is poisonous to humans while wet, do not feel pain, and can be harmed only by gold.

Theatre (amphi-theatre)	A semi-circular depression on the side of a hill, open to the sky, with tiers of seats carved out of the hillside and a stage at the bottom. Most cities built in the Greek style had a theatre.
urn	A large pot used for storage or for planting flowers and trees.
usurper	A person who wrongly seizes the throne. In Halicarnassos, Ada's supporters saw the Persian Satrap Orontobates as an usurper, even though he had married into the Carian royal family.
voting tokens	These were used for voting at a public trial. There were two kinds – holes in the centre (guilty) and solid centres (not guilty). The jurors were given one of each, and voted by depositing their chosen token in the voting urn and discarding the other token in a second urn.
water clock	Two urns marked with lines and fitted with taps. They were placed one above the

water clock cont.	other, so that when the tap was opened the water from the top urn would run into the bottom urn, giving a measurement of time. When the water ran out, the urns could be reversed and the process repeated.
Zeus	The most important of the Greek gods. He controlled the weather and threw thunderbolts.

THE WINNER OF
THE 8th WONDER
COMPETITION

is

Aysha Rashid,

who wrote:

The Eighth Wonder could be something
completely unique – The Future!
The Future would make the perfect final
Wonder because it's something secretive
and unknown; the Future is faceless. It is
unidentified and indefinite – do you
believe in fate? I believe we take our
own steps in life and these alone shape
what will happen tomorrow. Our heart
is the key to our own destiny, and the
human heart can be a powerful spirit. It
is this unpredictability and sensitivity to
these "trivial emotions" that make life
what it is: hopeful – and make the Future
what it is: eternal.

This is what

Katherine Roberts

had to say about the entries:

"I very much enjoyed reading all the entries. Sadly there can be only one winner, but I would like to give a special mention to Eloise Charig who continued the ancient Greek theme with the Trojan Horse, Callum Dawson who suggested a Viking saga featuring the Kraken sea monster, and Olivia Scott-Berry whose story took place inside the Great Wall of China. Well done to everyone who entered, and many congratulations to Aysha for her interesting approach to the topic."

THE
SEVEN FABULOUS WONDERS

THE GREAT
PYRAMID
ROBBERY

Magic, murder and mayhem spread through the Two
Lands, when Senu, the son of a scribe, is forced to
help build one of the largest and most magnificent
pyramids ever recorded. He and his friend, Reonet,
are sucked into a plot to rob the great pyramid of
Khufu and an ancient curse is woken. Soon they are
caught in a desperate struggle against forces from
another world, and even Senu's mischievous ka, Red,
finds his magical powers are dangerously tested.

000 711278 5

Visit the booklover's website
www.harpercollins.co.uk

THE
SEVEN FABULOUS WONDERS

THE
BABYLON
GAME

Tia's luck starts to change the moment she touches a
dragon patrolling the Hanging Gardens of Babylon.
At the Twenty Squares Club Tia wins every game –
could the dragon have given her a magical power?

But Tia discovers her lucky gift brings great danger.
While the Persian army prepares to attack her home,
she and her friend, Simeon, must fight their own battle.
Will Tia's magic save the city – or destroy it altogether?

000 711279 3

Visit the booklover's website
www.harpercollins.co.uk

THE
Seven Fabulous Wonders

THE
AMAZON
TEMPLE
·QUEST·

Lysippe is an Amazon princess with a mission. Her
tribe has vanished and her sister is fatally wounded.
Only the power of a Gryphon Stone can help, but
Lysippe has a problem. She has been enslaved by the
sinister Alchemist, and he is after the Stones too…

Lysippe and her friend, Hero, plan a daring escape
from the slave gang and claim sanctuary in the
mysterious Temple of Artemis. But can they decipher
the Temple's magical secrets before it's too late?

000 711280 7

Visit the booklover's website
www.harpercollins.co.uk

forthcoming titles...

THE STATUE OF ZEUS AT OLYMPIA

Persion terrorists, angry at Alexander the Great's invasion of their home, are targeting young athletes in this tale of treachery at the Olympic Games. Sosi has the power to save his friends, but first he must train in his brother's place and confront his own demons...

THE COLOSSUS OF RHODES

For years this titanic figure has guarded the harbour entrance on the island of Rhodes and kept watch over its people. But now a fatal prophecy foretells doom and destruction...

THE PHAROS AT ALEXANDRIA

In the days of the last Egyptian Queen, Cleopatra, the citizens of Alexandria fight for independence against the mighty Roman Empire. Their great lighthouse is the key to control of the port, but do they dare awaken the spirits of their ancestors...?

Katherine Roberts

I spent my childhood on the beaches of Devon and Cornwall, searching rock pools for weird creatures. My first stories, featuring some of these creatures with added magic, were told to my little brother at bedtime when I was eight. But it was another twenty-two years before I dared send anything to a publisher – initially short stories for adults, followed by my first children's book *Song Quest,* which won the Branford Boase Award in 2000. In the meantime, I went to university to study mathematics, worked as a computer programmer, exercised racehorses, and helped in a pet shop. I also learnt to fly a glider, morris dance, and ski down black runs… all these experiences creep into my books in fantastic ways!

The Seven Fabulous Wonders series grew out of my interest in ancient myths and legends and the creatures that inhabit them. Rather than re-tell the familiar tales, I wanted to explore what happens when legend meets history, and especially the gaps in between that nobody knows very much about. In this series, you will meet seven extraordinary young people who lived in a time when magic and reality were closer than they are today – a time that gave birth to the fantastic fiction I so love to write.

Katherine Roberts, Ross-on-Wye
www.katherineroberts.com

The Great Pyramid Robbery

"A grand tale unravels – ancient curses, magical powers, dangerous forces and spirits make *The Great Pyramid Robbery* a wonderful fantasy-filled read! Unearth this fab book."
Funday Times

"A terrific tale of plots, curses and evil forces set in ancient Egypt."
Sunday Express

"I did nothing for the rest of the day except read it... from the first moment, it grips."
Susan Price, author of *The Sterkarm Handshake*

"Murder, magic, power struggles, spirits, adventure and a desperate race against time... all combine to make this a good choice."
School Librarian

The Babylon Game

"Katherine Roberts is a children's author of genuine skill and imagination, and *The Babylon Game* is one of her most engaging titles."
Publishing News

"Fast paced ... and starts the action straight away. Really good – recommended."
 cool-reads.com

"Incredible story of adventures that twist and turn and will have you spellbound on every page."
Children's Book of the Week, South Wales Evening Post